CREDITS

J.S.D. who left me some unpublished writings.
C.S.D.B. who shared her experience as a new girl at Bishop Starchan School, Toronto.
Lynn Williams for typing the original draft, and for the gift of a word processor.
Elizabeth Taylor, archival assistant, avid internet researcher, for help with the family tree charts.
My husband Fred for hours of proof reading.
Audrey Tournay, David Neal, and Emily Duffield for illustraions.
Emily Duffield who has acted as editor and publisher.
My nephew Bill Watson for encouragement and literary advice.

Copyright 2014 Sarah Ditchburn Neal.
All rights reserved, not to be reprinted without written permission from the author or publisher.
Published in Canada by Shadow River Ink, 2015.
ISBN: 978-1-312-66714-3

Lynnehurst
BOOKS I & II
Liza's Story
&
Her Seasons of Summer

by
Sarah Ditchburn Neal

*Eliz, Happy memories
Love,
Sarah*

DEDICATION

To the spinsters who helped develop this country and who served their families and their communities as tutors, nurses, teachers, gardeners, artists, diary keepers, and as domestic engineers.

I make this dedication especially to:
A.B., M.J.W., E.W., E.R., K.L., A.C. and D.C.,

each of whom enriched my life as well as the lives of others.

FOREWORD

Lynnehurst is a portrait of a Canadian family reaching back to the early years of our nationhood and stretching forward into the twenty-first century. Lynnehurst puts the spotlight on a part of English Canada, the Muskoka Lakes District of Ontario, a setting which the author knows well. Though descended, on both sides, from old Muskoka families, I have not written a family history. No character portrays any particular person either living or dead. I have drawn from family stories and situations as well as from my knowledge of other families. However, imagination plays a major role.

The location is based on several Muskoka places. On your next weekend there do not exhaust yourself, dear reader, trying to identify Needles Point or Drayton Beach. Wherever you may be staying, they will be nearby. The wharf at your cottage or resort will feel just as warm and wonderful as the one at Lynnehurst.

As for the American sections of my story, several Canadian families have histories that straddle the "unguarded border." Precisely because of the American presence in Canadian history, I give an American experience to the Drayton and Brown families. My own childhood memories of Louisiana influenced me to position that portion of their lives in the Deep South.

Many of my friends and relatives have a mystic attitude to Muskoka. For those who love to escape there in the summer it's a Canadian Brigadoon. However, Lynnehurst Legacy is not a fairy story any more than it is a factual historical account.

It is fiction based on fact; fiction which reveals truth. I offer a tale, or rather a series of tales, linked together by relationship to a place. Muskoka is a legacy for all who visit and all who live there, a wonderful part of a great country still striving to identify itself.

Sarah Ditchburn Neal
Rosseau, ON
2013

JOSEPH DRAYTON
Born: 1820   m. 1848

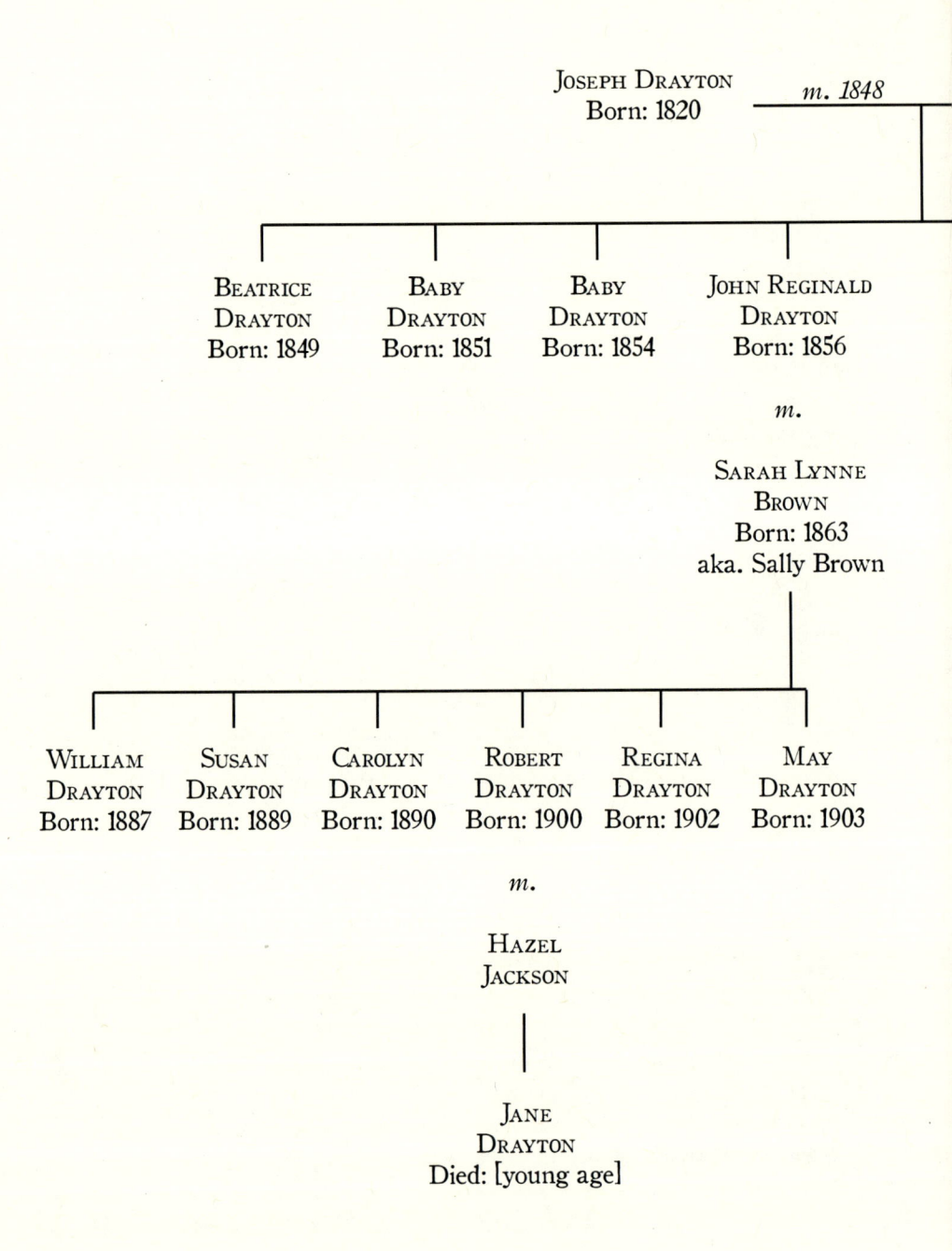

BEATRICE   BABY   BABY   JOHN REGINALD
DRAYTON   DRAYTON   DRAYTON   DRAYTON
Born: 1849   Born: 1851   Born: 1854   Born: 1856

m.

SARAH LYNNE
BROWN
Born: 1863
aka. Sally Brown

WILLIAM   SUSAN   CAROLYN   ROBERT   REGINA   MAY
DRAYTON   DRAYTON   DRAYTON   DRAYTON   DRAYTON   DRAYTON
Born: 1887 Born: 1889 Born: 1890 Born: 1900 Born: 1902 Born: 1903

m.

HAZEL
JACKSON

JANE
DRAYTON
Died: [young age]

THE DRAYTONS

CAROLYN ROBERTS
Born: 1827

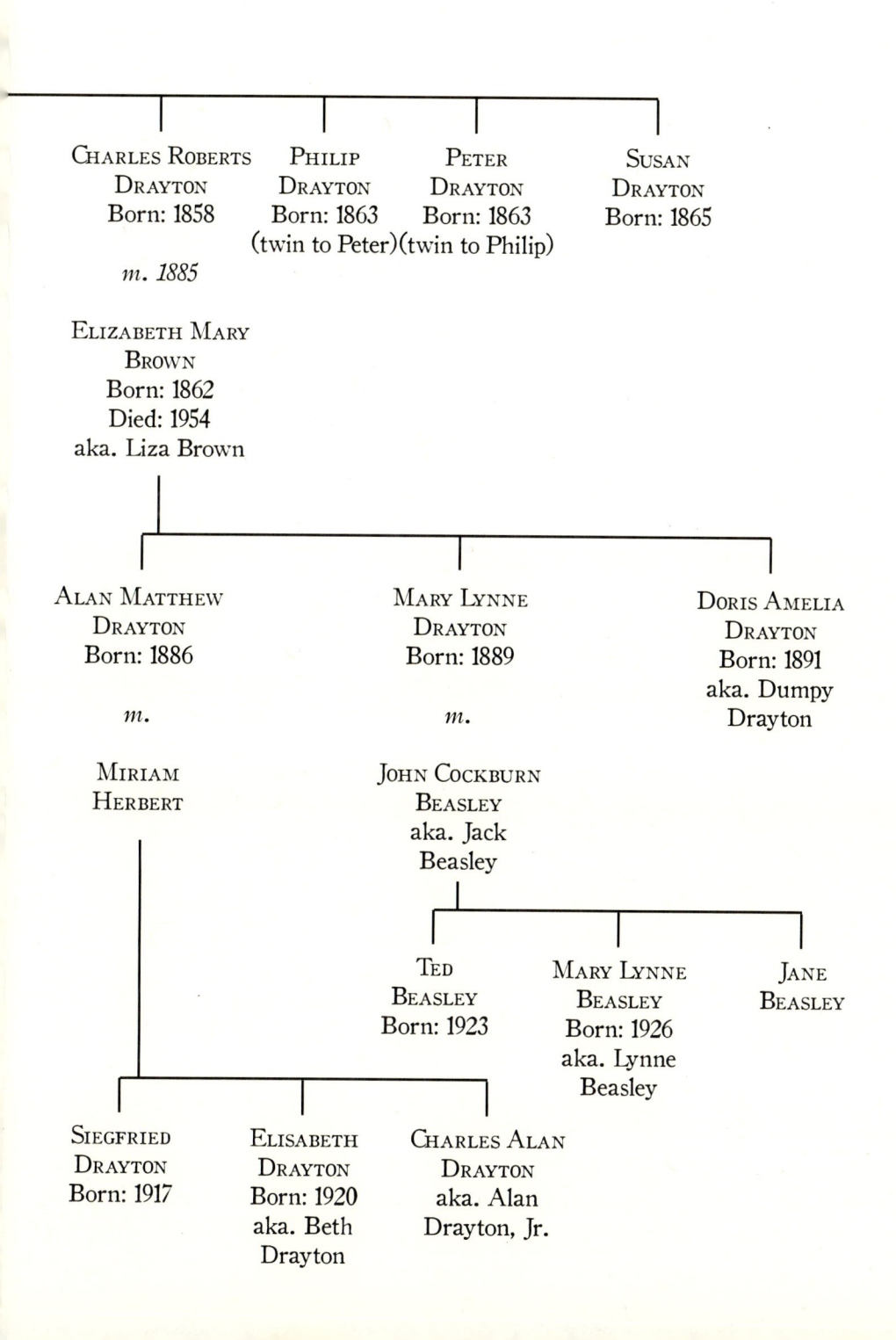

- **CHARLES ROBERTS DRAYTON**
  Born: 1858

  m. 1885

  ELIZABETH MARY BROWN
  Born: 1862
  Died: 1954
  aka. Liza Brown

- **PHILIP DRAYTON**
  Born: 1863
  (twin to Peter)

- **PETER DRAYTON**
  Born: 1863
  (twin to Philip)

- **SUSAN DRAYTON**
  Born: 1865

Children of Charles and Elizabeth:

- **ALAN MATTHEW DRAYTON**
  Born: 1886

  m.

  MIRIAM HERBERT

- **MARY LYNNE DRAYTON**
  Born: 1889

  m.

  JOHN COCKBURN BEASLEY
  aka. Jack Beasley

- **DORIS AMELIA DRAYTON**
  Born: 1891
  aka. Dumpy Drayton

Children of Mary Lynne and John:

- **TED BEASLEY**
  Born: 1923
- **MARY LYNNE BEASLEY**
  Born: 1926
  aka. Lynne Beasley
- **JANE BEASLEY**

Children of Alan and Miriam:

- **SIEGFRIED DRAYTON**
  Born: 1917
- **ELISABETH DRAYTON**
  Born: 1920
  aka. Beth Drayton
- **CHARLES ALAN DRAYTON**
  aka. Alan Drayton, Jr.

MATTHEW BROWN ———— m. 1855 ——————

HAROLD BROWN	JANE LYNNE BROWN	BABY BROWN	ELIZABETH MARY BROWN	SARAH LYNNE BROWNE
Born: 1856	Born: 1858	Born: 1860	Born: 1862	
	Died: 1860		Died: 1954	
m. 1888			aka. Liza Brown	m. 1855
ELSIE			m. 1885	JOHN REGINALD DRAYTON
			CHARLES ROBERTS DRAYON	Born: 1856
			Born: 1858	

THE BROWNS

MARY JANE LYNNE
aka. Polly Lynne

EDGAR BROWN	HANNAH MATILDA BROWN	BABY BROWN	ANNE REBECCA BROWN	BABY BROWN	ISABELLE BROWN
Born: 1865	Born: 1867	Born: 1868	Born: 1869	Born: 1871	Born: 1874 aka. Belle Brown

LYNNEHURST
BOOK I
Liza's Story

"That which happens is not past.
It is all part of our now."
Waln, *House of Exile*

Escape

It was a fine afternoon in June, 1875. Hauling two coaches, the Toronto, Simcoe and Muskoka Junction train rattled its way northward past small settlements and scattered farms. Sunlight flickered through the dust-coated windows of the first coach searching for a hero or even a heroine. Liza Brown sat facing southward, stiff and erect, beside her father. She had not removed her cape of moss green serge with its round collar trimmed in black velvet or her travelling bonnet that held her light brown hair so neatly. Her right hand gripped a small canvas valise on the seat beside her.

The rays of sunlight that played across Liza's features revealed a troubled look in a pair of grey-blue eyes. Liza was not concerned that she was heading toward a strange and largely unsettled land where wild animals and even indians might roam. Nor was she timid about a reunion with the Drayton family whose boys were known teases. Her concerns were all centered back in Toronto with her sister Sally and with her mother, still weak from a lengthy illness. Could these two really manage the needs of the younger sisters Tilda, Annie, and one-year-old baby Belle, as well as coping with kitchen work and the laundry? Would Tilda run errands to the greengrocers? Their Mother, an expert seamstress, could again take over the mending chores but would she notice that baby Belle's night dress needed attention before the tear got any longer.

During her mother's illness, Liza had been in charge of the household and the nursery. She did not regret these past six months. A little self pity did enter her sober head as she remembered having to leave school to help out at home and because Buppa could not afford both a doctor's care for his ailing wife and education for their five daughters. Book learning was a much coveted pleasure for Mary Elizabeth Brown, alias Liza. This was not surprising considering she was the eldest daughter of Matthew Brown, known to be a scholar and a Latin teacher.

Matthew Brown put down his book and casually took off his glasses.

Trying to read while the train swayed and jolted was tiring to his eyes. He stretched his back and turned to look at the precious daughter seated beside him. His movement did not interrupt her trance-like mood. He thought of his wife and the day in High Park when he had first called her Polly instead of Miss Lynne. Polly had endured much since their marriage, including a succession of births. Each baby had been welcomed with an abundance of mother love as well as mother's milk. Each toddler, in turn, had been lavished with attention, truly spoiled until replaced by a newer babe. Two of their children had died at birth and they had lost Edgar at the age of five years. Had Polly ever harbored resentments?

His teacher's salary rarely stretched far enough to pay for a maid. From an early age Liza had learned to cook and to clean the house. As well, Polly had taught her to help with the seemingly endless sewing and mending chores. Liza could mend a heel or an elbow so craftily that the repaired garment looked like new. She would make a good wife for someone some day, that is, if she lived that long.

"Liza dear, you must not fret yourself about Mother and Sally. They will manage."

"But Buppa, what if mother becomes in the family way again? Does Sally know what to do? She's only twelve years old."

"There will be no more babies." His words were flat but crammed with emotion.

Father and daughter lapsed into silence again. Once infected with worry, Matthew couldn't stop. Had it really been fair to Polly to remove Liza from the household? On the other hand, someone had to rescue this thirteen-year old whose cares and worries made her look twice that age. Had Liza ever had a childhood? A chance to visit their old friends the Drayton's and to see a new part of the province seemed a golden opportunity. Matthew certainly hoped this place called Muskoka would prove to be a blessing.

The train lurched to a stop. Liza slid unceremoniously off the seat and onto the floor, her valise on her lap.

"Have you injured yourself, my dear?"

"I don't think so," She rearranged herself on the seat, "What happened?"

"Washago; any one for Washago?" As he spoke, the uniformed

conductor walked to the other end of the coach to help a thin man in farmer's togs with a pile of boxes and bags.

Liza and Buppa peered through dust and glass at a cluster of small, unpainted houses and an insignificant hotel that made up the village of Washago.

"Do the Drayton's live in a house like those Buppa?"

"I don't think so. Theirs is a log house... Look over there to the left; see that water? It looks such an unusual aqua-green colour. I think it's the Severn River."

"Will the Drayton's lake be green like that?"

"I don't know; we'll have to wait and see."

The train started forward with a jolt and a jerk. It crossed over a creaking wooden bridge and entered a domain of rock, trees, lakes, juniper bushes, and wild berries. Liza was saying goodbye to her known world. As she approached the rugged beauty of Muskoka, a new sensation enveloped her. Her apprehension became submerged in an energizing sense of destiny.

Liza and her father disembarked several miles further north and stood, wonderingly, beside the railway track. The afternoon sun was still high in the sky; several hours of daylight remained before nightfall. Buppa carried a goodly sized bundle of luggage and Liza her smaller valise. The remains of lunch were in a fisherman's creel slung from Matthew's left shoulder.

A steamer from Gravenhurst would have been the easier way to progress, but Joseph Drayton had written about difficult landings in their bay during storms. Matthew thought it best to stick to land. He had not been precise about their day of departure so didn't expect Joseph or any of the Draytons to meet them in their jumper.

In high spirits, Matthew and Liza approached the small home of the designated carter. In the doorway stood a woman. Her skirts and legs were shackled by the clasping arms of a wide-eyed child. This forlorn woman announced that her husband had gone on another trip and wouldn't be back 'til morning.

"You'll want to sleep here," she offered, "The girl could bunk in with my Jannie and you, Sir, would be cosy on the bear rug affront our fire."

Liza was thankful that her father insisted on proceeding by foot.

"Oh well, suit yourselves. The road's clear enough." The woman indicated the direction with a gesture.

Matthew and Liza couldn't walk side by side; each had to pick a way along mud ruts. After a few minutes, Liza spoke.

"Buppa, I'm glad we're walking. I haven't gone further than market in many months. I do love a good walk."

An hour later, the woods seemed to press closer to the trail. Mosquitoes issued forth in droves. Having been forewarned of cool evenings, Matthew and Liza were well covered in clothes, but they found it necessary to fan mosquitoes away from their faces with their free arms.

Later, the skies shadowed to a paleness that reminded Liza of a poem she had studied at school... *This must be what Browning calls the "even coloured end of day,"* she thought.

A refreshing breeze sprang up. The insects lessened their attacks and the adventurer's rapid pacing provided escape. Liza shifted her load to the other arm and took fresh hope.

"It's a longer way than I anticipated," explained Matthew.

"There's no need to worry, Buppa; I feel I could walk forever. Do you not feel the same?"

"Oh yes, little one, but I'm concerned for you. There's a house; let us ask if we are close."

Fortified with the knowledge that they indeed were only "three, perhaps four miles this side of Drayton's Place," father and daughter renewed their determination to persevere.

Matthew watched his daughter carefully. Her pace was slackening but remained fairly steady. She. was a good little walker who reminded him of Harold, his firstborn.

Harold had been a day-scholar at the boys' school where Matthew taught, as well as being a son at home. The two of them had often gone together for treks in and around Toronto. At age nineteen, Harold now worked in Montreal and Matthew missed having his son at home. It was a different world raising a bevy of daughters.

As they trudged onward the light of day, so long lasting at that time of year, began to dim. They could see little but darkness on either side, but they could still determine the roadway by feel, if not by sight.

"It seems like more than three miles," remarked Liza.

"Yes, but perhaps it's only our desire to make it so," replied Matthew, coming to a halt. "I don't see any sign of a house or a light. I'm concerned that we could pass the place in the dark. Let us rest here a while."

The woods around them seemed eerie and empty. Liza drew closer to her father.

"Buppa, do people go to bed earlier in the north country?"

"Perhaps." He began spreading his coat for her in a shallow hollow beside the trail. She did not protest, merely added her load by way of a pillow before lying down. Matthew tucked the coat over and around Liza as best he could, all the while considering what he had best do with himself. In the end, he sat propped against a large log and asked his Maker to take care of any wild animals that might be around.

Thus comforted, he fell into a fitful sleep while remaining seated more or less upright.

༺༻

Morning came early and bright with dew. Matthew blinked several times, rolled to his knees, and stood to look along the roadway in front of them. He realized that he was staring at a crude signpost standing just a few yards away. Four winters of exposure had made the one word in capital letters indistinct. He hardly dared believe his first impression. Matthew stepped closer and traced his finger over each letter, carefully spelling out "D-R-A-Y-T-O-N."

With a shout he grabbed the sign as if he expected the small plank to turn into the old friend whose name it bore. In doing so, he discovered that the sign pointed to a narrow wagon trail, rough, but obviously well used, leading to the left through the woods.

"Liza, Liza, come look!" he called, his voice swelling with excitement. It took longer for Liza to shake sleep from her body. More muscles than she ever dreamed her body could contain were aching in unison with a singy sensation.

She got to her feet, wobbled, and sat down again. In time, she came to understand her father's elation.

"How did you know, last night?"

"I didn't know. That's what is so amazing. If we had gone even a few yards further last night we would have missed our target altogether."

They quickly ate the remains of their bread and cheese, straightened their clothing as best they could, then set forth with renewed vigour along the indicated trail. After almost a mile, Drayton Road left the woods and wound its way into an open area. Matthew and Liza halted to let their eyes accommodate the change.

Almost dead centre, but several yards down the gentle slope, a female figure was bent slightly, working with a hoe in a tilled field decorated with old tree stumps. She was singing a high lilting tune, interrupted from time to time as she bent groundward to handle some stubborn clod of earth, coaxing from it a burden of weeds. Her dress, though somewhat tattered, bore the unmistakeable lines of a ball gown fashionable in a previous decade.

"It's Caroline Drayton!" exclaimed Matthew, "I didn't know she could sing. It must be the Welsh in her."

Drayton's Place

WHEREAS MANY MUSKOKA PIONEERS chose locations near a road and away from winds, Joseph Phillip Drayton and Caroline Roberts, his wife, had the aesthetic sense to place their pioneer homestead in full sight of the lake. Drayton, a once prosperous dealer in fine furniture, had sold his Toronto holdings to pay off debts incurred by his less astute business partner. Sufficient funds remained for the purchase of some partially cleared land offered after the original settler had suffered an accident and was not able to complete the terms of the government land grant.

Drayton had been able to hire local men to help him, his wife Caroline, and their four sons and two daughters as they strained their minds and muscles to master pioneer ways and to clear and cultivate several acres of wilderness. Drayton even risked $10 to have a rough mile-long roadway carved through the thick woods from the main road to the site of their farmstead. After four years they had made their holdings and their log home blossom into a semblance of civilization amid surrounding forests.

As Liza gazed at the panorama of clearings and buildings spread out before her, feelings of amazement, delight and love welled up inside her weary self. Down the slope from where she and her Buppa stood lay a large log home framed by a maple tree at one side and a cluster of white birches at the other. Yellow day lilies and peonies of every shade hugged the rough walls. If this was the back of the house, what glories might they find in the front?

"If ever I have a home," Liza wondered, "will it be like this?"

Matthew's eyes hardly noticed the flowers. His had focused on a hillside of grape vines neatly marshalled into straight rows on rough fencing. Nearby, also on the south side of the house, were a few young trees that looked remarkably like plum, pear and apple. To the north, two sheds were huddled together, and beyond them, a new and larger structure was being constructed... possibly a barn, thought Matthew.

A distant lamb's bleating joined in the chorus of Cym Rhonda. Neither Liza nor Matthew could detect the direction or source of it. To Liza, the crowning glory to this moment was the lake, which lay beyond the house. Calm as glass, its stillness reflected the blueness of sky. The nearer shore was trimmed with a thin line of sand beach. Everywhere else was rocky and irregular.

Huge evergreens, later to be identified as hemlocks, pines and spruce, marched down to the water from various points of land. Maple, beech, birch, ash and others of the deciduous family, followed, providing lighter tints of early summer greens. *It's a rainbow of greens, blues and yellows,* thought Liza. Every shade and tint was related to the next one. The missing, warmer colours of the spectrum were not needed. As Liza's body absorbed the sun's warmth she felt a wholesome contentment. She offered thanks, even for the stiffness and aches of the night, so good was it to allow the sun's caresses to heal and iron out the wrinkles of her whole being.

The magic could not last forever. As Matthew and Liza approached, Mrs. Drayton stopped singing. Her stunned silence was followed by recognition and a jumble of greetings, embarrassments, explanations. Caroline Drayton, usually fearless in the face of local criticism, was upset by being caught in ridiculous attire by friends from her former city life. The gown had been part of a shipment sent by well-meaning members of the Roberts family back in England; they hadn't the remotest idea about life in the backwoods of Muskoka.

"The Welsh in me won't let me waste anything, so I wear it for working while the simpler dresses I save for Sundays and social occasions," Caroline laughed, in an effort to make them feel more at ease while Matthew apologized, again and again, for surprising her at such an early hour of the day.

They might have gone on like this, laughing, explaining, and repeating themselves if Buster hadn't joined them to announce, with much barking, that it was time for breakfast.

"There, there, Buster." Mrs. Drayton patted the dog's head as she spoke. Then turning to Matthew and Liza she exclaimed, "I'm forgetting myself. You must be tired and hungry. Do come in and unload your bags."

Inside the house, more explaining went on. Joseph was abed with gout. He might even have to remain there. Son John was in Toronto looking for employment. The twins, Philip and Peter, were staying with friends by the name of Beasley so they could be part of a long-promised fishing expedition in the deeper bush. The Drayton maid of all work had left suddenly so son Charlie had gone off girl-hunting. Since he had not returned, his parents assumed he must still be looking and probably was staying with friends. Their youngest, Susan, was out in the sheep shed looking after her lambs.

As Caroline spoke, she put a stick of wood in the stove and pulled the kettle forward.

"There's bacon here and eggs. What else? Oh, yes, we could easily stew some rhubarb." Caroline was thinking out loud. Then she added, "We have no bread. I was never taught how to make it. The girl always did that for us."

"If you have flour and soda I could make quick biscuits." offered Liza.

"That would be good. I'll put some preserves on the table too."

In time, they had a sumptuous breakfast. Encouraged by the sound of friendly voices, and feeling improved after his night's sleep, Joseph Drayton was able to join them at table. Susan appeared and was introduced. Both Matthew and Liza thought Susan to be a replica of her elder sister, Beatrice.

"What do you hear from Beatrice, these days?"

"We don't hear often. She and Sam moved further west to British Columbia after burying their two little ones somewhere on the Prairies." Caroline was at a loss for further words. Joseph began asking about former friends in Toronto.

Liza was enjoying her biscuits with wild strawberry jam and a good cup of tea with thick milk. She would have liked the meal and conversation to continue.

Shortly, Mr. Drayton stood up and insisted that Matthew and Liza inspect the vineyard. They had to hear how much pruning and cultivating went into the miracle of producing grapes so far north. Their friend had to share his hopes and dreams concerning the small orchard he had planted. He even instructed them about hot beds, made of wooden frames topped with storm windows from the house.

"I can start my seeds early in hot beds. After the Queen's birthday, I have plants big enough to transplant."

"Your methods must be correct ones," answered Matthew, as he gazed in admiration at a very healthy vegetable patch.

Liza and Susan left the vineyard to check two hens for eggs, then went to the sheep shed.

"I worry about these four lambs," explained Susan. "Lambs are so fragile at first."

In the absence of Charlie to work the big hand pump, Susan and Liza fetched pails of water from the lake. They filled the kettle, then began to wash the breakfast dishes. Liza enjoyed handling the Drayton's fine china. She dried each piece carefully. Mrs. Drayton busied herself with numerous chores around the house. It was a challenge to make space for her guests.

The log house was large enough, but starkly primitive in comparison with the former Drayton home in Toronto. Fine furniture which they had brought with them seemed out of place. However, a row of windows facing the lake gave the house more graciousness than most pioneer homes. Liza let her eyes explore the whole setting, especially the view of the lake. She thought it must be wonderful to live with such a view.

☙

Dinner at noon brought them together again. They were still at table when Buster heralded the approach of other people.

"It must be Charlie," exclaimed Mrs. Drayton as she rose and rushed to the door. The others hesitated, then trailed behind her.

Coming through the field of stumps was a tall, lanky lad. Beside him was a large, big-boned girl. Her square face bore a ruddy complexion. Liza thought the new girl must be not much older than herself, but about three sizes larger.

Charlie Drayton introduced Betty Tullis to his parents, then welcomed Matthew and Liza to Muskoka. Liza had grown so much Charlie wouldn't have known her had her father not been with her. Liza did not like to admit that she had no clear memory of any of the Drayton boys. They lodged in her mind only as a group demonstrating boyhood energy, but lacking individual qualities. Not knowing what to say, she remained silent. The others had plenty to talk about and did not notice Liza's silence.

Charlie, a great favourite with his sister, joyously lifted Susan for a whirl in the air. This twirling seemed to be their special ritual.

Mrs. Drayton took Betty off to learn the ropes. Mr. Drayton followed them into the house. He needed an afternoon rest. Charlie, who seemed relieved to be free of his responsibilities for Betty, claimed that he wanted neither food nor rest. He offered to take the Browns on a tour of inspection of the lake. They readily accepted.

Susan followed them along to the beach. The row boat was quickly fetched from its crude shelter under some trees.

Charlie shoved it into the water beside the primitive landing stage. He gave brief directions, placing everyone according to where their weight would best balance the boat, Susan in the bow and Matthew on the second rowing bench. Charlie took charge of rowing and placed Liza in the stern facing him, asking her to manage the rudder.

"I don't know how," she protested meekly.

"It's easy. Pull on the starboard, the right hand rope, and we turn to the right. It's the same with the left."

Liza had to try a few times but quickly got the feel. Charlie never told her that he didn't need the rudder; he could manage the steering quite handily with the oars.

Charlie pushed the boat away from the dock and let one oar trail in the water while he twisted his body around and indicated with a sweep of his arm past the bow.

"See that bare rock bluff over there?"

"The one with the dead pine tree on top?"

"Yes, we call that Little Bluff. Steer toward the tree. I want to show you the shore between here and Little Bluff. It's beautiful, but useless for cultivation because there's so much rock."

Charlie rolled up his shirt sleeves revealing a pair of wellshaped muscular arms. He clasped both oars in his practised hands and, leaning forward, began to take long, strong strokes.

Liza was surprised how easily the light craft moved over the smooth surface of the water. She held the steering ropes firmly and was relieved to have a responsibility.

The need to focus on the rock bluff freed her from having to stare all the time into Charlie Drayton's hazel eyes and tanned face. Those eyes were remarkable. There seemed to be so much going on behind them. Liza marvelled, also, at his relaxed confidence. She wondered if she would be as composed as Charlie by the time she reached age seventeen. Charlie chose a flat, grassy place below Little Bluff for landing.

"The Miskoko Indians used to camp here in the old days. Now we use the flat area to stack wood for the steam boats They can land here more easily than at our beach." Waving his arm to indicate direction, Charles continued: "John and I cut timber in there behind Little Bluff."

Susan was the first out of the row boat. She took the 'painter' rope with her and then held the boat while her brother shipped the oars. Back in the woods a flock of crows rose noisily-from their tall oak, only to roost again on higher branches. Liza eyed the birds quizzically. Their loud cawing sounded dreadful.

"Pay no attention to them," said Charlie, laughing. "They think they own this place but they won't hurt us."

As he spoke, he was helping Liza and her father disembark.

Liza realized that some of the stiffness and aches from the previous night lingered with her. Her father must be feeling the same. Once on shore, he arched his back and stretched his arms. He didn't notice that Charlie had only Susan to help pull the row-boat up over a log. Liza noticed but felt unable to offer assistance. She stood watching, envying their easy skill in handling the craft.

"I love this place," said Susan, "Mother sometimes lets us pack a cold supper and bring it here to eat. Then we go exploring."

"Yes," added Charlie, "but there are too many mosquitoes for exploring this time of year. Mother sometimes comes here, too, to see the sunset. We get a better view of it from here than we do at home. Father only comes if he has something to say to the men stacking wood for the steamers. He says it's too dark in there behind the bluff to suit him. I think what he means is that he couldn't put a decent garden over there. He's not really suited to farming, but he is a wonderful gardener. Did he tell you about the strawberries he grew last year?"

"No he didn't."

"One was four inches in diameter. He's hoping to increase his crop this year. Summit House will likely buy berries for their summer guests, or he might send them by steamer and train to Toronto. We hear the railroad will reach the docks in Muskoka Bay; then it'll be no trick for the steamers to connect with the train. We could have our fruit for sale in Toronto the day after we pick!"

The two men perched themselves on a log near the water where a light breeze kept mosquitoes away. The two girls stood behind them.

Charlie continued, "there've been some real changes since Father moved here. When we first came, we had to get off the train at Belle Ewart. Then it was a steamer and another boat, some of shanks mare and carts. Now the train is already past Severn Bridge. The biggest change is the locks at Port Carling. There are more steamers on these lakes too. The more steamers, the better for us. They bring our supplies and buy our wood for their fuel. Maybe I'll be able to start a business myself, right here in this heaven."

Matthew chuckled, "It'll be a few years before that can be. It's strange, too, that you desire to develop a business when your father came here to escape the hurlyburly of the business world."

"Yes sir, that's true."

Charlie didn't let the older man's words dampen his spirits. His response was polite enough, but in his own head he went on planning and dreaming.

All were silent for a while. Then, despite mosquitoes, Matthew decided to explore further. Susan volunteered to show him her private trail to the top of Little Bluff.

"You have to start on the other side where the trees are still thick," she explained.

Liza couldn't seem to move. She just stood staring at the lake. Charlie stayed with her. He wondered how long she would remain silent.

At length, he heard her exclaim softly, "It's absolutely beautiful." Then, turning to Charlie, she asked, "What's that white thing?"

"Where?"

"The other side of your place, but further along." Liza pointed to a blunt point of land whose tip consisted of bare rock, bulky but not nearly as high as Little Bluff.

"That's Hunchback. Some new people by the name of Webster have settled there. They don't intend to farm much. They want to build cottages where people can come in the summertime. It would be cheaper than hotels and the visitors could stay longer."

"But the white part is moving. It isn't rock."

They both stared. The white shape kept changing and wobbling, then got larger and disappeared altogether for a few seconds. When it emerged from the other side of Hunchback, it obviously was a large, graceful sail poised on the mast of a long, slender, white boat.

"A sailboat!" Their voices were in unison. Liza didn't know how sailboats worked. Charlie did, and proceeded to tell her in great detail, ending with a triumphant pledge to himself that some day he would own one.

The calmness of the early morning gradually vanished as the day progressed. Now, in mid afternoon, a sprightly breeze was sending the white sailboat along at a good clip. They watched as it headed for the opposite shore and then turned more in their direction.

Charlie had fallen in love with sailboats when he was quite small. He remembered Toronto Harbour. He and his brother John would go down there as often as they could. The sailboats on Lake Ontario were larger than this one. Once, someone had taken the two boys out on the harbour as far as Toronto Island. His memory was hazy about the details but he had learned much by reading books about boats.

"Liza," he said suddenly, "when I get my sailboat, I'll take you out in it."

※

The row-boat ride back to Drayton Beach through the now choppy waves seemed excessively long. Suddenly, Liza's lack of sleep and fatigue caught up with her. Back at the house, she gratefully accepted Mrs. Drayton's suggestion that she go straight to bed after a supper of hot milk and biscuits.

Next morning, Liza woke to the sound of rain gently throbbing on the roof shingles. She stretched, turned, then snuggled back to the cosiness of flannel gown and comforter. Susan's cot by the window was empty. The little girl evidently was already out with her precious lambs. Liza made no effort to arise. She lay there watching raindrops slide down the window panes. The apple tree and the out-buildings beyond were dark with wetness. A fragrance of wood smoke reached her nostrils.

Immediately, she was aware of a great hunger. Liza got up and dressed. For two weeks, wet and chilliness hung over Drayton Farm and all its occupants. Liza did not mind. She enjoyed it all. The wet forays with Susan to sheep shed and chicken coop were pure adventure followed by a welcome return to hearth and comfort. Between rain showers, they went down to the lake for bathing. With a whole lake of soft water and the grey sky above, Liza felt she was experiencing a tender luxury such as would be impossible in the Brown bathing closet back in Toronto. She relished the intimacy with nature that made her feel more alive than ever before.

Even in the house, the closeness to nature was ever present. During many hours spent indoors, Liza was never far from a window view of earth, woods, sky and water. The freshness of Muskoka's wonderful air stayed in her nostrils. Best of all was a new found vitality within her.

Liza began helping Mrs. Drayton alter some of the clothing that had come from England, making it into more suitable attire. With Liza's skilful hands helping, Caroline Drayton's mending pile was quickly reduced. Susan watched Liza carefully, trying to follow her example, but her fingers soon relaxed as her thoughts wandered.

Caroline was only too glad to leave the mending to Liza. Needlepoint was so much more satisfying. While the women kept their fingers active, their tongues would be busy as well. Liza loved to listen to conversation or to one of the men reading aloud.

One night, Charlie was reading Mr. Whittier's *Snowbound*. Liza was enthralled. Whittier's family group resembled, in spirit, the present circle of good folk around the Drayton hearth. She solemnly looked around as the firelight lit up their faces. There, on the bench beside the fire, were the Drayton twins, Philip and Peter, who had rejoined the household when their fishing trip had been drowned out. Their boyish faces were sweet with drowsiness. It was well past their normal bedtime. The indomitable Betty Tullis, her face redder than usual in the fire's glow, seemed untouched by the spell that Whittier's words were casting on the others. Indeed, Betty was on her feet in a short while shuffling off to her little bedroom behind the kitchen.

Susan's head was upon her mother's lap. In total contentment she drifted off to dreamland. Mrs. Drayton ceased her hand work. The two boys, Philip and Peter, blinked and made a greater effort to look awake. Buppa and Mr. Drayton next in the circle sat motionless and thoughtful. Her father's squarish face and rosy cheeks were so different from Joseph Drayton's paler skin and egg-shaped head. Buppa's hair was thick with brown woolly curls. Mr. Drayton was almost bald. Would Charlie resemble him later, Liza wondered?

When Charlie stopped reading, there was total silence for a space of time. Charlie, himself, broke it with, "someone ought to write an epic poem and call it 'Rainbound in Muskoka'."

Near the end of the rainy spell, Betty Tullis left Drayton Farm to visit her family for two or three days. During her absence, the evening conversations seemed to flow more freely. Caroline recalled Betty's first day with them.

"She said she could make bread and she seemed to have a good knowledge of food preparation. Housework, she dismissed as a mere trifle. However, I pressed my good fortune too far when I asked her if she knew how to serve at table. She did not understand. When I explained, she looked aghast and exclaimed, "don't you do your own reaching?"

"Well, my dear," remarked Joseph, "we've worked out a nice compromise. She does a little serving and we do some reaching. All in all, I think we're most fortunate."

"Yes, indeed."

"She certainly is a hard worker," added Matthew, "but, then, I don't suppose anyone could be lazy and survive in this country."

"Oh, we have some lazy ones," Joseph replied with a hearty chuckle, "I remember our first winter here when I needed some stove wood. Two brothers, who shall remain nameless because you met some of their relatives at Sunday worship, agreed to supply enough to get me started. You understand that wood is sold by the 'cord,' which is measured after the wood is stacked."

"It is any pile that's eight by four by four feet," interjected Matthew.

"That's correct. Now these brothers thought they could get the better of me by stacking the wood so that there were many air spaces in between. They took a long time and achieved this so well that the whole lot fell over just as they finished stacking. Well, sir, I put some distance between me and them while they restacked the wood. I warned Caroline to keep Susan out of earshot because the language those men used was not fit for ladies nor children to hear."

"Then there was old Job," Caroline reminded him.

"Yes, but I don't think laziness was Job's problem. He was fine as long as you told him exactly what to do. If you asked him to split log chunks into stove wood size, he'd do it 'til the indicated pile was gone. Then he'd sit there and stare at the horizon 'til someone got him going again. I'm glad Charlie and John have learned to split wood, but, as you know, they were still at school in Toronto our first years here."

"I've known Job to sit, staring for two hours straight," added Caroline.

"What became of Job? Have we met his relatives, too?" asked Matthew.

"I don't think he has any relatives, poor man."

"He went further north. Someone up there was clearing land. They had plenty of routine jobs for him and didn't mind getting him started over and over again. The good side of him was that he had few wants. They wouldn't have to give him any money; he'd only need a place to come in out of the weather and some food. As for me, I didn't have the patience to deal with him. He got on my nerves."

"It takes all kinds to make a world, doesn't it?" observed Matthew,

"Indeed. It has taken all kinds to pioneer in Muskoka."

"We knew what to expect," added Caroline, "Some people came here with such high hopes. Think of our two English friends who arrived in August of '69 with only summer clothes and the few possessions they could carry."

"You mean the Raeburns? They had absolutely no woods skills. Straight from London, they were… had romantic notions about adventure in the new world."

"Very well-educated Londoners; used to every comfort."

"They settled into a little cabin some surveyors had left. That was the year the snow fell and stayed on the ground from October 15th. Until the carter got their trunks to them in November, they were miserably cold."

"Did they stay in Muskoka?"

"They stayed, hunting and fishing and working at keeping warm through the winter. Then they tried Toronto for awhile. Now they've returned to help at the hotel. Once you've been here, it's hard to forget Muskoka. We often see the Raeburn brothers in the winter. When the ice is thick they walk here across the lake. They cheer our long winter evenings."

"John Raeburn plays the violin. He's entertained us many a night. His brother, Tom, recites poetry and is a good story teller. Tom, who has memorized the whole of Dickens' *Christmas Carol*, treated us to a dramatic recital of it last Christmas."

"Last July, John brought some visitors from the hotel who wanted to paint scenes of Muskoka to sell back in New York City. They admired our situation."

"Did they paint views of the lake or was it the quaintness of the log house that attracted them?"

"Both, and the flowers that Joseph tends with such care." Caroline paused, then began to chuckle.

"What has amused you, my dear?"

"I was thinking how ridiculous I must have looked to Matthew and Liza that first morning. Do you think our artistic people would like a painting of me in my ball gown working the soil?"

"Maybe those American customers would take pity and send us parcels of clothing."

"More likely, they'd decide that Canadians have peculiar customs. But if you think I'm strange, what about Mrs. Beasley's mother?"

"What about her?"

"They tell me that back in England, she was used to changing her attire every evening. Here, her wardrobe has dwindled to one dress. Apparently, she takes it off every afternoon and hangs it somewhere to air while she rests on her bed. When she gets up, she puts the same dress on again."

Liza could have listened to the Draytons and her father talk every evening. However, Mr. Drayton wasn't always content, just with conversation. Some evenings, he asked for a game of whist. Matthew would join him. Liza was glad that she could use Mrs. Drayton's mending as an excuse to avoid any card game. She sensed that Charlie didn't enjoy cards either. Philip and Peter were happy to oblige their father by learning to play—anything to delay bedtime. Caroline enjoyed a game now and then, but she preferred to save card playing for the long winter evenings.

"My eyes tire of needlework. Lamplight dulls my senses, too," Mrs. Drayton explained to Liza, "Cards take less effort."

Liza tried to visualize those long winter evenings to which the Draytons alluded. Were the hours longer here than in Toronto?

"Can you play Patience?" Mrs. Drayton suddenly asked Liza one evening, "No? Let me teach you. You might find it useful someday."

Liza could not imagine cards ever being useful. She suspected that card games were closely allied to idleness and, therefore, a chance for the devil to tempt people.

On the other hand, the Draytons must be good Christian people. Liza politely let Mrs. Drayton teach her Patience. After all, the name, itself, was one of the virtues.

Eventually the rain lifted. The Brown's were persuaded to lengthen their stay.

"You haven't seen Muskoka at its best yet," was the argument given whenever Matthew protested.

Indeed, the second half of their visit was idyllic. Delightful breezes blew away both wetness and mosquitoes. The days were long and sunny. Produce from the garden became more abundant and of greater variety. Liza's days were filled with happy activity. She helped Susan and the twins with the livestock. She picked wild berries. She made herself useful in the kitchen. When Charlie needed company in the rowboat, as he went out to meet the steamer, she and Susan gladly volunteered. Both girls learned to row and to hold the boat in position while Charlie off-loaded crates of food, bags of grain, smaller parcels, papers and letters from the larger vessel into their own sturdy craft.

Swimming was the best of all. Peter and Philip were skilfully at home in the water. They were even more practised in the arts of teasing and showing off. For this reason, the girls were thankful that the twins did most of their swimming out in the deep water.

Liza Brown's first swimming lessons were given by Susan, who simply said, "keep kicking and use your arms. If I can do it, you'll be able, also."

It was reassuring to know that Drayton Bay was shallow so the lake bottom was never very far below. They invented bathing costumes for themselves out of garments from "The Roberts Treasury Box," as Mrs. Drayton called her trunk of hand-me-downs. The makeshift outfits were not suitable for city use but Mrs. Drayton declared them to be perfectly modest. Liza found that so much cloth impeded her progress in the water, clinging in a dreadful way when it was wet. On shore there were always uncomfortable moments until the sun did its duty of drying. To speed up the drying process, they invented games of tag and ran along the beach vying with the waves for playfulness.

Peter and Philip laughed at the girls and told them how ridiculous they looked, but the boys were not above joining in the games of tag.

One day, Charlie Drayton declared a holiday from farming duties and instigated an expedition to Little Bluff so that Liza could try swimming in deeper water.

"It's not good in our bay because the bottom gets in your way. Over there, we can jump in and not hurt ourselves. It's much more exciting."

Liza wondered if deep water really was superior but she trusted him. Into the boat they all scrambled. The twins shared a seat and the second pair of oars. Their irregular strokes were a hindrance rather than a help to Charlie. Some of Betty Tullis' home made bread and chunks of local cheese accompanied the young voyagers.

"Just in case," explained Charlie.

It proved to be a wonderful outing. Little Bluff welcomed them back, offering all the enchantments of privacy, peace and nature. A crow cawed in the distance over the tree tops; the lake chatted with the shoreline, punctuating its pleasure in wavelets.

Otherwise there was solid silence.

Charlie got in the water first. Peter and Philip were not long after him. Susan waited for Liza to be ready. Noticing Liza's reticence, Charlie returned to help her over the stones into deeper water. Susan jumped in, shouting her glee. Once in the water, Liza gained confidence. She became daring and, leaving the others behind, headed out towards the middle of the lake. A gull circled overhead, the sun brightening the tip of its wings.

Charlie called Liza back towards the landing, "It's just as wet by shore."

Obedient by nature, Liza complied, but empowered with new strength, felt she could have gone further. Surely she could reach the horizon itself so long as there was enough water to hold her.

At length, the children scrambled out on the rock-covered shore to dry off before eating their provisions.

"We should have brought more," complained Philip.

"I think a rock is nicer for drying out than the beach," said Liza.

"I agree." This from Charles.

By the time they got back in the row boat, Liza's new found strength had mellowed into a healthy, happy, tiredness. She was grateful that Charlie's rolled-up sleeves exposed a pair of brown arms that showed no sign of fatigue. He plied the oars steadily. She did not realize that she was neglecting her duty with the rudder. Perhaps her subconscious knew it didn't matter.

For all of them it was early to bed that night.

Liza slept soundly and woke with the birds, ready for new adventures, only to be confronted at breakfast by Buppa announcing: "All good things must come to an end. I've made arrangements with Captain Beasley to take us on board tomorrow morning," turning to Caroline Drayton he added, "I do thank you. The change of air has done wonders for us both. I'm especially happy that Liza has been able to be a child again. You can't know how much she needed this vacation."

Liza suddenly realized that her happiness in Muskoka had eclipsed concerns about her mother and her sisters left at home in Toronto. Feeling guilty, she made no comment about her father's dictum, but stoicaily remarked, "We'll have to rise early tomorrow." Then she added her warm thanks to Mrs. Drayton for the way in which she and her father had been taken in like members of the family.

"You must find a way to come back. I'm sure your mother and the girls would like Muskoka too," insisted Caroline.

Hunchback

Frank Webster had just finished painting the window trim on his newest cottage when his wife, Emily, appeared, carrying a pile of blankets on her arm.

"I thought they were bringing their own bedding."

"Yes, but I said we'd have a few blankets and some pillows. Have you put the mattresses in yet?"

"Only the small ones. Can you help me with the big one?... Tell me, again... the name... Smith?... Jones?"

"No, Brown; and they have five daughters."

"The second bedroom is small. Will they all fit?"

"The youngest is small and can use the cot in her parents' room. One will be staying with the Draytons."

"I'm glad our cottages are so popular with city people. We should build more."

"Don't forget that your father is coming on the same steamer. He'll want to go sailing right away."

"Yes, I know. He's probably annoyed to be arriving this late in the season. I want to put a second coat of paint on the boat. Then he can help me launch and rig it... oh look, Emily, there are some shavings and old leaves in this new cabin. Could you go over the floor again with your broom?"

Charlie Drayton was on hand to meet the steamer which landed seven Browns and one Webster at Hunchback. He had orders to transport Sally, the second eldest Brown daughter, back to Drayton Farm. The summer visit would be a trial period to see if she would like to stay all winter.

Charlie saw Liza first, not Sally. With something like a shiver down his spine he realized that in the three years since he had last seen her Liza had become a young lady.

Her face alight in recognition, Liza came towards him.

"Charlie, please thank your mother for inviting me to come to Drayton Farm. I would love to stay there but my own mother can't do without me yet. I'm sure Sally will be helpful. She knows how to do everything and she's a very cheerful person."

"If she's half as nice as you, Mother will love her... Oh, yes, Mother said to invite all of you for dinner tomorrow noon."

"Thank you... Will I be able to check on the chickens and lambs? Can we go swimming at Little Bluff? I've made proper bathing costumes for all of us."

Liza's face fell as she remembered swims with Susan, Charlie's sister.

In a softer voice she said, "I was so sorry to hear about Susan. She seemed so well when we were here before. What happened?"

Her question hung unanswered for a few seconds. Charlie's hazel eyes were confronting her again, this time with a steadiness that seemed to invite consolation.

"Our Muskoka summers are one thing," he began, "our winters, quite another. She stepped on a rusty nail last September and her foot became infected. Mother and Betty cleaned and bathed the wound often but some infection remained. They tried bleeding her but she just became weak. Poor girl, she tried not to complain. Then she caught cold and it turned to pneumonia. She had no strength to resist."

They were interrupted by Matthew's approach and greeting. Soon all seven Brown's surrounded Charlie, exchanging greetings. Matthew invited Charlie to come with them to inspect the Webster cottage that would be their home for the next six weeks.

The next three weeks were a jumble of good times. Sally happily took over Susan's role with the chickens and lambs. Matilda plunged into berry picking treks and cliff climbing with Peter and Phillip. Whether at Hunchback, Drayton Farm, or Little Bluff, Annie found much to stimulate her vision and activate her paint brush. She produced several water colours. Belle tagged along with whoever would include her.

Matthew divided his time between fishing and having long talks with Joseph Drayton.

Gardening was a great bond between the two of them. Polly was happy to be reunited with her friend Caroline. They enjoyed their almost daily visits at Drayton Farm. The whole Brown family enjoyed swims and meal times every day. Annie was eating much better here than in the city; indeed they all seemed to have developed enormous appetites.

Liza was immensely satisfied to observe her beloved mother and sisters gaining in health and happiness.

Liza Brown and Charlie Drayton often were together when his farm duties permitted. One day when their families were picnicking on the grassy flat by Little Bluff Charlie asked Liza not to join the younger members on an exploration of the area behind the bluff.

"Please, let's sit here on the rock and watch the waves. I have something to tell you."

"All right. It's too soon after eating to go swimming again."

"Liza, you know John and I have been writing letters to each other. He's not totally satisfied with his job in Toronto at Perkins' Furniture Store. He doesn't have Father's interest in fine furniture but felt at least one Drayton should be in commerce to help support the family."

"What would he rather do?"

"Farming. Without telling any of us, he's been taking courses in Agriculture at the University. He even took the train a few times to hear lectures at the new campus in Guelph. In his most recent letter he told me he's been offered a position in a small shipping firm in the United States. Mr. Perkins has an English business connection whose growing business in New Orleans needs an accountant. Mr. Perkins would be glad to recommend John. John proposes that I go instead."

"You!"

"I'm going to Toronto tomorrow and to the South as soon as arrangements can be made. There's a need for someone right away, to learn the ropes before the busy fall season begins."

They talked at length about his plans, Liza trying to keep calm. John would come home to take over Charlie's responsibilities at Drayton Farm. The best part was that the shipping business usually was slack during June and July. Charlie could look forward to spending his summers in Muskoka.

"New Orleans? Isn't that the place that had those dreadful yellow fever epidemics?"

"Yes, but that was long ago. They don't expect any more outbreaks.

The city's cleaner since it's been modernized."

The young explorers' return interrupted Charlie and Liza's dialogue. It also heralded swim time. Places to change were assigned in one direction for men, another area for women. Liza helped Annie and Belle into their bathing clothes and later supervised them in the water. Charlie kept his brothers, the twins, from pushing or splashing too much. He suspected Tilda was taunting them into this mischief but he thought some decorum should be maintained.

After everyone had been thoroughly refreshed from their exercise in the lake, Charlie and Liza, sitting on a rock to dry off, got a chance to continue their conversation.

"Liza," Charlie paused, searching for the right words.

What could he, an unestablished young man say to this sixteen-year old lady?

"Yes?"

"When I make my fortune, I'm coming back to buy that sailboat. I haven't forgotten my promise to take you sailing."

"I'd like that," this time she was able to look steadily into his hazel eyes.

The next morning when Charles Roberts Drayton boarded the Medora, he took with him this memory of Liza's grey-blue eyes.

Sally

SALLY BROWN SPENT NOT ONLY THAT SUMMER, but as well the following three winters at Drayton Farm. Caroline Drayton, having grieved over the death of their daughter Susan, had readily accepted her husband's suggestion of a 'companion' for her. Sally took over care of the chickens, counting the eggs carefully each day, not a hard job when, at first, even one egg was cause for rejoicing. Caroline always recorded the egg count in the family diary, an account that documented an increasing flock year by year.

Sally, less serious and more fun-loving than her older sister, was as skillful as Liza in the domestic arts. She took over the Drayton mending pile. Using the latest batch of ballroom finery sent from England by Cousin Mary Roberts, Sally added such refinements as curtains and decorative cushions to the Drayton home. Betty Tullis taught Sally how to make bread; Sally soon surpassed her teacher in the art.

Each year some of Sally's adolescent awkwardness left her. She became more poised and her homely, freckled, pixie face developed into one of striking beauty. Her four sisters seemed to have been made out of the same mold, but Sarah Lynne Brown had a style all her own. Joseph Drayton observed Sally's development, making note of her favourable features in the family diary. He also noted that John Raeburn came to visit Drayton Farm more frequently after Sally joined their household. Sally was sensible to John Raeburn's attentions but it was John Drayton she favoured.

John Drayton's friendship with Sally Brown blossomed into a marriage proposal. Following a simple wedding he and Sally moved into a partly built new home up the hill to the south and about a third of the way between Drayton Homestead and Little Bluff. John himself had created the house, with some help from his brothers and from his father's hired man. As for Sally, she had done much holding, picking up, and running to fetch. John, the only Drayton who intended to make his living by farming, took over the bulk of his father's land. Joseph settled shore lots for Phillip and for Peter, side by side, to the north of the original homestead. Charles was allotted some rocky acreage to the south, beyond the Little Bluff property.

Each summer, Charles Drayton returned home from New Orleans for his vacation, much of which he spent with the Brown family. He was doing well in the South and was able to help keep Philip and Peter in a Toronto boarding school. As yet he had no sailboat.

Any or all of the Brown sisters were happy to accompany Charles for outings in one of his row boats. Little Bluff was the site of several picnics. In berry season, the young people ventured as far as Needles Point. Over the years they continued to explore neighbouring islands and points of land.

Act One

In the spring of 1885, Matthew Brown was ready to start his own Muskoka summer home. Frank Webster, now considered a worthy builder, agreed to oversee the work.

As Frank, himself, said, "I know many ways not to build. Experience teaches that much."

Mr. Drayton had been happy to sell his friend four acres he considered unsuitable for farming. The Brown purchase included Little Bluff and the flat landing place which shortly became known as Brown's Landing. Under the agreement, the Draytons could still cut and stack firewood on the landing to sell to the steam boats.

The Draytons also would build a large steamer wharf for the benefit of both families.

Under Webster's direction, workmen came and went. Captain Beasley carried messages between Webster and the sawmill. Sometimes his steamer brought supplies.

More often, a little steamboat named the *Ella Alice* towed a scow loaded with lumber for the building site. Weather conditions often interrupted construction but, by haying time, the foundation was complete and supported a two-storey skeleton of two-by-sixes.

Both chimneys were in place. The house could not progress further until every settler's hay was snugly tucked into all available storage places.

Haying season was whenever the hay was ripe and the sun, ready to shine. If a sunny spell did not last long enough, the cut hay had to wait for the next dry spell when the process of turning, drying and re-stacking would start again. Thus it was that during a good August hot spell, men became slaves to their hay for the sake of their animals who, after all, spent most of their time working for the men. No one questioned this agricultural tyranny. Every able bodied man or lad simply got on with the job, neighbour helping neighbour, bearing up against the heat as best they could.

The women supported haying operations with hearty, collective meals. Sometimes a rake or a harness, a pot or a plate went missing, but generally it turned up whenever and wherever the need was greatest.

It was the end of August before any men were ready to resume work on Mr. Brown's house. By this time Polly (Mary Lynne Brown) had suggested the name "Lynnehurst" after the Lynne ancestral home in Hampshire.

September that year was blessed with more than its usual quota of wonderful golden days. Early morning mists shrouded the lake and low lying land areas, protecting all with an immense stillness. Then, as if ordered by some unseen stage manager, the wispy whiteness would lift and dispel itself into nowhere. A world of modest wonderment and serene silence lay revealed upon Muskoka's stage.

Often, Frank Webster and his dog, in the Webster row boat on course to Lynnehurst, were the only audience. Frank was not insensible to surrounding beauties. He enjoyed watching his boat's wake disturb the lake's glassy surface. The morning bird songs cheered him and the sun's warmth felt good on his back.

How fortunate I am, he thought, *I have my back to the sun both coming and going.*

The arrival of the workers at Lynnehurst, heralded by raucous cawing in the old oak, seemed to tell the lake it was time to get moving. Breezes danced out from each bay, making grey-blue streaks on the lake. Before noon, the lake was alive with dancing waves. The men, too, quickened their pace. Noises of saw and hammer advertised their activities to anyone around and across the lake. Each day followed a similar pattern. Plank by plank, the walls grew. The roof went faster. Windows and doors took longer. It was a pleasure to work like this; no mosquitoes to slap off or bites to scratch, lots of invigorating air to breathe and always, the satisfaction of creating an edifice that was intended to endure the tests of time. Only the crows seemed unhappy.

Ten year old Alfred Beasley considered himself most fortunate to be part of the crew. This was more exciting than any childhood game he'd ever known. Mind you, the Christmas Drama that his teacher father had written and directed had stirred his imagination. He had loved the jovial faces and vigourous hand clapping of the community audience crowded together in the one room school house; but this Lynnehurst drama was real and would continue, even after the house was complete.

Alfred was too young to know that no house is ever "finished" or that modifications, improvements, extensions and repairs go on and on. Alfred vowed within himself to visit Lynnehurst every summer of his life. He would grow up to be a builder. Perhaps he would build greater places but always he would return to this place and applaud. For him, it was Act One.

One especially golden day, the workers were there in full quota spurred on by a cold touch to the air as well as by the feeling that the job was nearing completion.

Everyone wanted to witness the finish. It went without saying that they shared a great pride in their achievement. Only Alfred felt sad. He was not ready to stop. Just then, a mournful hoot split the air. A chorus of cawing crows responded as the workers stopped hammering, lifted their paint brushes, and turned to watch the Ella Alice emerge round Point Caroline, a load of lumber atop her trailing scow. Clearly, someone had miscalculated.

Frank Webster placed his left hand over his mouth, a sign that his mind was considering something. The men, sensing Frank's state of embarrassment, politely resumed activity. Frank thought of blaming a Beasley message taker but dismissed that as unfair. Could he blame the mill for a misunderstanding? Would Mr. Brown notice an extra pile of lumber and question an added cost to the bill? In the end, Frank decided to accept the blame and try to work out a solution later.

By the time the little steam tug had brought her load alongside, Frank, followed a few steps behind by Alfred and the Webster dog, had sauntered deliberately down to the landing to engage in a cheerful exchange of greetings. Local news, opinions and weather prophecies were exchanged. Helping hands transferred the lumber ashore.

Alfred Beasley knew at such times his job was to keep out of the way and to listen.

"Your house is coming along pretty good, ain't she?"

"Yes, thanks, we're nearly done."

"Sorry we didn't get this to you sooner but we had to wait 'til Chadwick's order was ready, so as to make only one trip this way."

"That so? Well now, how is the Chadwick place progressing?"

"It's something wonderful to behold; three stories high in the center with a two-story wing to one side, ya' know. Some of this here lumber was for the inside, all planed smooth for panelling, ya' know. The missus there has fancy ideas. She wanted what she calls a conservatory room put right beside the dining room. Don't know where young Chadwick gets his money."

"No, nor where he'll get it in the future," added another voice. "He plans to raise race horses. Who's gonna buy them things around here?"

Presently the Ella Alice pushed off and, with a friendly toot, headed back down the lake.

The Lynnehurst workers came and stood around Frank, but at a sympathetic distance.

Finally, Mr. Jacob spoke out: "Don't Mr. Brown want an ice house?"

"Well now, it could be ... but there's enough of this lumber for three ice houses."

"How about a boat house?" offered Ted Beasley, Alfred's bachelor uncle.

"Summer people like boats. I think they use them more than settlers do."

"Mr. Brown didn't say anything about a boat house and I don't know where he'd like it."

"The best place would be back in the corner there; wouldn't need much crib work. We could find a couple of logs easy enough and a few stones. Most of it would be on the shore anyway. It'd last a hundred years in that spot. The ice shove can't reach it."

So it happened that they made a decision for Mr. Brown. While the good weather lasted, an ice house and a boat house quickly went up.

Uncle Ted told Alfred to fetch stones for the crib work. "We don't need too many big ones like I used for your father's dock," he explained, "That was deep water. Small rocks will do nicely here."

"I can lift big ones!"

"Don't lift big ones. Your back isn't fully formed yet. You don't want to make a cripple of yourself for life. No bigger than this," commanded Uncle Ted, lifting a sample size for inspection.

"Yes, sir," was the disappointed reply. Alfred, doing as he was told, soon was happily scouting the shore and the wooded area for stones.

Frank, meanwhile, took his rifle and headed toward the crow-oak.
"If you were my crows," he shouted, "I'd shoot every last one of you."
Pow, went the rifle, *Pow, pow.*
Caw, Caw, Caw, came the response.
Frank was not a good shot.

༄

A month later, Frank's note to Matthew Brown said simply:

> Dear Sir,
> Your house, ice house and boathouse are complete
> as per instructions. I enclose the invoices and the hours
> of work. The scraps of lumber are piled on your front
> porch. You have enough for cupboards and shelves.
> Sorry to hear that your wife's illness prevents you
> from coming to see for yourself.
> Emily and I and the young one are well. Please
> give our regards to Mrs. Brown and the young ladies.
>   Yours Truly,
>   Frank R. Webster

"There," said Frank to Emily as he signed his name with a flourish. "I said, as per instructions, but I didn't say whose instructions."

"Mr. Brown is a reasonable man, dear. I'm sure he'll be glad of the extras. Did you suggest we would get some sawdust for his ice house when we get ours and the Drayton's?"

"That's a good idea. I'll add a postscript. John Drayton and Joseph's man can help us cut some ice for the Browns, too."

Annie

It was Annie's health more than Polly's that concerned the Brown family that winter. She had always been the frail one but now, more than ever. They knew she was often in pain and guessed that it was so, more frequently than she let on. At Bishop Strachan's School, the teachers noticed her inability to concentrate. History, English Grammar, and Latin were complete losses. Mathematics was sometimes excellent and at other times, not.

Only in Art class was Annie really able to achieve. The mistresses agreed to let her remain there most of the morning. Her sketching showed promise but she loved water colours the best. She liked Religious Instruction and Catechism too, but they were scheduled in the afternoons which she often missed, being too weary to return to school after noon time family meal at home.

One evening after tea, Matthew noticed that Annie seemed not only sad but was positively shuddering. Polly said that Annie had been upset all afternoon.

"Little one, what is disturbing you?"

"Oh Buppa, I have sinned and will spend eternity being burned."

"My dear child, God can forgive you, but I can't imagine when you could have committed any heinous sin." He reached a hand out to console.

"I thought evil things about Maria at school today and it says thoughts are as bad as deeds."

Handing Matthew a little pamphlet, Polly interrupted, "She has been reading this tract."

"A man came to visit Catechism class yesterday and gave each of us one of those."

Matthew turned the pages over thoughtfully. Presently he spoke to the waiting wife and daughter:

"My dear, this was written by worthy people but it was not intended for you. Do you believe that I love you?"

"Yes."

"Well then, I tell you God loves you a thousand times more. He knows you are sorry for any mis-doings. Would such a God let you burn?"

"No, Buppa." But Annie was quavering as she spoke. Her sensitive soul caught the tone of vexation in him even though Matthew tried to speak calmly. She wondered if Buppa was bad too. Wasn't there something about a wolf in sheep's clothing?

Annie was too old now to be tucked in or to have her prayers 'heard' by anyone. Nevertheless, Polly felt Annie should have a bed time visit on this occasion.

"Are you still worried, Annie?"

"Mother, I know I'm going to die soon. Maybe there' ll be sin in me when I do."

"Jesus told us there is nothing to fear. We trust him."

"But I must do something about my sin. What must I do? Polly was stunned by such a question. Liza, who had joined them, spoke.

"Annie, I think you should pray for Maria. Mother and I will pray for you."

Polly looked at her oldest daughter. No wings or halo were apparent. It was just Liza standing there. Then quietly, Polly found herself saying, "I will pray for you, Annie, every day."

There were kisses and hand pattings. Finally, Annie's head sank peacefully to her pillow.

෴

Dr. Rosseter confessed that he could do little more for Annie, "Her health has deteriorated over the years. We have no skill to stop that. The best thing would be to take her to the country for fresh air and good food."

"Would bodily exercise help?"

"If she feels like it. Let her do whatever she wants."

"How long do you think she will live?"

"I don't know. If she were an older person, I would say not more than a year. Annie's youth is against her... that is, she will have longer to suffer. I don't want to start her on morphine too soon. Here is some chloral hydrate, if she needs something to help her sleep at night."

Brown's Landing

THEY HARDLY NEEDED ANNIE'S HEALTH AS AN EXCUSE to head for Muskoka early the next Spring. Matthew went up during the Easter break with some household furnishings they had culled from the attic, from second hand sales and from kind friends. Matthew felt a twinge of pride when he bought his train and steamer ticket. The destination read "Brown's Landing"!

Sally and John were there soon after the steamer landed. They had heard the toot.

"How was your trip?"

"You don't look tired at all."

"Here, I'll give you a hand with some of these things."

"We've been over the last three days to light fires so the worst of the chill is off the house. but you can stay at our place if you prefer."

"Thank you, the journey went well. The only mistake was buying a cup of tea at Allendale. Those people don't even try to make anything taste good there. But let us not dwell on that."

They chuckled sympathetically.

"The best part of the whole trip," he continued, "was coming round Point Caroline. Suddenly, there was Lynnehurst, just as I had imagined it. It's a miracle!"

Matthew stayed that night with Sally and John and next morning over breakfast enjoyed a good chat in their warm kitchen. As soon as a little box stove was installed in Lynnehurst's kitchen, he wanted to be in his own place as much as possible.

He made two double beds out of some of the left over lumber and screwed the pieces together securely. It was a very basic design embellished only with a quick coat of yellow paint.

"If fortune allows," he told himself, "we'll replace these with proper beds; in the meantime…"

"Meantime" proved to be a long time. In fact, those first two beds were still being used by Brown descendants one hundred years later!

Matthew constructed a single bed to fit the good mattress he had brought with him for Annie. Belle could use the canvas cot. Meticulously, Matthew made a list of items the ladies could bring when they came in May. Back in Toronto, Polly was making a list also. Neither list contained the word 'curtain'. In the middle of the woods, who needs curtains? Furthermore, it would be an insult to the Creator to block out even one square inch of nature's beauty that greeted occupants at each window.

John Drayton showed Matthew how to convert an empty packing case into an ice chest.

"You'll need some sawdust 'round the block of ice to slow the melting Then you place the milk and butter here, close by. Eggs would be all right over there. Mind you, some people use two crates, a small one for food inside a larger one in the sawdust. That makes your ice last longer."

"I don't need an ice chest now. The pantry's cool enough."

"True, but you'll need one in the summer. Remember how hot July can be!"

Matthew's ten days at Lynnehurst went all too quickly.

☙

Back at the college, Matthew found himself daydreaming frequently. Sometimes, he did not hear questions his pupils asked. Often, they had to repeat themselves.

The next trip north was made by the six Brown women, including Belle, the only one still in school. Belle didn't mind leaving her studies early. Matthew stayed behind in Toronto to finish the school term.

Liza had much on her mind during the train ride to Gravenhurst. She thought back to her first trip and noticed all the changes since then. Passing settlements had grown into small towns and villages. More wooded areas had been chewed away by axe and cross cut saw, leaving open areas and rough fields. Older fields looked quite tame with neat rows ready for wheat, corn and vegetables. She loved the tidy kitchen gardens near each homestead. Everyone had lilac in clumps or hedges, often near an outhouse. Rhubarb and chives were visible already. Narcissus were showing in clumps and several wooded areas were carpeted in white trillium. Around many of the isolated farm houses there were cultivated flowers.

Muskoka granite north of the Severn River still marked a dramatic change in the landscape. Seeing the invincible shield rock charged Liza with a feeling of security, a feeling she welcomed, for not only was the view out the train window full of transition, so was her life. Would she love Lynnehurst as much as Buppa seemed to, or would she be upset because a portion of those dark and wonderful woods had been destroyed?

Would Little Bluff and the Landing hold the same magic for her if she lived with them every day?

Just as her first trip to Muskoka had been like the beginning of a new life, would Liza find this trip another new beginning or, perhaps, an ending? Would it be the end of her childhood and youth? On her next birthday, she would be twenty-three and not married.

The thought of spinsterhood occupied Liza's thoughts for several more miles.

Mother didn't need her so much any more. Matilda was very capable. Annie seemed better. She should be learning to be responsible. Perhaps John and Sally would have children one day. They might welcome help with their household and farm. Perhaps she might live with them.

Thinking about these possibilities made Liza realize how much she missed Sally. The thought of seeing her favourite sister again brightened her mood. Another enlivening thought was that Charlie Drayton had written Buppa to ask permission to store his new canoe in the Brown boathouse. The ice shove last spring had badly damaged the Drayton Boathouse. John and Mr. Drayton had pulled the rowboats out the back door to safety just in time. Clearly, Drayton Beach was a vulnerable location.

Charlie's canoe would be delivered in June in time for his holidays in July. He hoped the Browns would try the canoe themselves before he arrived.

At Gravenhurst, Liza's thoughts were interrupted by the hustle and bustle of people and the transferring of bundles and trunks from train to steamer.

At Port Carling the Browns watched the process of "locking through."

Then, at Port Sandfield, Liza watched from the foredeck as passengers disembarked for the new hotel. To Liza's eyes Prospect House looked naked. She missed the slain trees.

The Brown ladies became quite talkative for the rest of the lake trip, staying on deck so as not to miss the first glimpse of their new domain. At last they drew near.

"There's Needles Point."

"There's Chadwick Bay."

"The Chadwick's house must be right at the end. I can't see it."

"Buppa says it's a mansion, but he hasn't seen it either."

Suppressed silence.

"Point Caroline!"

"No it isn't."

"Yes it is. Over there... not there!"

The steamer's toot drowned out their clamour as around the point, Lynnehurst burst into sight.

"It's unbelievable!"

"It looks like it belongs there."

"Is it really ours?" asked Belle.

Tucked in beside Little Bluff, their new home nestled among the trees, as if it had always been there. It was a typical two-story country house with an open porch on the front. Above, the second story boasted three windows, all facing westward toward the lake. Liza gazed with love in her heart.

The west wind raised waves that were bright blue and brisk. Knowles Webster, out in his sailboat, seemed to be daring the bigger boat to change course. He knew the rules. Sailboats always had the right of way. Just as Annie started to scream, the little white dingy went about-ship, dashing northward and well away.

The big wharf was not yet built. Brown's Landing had a make-shift jetty to keep the steamer in deep water. The crew cast ropes around trees to steady the boat while people, bundles and trunks were trundled across a gangplank onto the grassy landing.

John Drayton was out in the field with the horses but Sally was there at the Landing. Joseph Drayton and young Philip were soon on hand to assist. The Browns and Draytons were not demonstrative people. Adults did not kiss or hug each other.

Their joy at reunion was expressed in lively converse. Belle danced around, tripping over luggage, demanding attention from everyone. Soon Liza was totally absorbed in family chatter, asking about everything. She had many things to tell dear Sally. She and Sally each picked up a small load and headed toward the house, tongues wagging all the way.

As usual, Annie held back. Philip, who had been teasing Matilda about her good looks, noticed Annie alone and went over to her. He coaxed a little conversation out of her as he picked up a nearby bag to carry. She, clutching her paint box and portfolio of paper, followed.

The men made several trips between landing and house while the women unwrapped themselves and located bedrooms. In the dining room Sally had spread a cold collation on a makeshift table of planks mounted on saw horses. She had a big pot of soup and a kettle on the box stove. A pail of drinking water stood nearby.

After a period of settling in everyone was ready to gather around the festive board. John Drayton joined them. Not everyone had a chair. Matthew's bench held four Brown sisters. Belle fit nicely on a stool. The men stood or perched on boxes.

Soup was issued in either a mug or a bowl with enough spoons to go around. It was Lynnehurst's first happy banquet. There were many more to come.

Daisies

In June Matthew Brown arrived from Toronto to join his women folk. By July, Lynnehurst was looking like home. Two rocking chairs had been found for the front porch. A hammock swayed gently between two porch posts. A Matthew Brown picnic table with it's accompanying benches occupied one end of that same west-facing porch. Now that the mosquito population had diminished, they could eat their meals out there. Polly still fretted about flies and other airborne visitors. On windless days, dishes of food had to be covered with lids; milk and cream jugs were festooned with cloth doilies.

One perfect evening, just as they had finished cleaning up after tea, Belle rushed into the house on her way back from the out house, a place she always managed to need during dish-washing time.

"Here comes Charlie Drayton. He wants to try out his new canoe."

Charles Drayton had arrived the day before and was staying with his parents.

Belle dashed off to freshen up and fetch her wrap. Presently, Polly noticed Liza, Charlie and Belle headed for the boat house. Polly and Matthew both wondered if Charlie had really invited Belle to be part of the expedition. They did not have to wonder long. Shrieks from Belle could be heard as she re-appeared, sopping wet.

"I fell between the dock and the canoe," she wailed. Charlie said I must learn to be more careful, but I was being careful ... really I was. Why did he laugh at me?"

Knowing looks were exchanged around the family circle. Tilda took a long time helping her little sister get into dry clothes but, at last, she could restrain her no longer. Belle once more went skipping over stones and around trees along the route that later became a wide and well-worn path to the lake. All too shortly, she was back expressing her juvenile wrath in wails and words.

"They didn't wait for me! Why didn't they wait for me?"

Matthew, who had seen the canoe disappear around Point Caroline, said nothing.

Annie, who was with him, spoke. "It's such a lovely evening. I wish I could reproduce those gentle colours with my paint brush. How can I know what I'm seeing when they move and change imperceptibly all the time? I want to capture them and the feeling of peace they produce."

"I think you should try, dear," said Polly, "Belle, you run and get Annie's paints and paper. I'll find a piece of paper for you too; you both can try."

Belle rallied to the challenge. The porch became an art studio as the two sisters worked at the picnic table. There was still enough light for them and for Matilda, who was reading *Pilgrim's Progress* while lying in the hammock. Polly took her needlework to a rocker but her hands remained motionless while her eyes fed upon the peaceful scene.

Meanwhile, Charlie Drayton had found a perfect little cove along the south-facing shore. He let his paddle trail idly in the water. Liza was seated, facing him on a cushion and leaning against a wooden back-rest supported by the middle thwart. They could not see the sunset from there but the reflection of it on the lake's surface, coupled with the interesting play of evening light on the far shore, were romantic enough for Charlie's purposes. He was not as sure of his position with Liza as he had been earlier, but the time had come to speak. She was avoiding his eyes, appearing to be absorbed in the surrounding loveliness.

"Liza," he ventured at last, "I know this isn't the sailboat I promised, but that will come in time. You know I helped father send the twins to the College."

Liza said nothing. Emotions of joy and expectation welled up inside her but fear of being mistaken strangled her voice.

Charlie paused, groping for direction.

"Liza, I've always admired you since the time you and your father first visited Drayton Farm... even before that, in Toronto... when you were a tiny girl... Liza, stop me if I'm on the wrong tack. The fact is I love you, love you very much... but I've heard that there is a young school master that visits the Brown home often and... oh Liza, tell me."

She had never seen him so unsure of himself. Usually he was the one in control. Perceiving his discomfort, her fear left her.

"Charlie," her voice, barely audible, was steady. "I will do anything you ask. Please ask me."

A canoe is a romantic craft, but there are times when it is predicament more than enhancement. The best she could do was to lean forward and reach out a hand.

They were conservative people and lived in conservative times, but he yearned to do more than just hold that precious hand and kiss the fingertips.

At Lynnehurst, the light finally grew dim. The family abandoned the porch and went inside. Belle, reluctantly, went to bed. Her worries that something dreadful was happening in Charlie's canoe kept her awake for only half an hour. Polly, Tilda and Annie voiced concern to one another but were not truly worried. Matthew did not even pretend to be concerned.

"Charlie may have a lantern with him or, if not, he knows enough to stay close to the shore."

"Yes, that's true."

"I'll wait up for them like a proper father. I have a good book to keep me company."

"That would be good. I'll get a kerosene lamp for you and if you sit by the window, they'll notice the light."

"Thank you, my dear..."

It was quite dark when the happy couple appeared. Charles apologized to Matthew for causing concern. Explanations followed. In the end, they had gone as far as Needles Point, telling themselves the sunset could be viewed better from there.

They also had taken the opportunity to plan their entire lives, providing Buppa's consent could be obtained. The only question remaining was whether the wedding should be that coming September or next July when the daisies would be in bloom again. With Matthew's encouragement, they decided on September.

As Charlie pointed out, "we can always celebrate our engagement with daisies. We will start a new tradition... engagement anniversaries rather than wedding anniversaries."

On Saturday, September 12, 1885, Holy Trinity Church, in the heart of Old Toronto, was comfortably filled with friends and relatives to witness the Marriage of Miss Elizabeth Mary Brown to Mr. Charles Roberts Drayton. Sarah Lynne (Brown) Drayton was Matron of Honour, preceded by the Misses Matilda and Anne Brown as Bridesmaids, and Isobelle Violet Brown as Flower Girl. John Reginald Drayton was Best Man. The newlyweds left immediately for New Orleans where Mr. Drayton had recently purchased a home in the Garden District.

On July 2nd, the next summer, Liza and Charlie, still known as the bride and groom, found themselves dividing their holiday time between Old Drayton Farm and Lynnehurst, Muskoka. Charlie went out into the fields and gathered a large bunch of daisies which he presented to Liza, as promised, an attention he continued to give for the next forty-two Julys.

Belle picked daisies too. Tilda helped her braid them into a circlet with which, at teatime, Liza was crowned by her sisters in Lynnehurst.

Years later, the grandchildren would gather daisies for Granny Liza on July 2nd, the anniversary of her engagement. Even today, daisies are a cherished reminder to some descendants of Charlie and Liza.

LYNNEHURST
BOOK II
Her Seasons of Summer

Golden Years

CHARLES DRAYTON'S BUSINESS EFFORTS in the American south bore results. After four years as an accountant with the English firm, he established his own business, C.R. Drayton & Company. He and Liza were blessed with children, first Alan Matthew, and later two daughters, Mary Lynne and Doris Amelia.

Each summer Charlie and Liza took their family to Muskoka to vacation at Lynnehurst. They talked of building their own cottage on the south shore lot given to him by Charlie's father. Instead they purchased Lynnehurst, thus providing Matthew Brown with financial security in his retirement years.

Tilda's marriage to Tom Armstrong and Annie's death reduced the number of Browns at Lynnehurst to three: Matthew, Polly and Belle. This left room for Liza and Charlie, their three children, and frequent house guests.

A summer home is a joy forever, but it is also much work. Charlie enjoyed splitting wood for the stove and fireplace. He taught Alan to split kindling with a hatchet. In the fall the Websters cleared underbrush; in the winter they filled the ice house. In the summer, one of the Webster girls came to help out with kitchen and laundry chores. Liza had time to enjoy her children.

Between golden summers in Muskoka came winters almost as golden in New Orleans. There Liza benefitted from black Mammy's help with household duties and with care of the children.

Alan, Mary and Doris received education from various sources. Each had the experience of a dame school in the Garden District of New Orleans. At home they were included in the family's evening habit of reading aloud. Their father did most of the reading until Alan began to take his turn, at a young age. Liza endeavoured to combine this activity with instruction for the girls in handwork. Mary had no taste for sitting still but did learn to knit. When the book being read was of particular interest, her fingers ceased to function as her mind became totally absorbed.

Doris (or Dumpy as she was called) became the biggest bookworm of all. She also enjoyed learning to embroider, especially floral designs with delicate colours. The finished project, be it on a pillow slip, a garment, or a piece of table linen, would remind her of whatever book she had been listening to while sewing that item. Her memory was clear, controlled and nearly always accurate in detail.

The Draytons became accepted by the old Louisiana French more readily than many 'Yankee' families who had moved south after the Civil War. Madame Renee Du Bouvier often invited Charlie and Liza to her soirees at which most of the guests spoke French. These soirees included poetry reading, sometimes a musical presentation, and always appreciation of the classics. When someone offered an original composition, be it a play, an essay, or a musical selection, it was politely received. Only if criticism was invited by the composer, was it graciously and intellectually provided, not otherwise. Above all, the art of felicitous conversation was practised both in English and French, a skill that impressed the Draytons.

As they grew older, Mary and Dumpy were included in these soirees. Madame took a special interest in her youthful Canadian friends. At first she was horrified that the girls' straight hair was cut short. Practical Liza wanted to make it easier for them to keep their hair clean and free of lice. Madam Renee took on the task of instructing the Draytons in the art of hair care. She urged Mary and Doris to use one of her recipes for the control of 'babites' and to massage their scalps by sliding the skin back and forth in circular movements over each section of the skull. Madame believed this exercise would enhance the healthy growth of their hair. Certainly, her own daughters had glorious waist-length, golden tresses which they wore piled high in elegant scoops. Mary did not have the patience to perform the elaborate massage techniques. She secretly thought that the Mesdamoiselles Du Bouvier's coiffures were so perfect because the daughters were endowed with thick, naturally wavy hair which was much easier to manage than the slippery, straight strands she and Dumpy had inherited.

Mary, who longed to have long hair. was granted this privilege at age twelve. She promised to brush one hundred strokes daily before making rolls each side of a central part. At first, the two rolls terminated in braids. Later, the braids became looped and were adorned with bows of stiff taffeta ribbon. Later, the braids criss-crossed Mary's head like a crown, and eventually she abandoned braids in favour of one single knot at the back of her head.

Dumpy paid careful attention to Madame Renee's advice. She shampooed and massaged meticulously and brushed the prescribed one hundred strokes. Through the years she followed the same phases of hair styling as her older sister. When Dumpy reached the looped braid stage, Madame Renee regarded her critically one day and sighed:

"You have les yeux beaux and good features of the face. If only you had the hair, you would be fabulous. Alas, you have brains. That will have to suffice."

To this, Dumpy quickly responded, "Madame Renee, do you really think I am intelligent? Merci beaucoup. I always feel so ignorant, so stupid when we are at your soirees. Your friends know so much and are so clever."

"Nonsense child, you are more than bright. It is because you are young that you feel stupid. Mais, ma petite, do not rejoice in your brains; for a woman, they are no asset unless disguised. Men despise clever women, especially those who may be tempted to compete. I, myself, find competitive women unbecoming, so gauche... so uninstuit! You must appear fragile, tender, a little helpless if you wish to have a man adore you. Ah, ma petite, it is something wonderful when a man adores you."

Dumpy tactfully allowed a period of silence as Madame indulged in sweet memories. Messieur Du Bouvier had died but a few years previous.

Then, speaking thoughtfully, Dumpy announced: "Madame, I do not want a man unless I can adore him."

"That is nice, ma petite Doris, but not necessary. Even if your man is a silly goose, it is all right so long as he worships you. Your job is to make him feel he is the grandest gander of them all. Do you understand?"

"Not yet... but I am young," replied Dumpy, her blue eyes twinkling sweetly.

That same day, Dumpy confronted her sister and her mother with some of Madame's theories.

Liza soberly considered before offering her own thoughts, "Madame Renee knows a great deal, but her ways are not necessarily our ways. If you are seeking a husband, I think it is important for him to be someone who can be your friend every day of the week. I hope you will find romance as well as friendship, but friendship and trust are important and more lasting."

Mary Lynne decided to get a masculine opinion. As soon as her father came home, she approached him with: "Father, do men avoid women who have brains?"

Charles, newspaper in hand, was headed for his favourite chair. He answered quickly with a quote she was to hear many times, "Be kind, sweet maid, and let who will, be clever."

Alan remained aloof from his sisters' concerns. If he knew the answers to their questions, he never let on. Nor did he attend Du Bouvier soirees as often as they did.

He certainly had no hair problems. No one ever heard him admit difficulty learning to shave. By nature and inclination close to his mother, as a child Alan learned some of her domestic skills including embroidery, an interest he later gave up in favour of mathematical puzzles and amateur inventions. His own children were to become scientists and engineers, but Alan followed in his father's footsteps as an accountant, then a businessman.

New Orleans provided advantages for the Drayton family. As Alan, Mary and Doris grew up, their life was pleasant, easy and far from humdrum. However, all three agreed that summer in Muskoka was the best part of the year. They eagerly looked forward to the long train trip, broken briefly in Chicago and again in Toronto.

They especially loved the last part of the journey by steamer from Gravenhurst to Brown's Landing. At Port Carling, they would beg to get off and "help" the men turn huge screws that manoeuvered the lock gates. Alan helped by keeping out of the way.

He watched, observed, and remembered. The girls wanted to be involved. They knew that if "Old Mac" was on duty, he would let them hold a rope.

"My arthritis is bad today," he would say, "I need your help. Keep turning that rope. That's a girl."

At the same time, Mac would be bending his full muscle to the real work of twisting the heavy lock apparatus. His good humour was rewarded with a shy smile or a shriek of delight from his young helper.

There was one lock keeper who liked neither children nor inquisitive adults.

"Get out of the way!" he would growl, fearing an accident. When "Cranky Stan" was in charge, Mary Lynne and Dumpy would stay close to Alan or go back on board.

By the time the steamer reached Port Sandfield, the children were usually tired, content to lean on deck railings and watch summer guests move to and fro at Prospect House. Dumpy was fascinated by the long skirts swaying as women paraded on dock or grounds. Each year she focused on changes in fashion, noticing subtle differences in style between Louisiana and Muskoka.

Tired or not, all five Draytons would surge forward on deck when it was time to catch a glimpse of Needles Point. They knew then that the boat would soon approach Point Caroline and Lynnehurst. Dumpy always stole a glance in the opposite direction towards Chadwick Bay. Although it was not possible, sometimes she thought she saw Chadwick Manor with its air of mystery and its cool, damp walls. Would Henrietta Chadwick be looking out for a glimpse of the steamer? Dumpy and Henny were almost exactly the same age. Dumpy couldn't remember a time when they had not been best friends. In their pre-teen years, however, they usually felt an initial shyness each June when they met. Each had to measure the new height of the other in the mind's eye. Each wondered if the other still wanted to play the same games as the previous summer. Quietly, one or the other would make a gesture of renewed friendship. Arms linked, they would head for the barn if the reunion took place at Chadwicks or if at Lynnehurst, out to inspect Dumpy's jungle gym. Buppa Brown had made a wonderful set of contraptions on and between the maple trees beyond the parkland where the Lynnehurst hammocks hung. He felt a healthy alternative to reading was needed for Dumpy, his physically delicate grandchild.

As the steamer drew near Brown's Landing, Dumpy would be reliving her memories of the jungle gym or of Henny Chadwick when someone, generally Mary Lynne, would shout and wave as Lynnhurst came into view: "There it is, it's still there!"

Liza, her soft eyes gazing affectionately at their summer home, would say a silent prayer of thanksgiving. As the psalmist expressed it, her cup was full to overflowing... Liza felt duty-bound to express her appreciation for all the Divinity's blessings in connection with Lynnehurst and all of

Muskoka. Nothing else provoked wells of love within her so poignantly.

At Brown's Landing wharf, the big hull cruised to a parallel stop dockside. The children restrained themselves as they watched two huge ropes being thrown out and looped securely on iron bollards. As soon as the gangplank was laid down, the purser would help Liza. Although nimble enough to walk off by herself, she graciously permitted assistance while clinging securely to her knitting bag and shawl, all the time admonishing her children to be careful.

Masculine hands helped with the luggage. Trunks were serious business. They were large, filled with household items, pantry supplies and much clothing. Even summer clothes were bulky. The food order from Michie and Co. of Toronto would have arrived on an earlier steamer. The steamers were continually active, carrying people and supplies and making golden years for the Muskoka Lakes Navigation Company.

Once allowed to disembark, Alan, Mary Lynne and Dumpy would rush onto Brown's Landing wharf and into the arms of whichever relatives were gathered there to greet them. Grandmother Brown, short of breath and stiff with rheumatism usually saved her welcoming for their appearance in the house itself. But Buppa Brown was always on hand, his thick white curls and rosy complexion clearly identifiable even from a distance. There was competition to see which granddaughter would reach him first. Alan was sorry as he grew older that his grandfather's hugs gave way to a manly handshake. Aunt Belle Brown, a younger, feminine replica of Buppa, was often there as well. Farm work kept Uncle John Drayton from being part of the landing ceremony but Aunt Sally usually came, bringing her children, the Drayton cousins, Willie, Susan, Carolyn and, in later years, Bob, Regina and May. Aunt Tilda (Brown) Armstrong with attending young ones, a visiting Beasley, or a Webster often were there too.

For the family of Charles and Elizabeth Drayton these were Golden Years.

Jack Beasley and the Drum God

MOST PIONEER FAMILIES REMAINED IN MUSKOKA both winter and summer. Three Beasley brothers, forsaking a family law firm in London, England, had migrated to Canada. One became a steamer captain, a second worked in summer hotels. The third, Thomas Alfred Beasley, became a teacher of the young and a friend-in-need to the illiterate. He could be counted on as a source of cheer. Thomas married Mary Jane who had been reared in a backwoods log shanty. She was known for her practical help, especially in times of sickness. Although life wasn't easy for the Thomas Beasleys, Mary Jane managed their large family on a meagre income. Some people said she surpassed Thomas in intelligence.

One July eleventh, the eve of Orangeman's Day, the Beasley's youngest son, lay sprawled on his stomach, a wooden toy soldier clasped firmly in one outstretched hand. The sun's rays slanted through wavy glass panels in the parlor's french doors enlivening the maroons and dull browns of the faded oriental rug into scarlet and gold riches. Jack envisioned his soldiers' brave deeds. Yellow and orange clouds became crags and boulders high in the sky. Every cloud-niche held a cannon. In dark cloudcaves courageous horsemen on prancing steeds waited with lances at rest or sabres drawn, eager to gallop forth through forests of yellow gauze to charge to their death in the burning furnaces of the sun.

"Ted," whispered Jack to his toy soldier comrade in arms, "Can you see that big cloud riding high in the sky?... That's King Billy... and there's the fife I don't see the drum... Don't worry. It'll be there tomorrow."

Tomorrow would be the Glorious Twelfth. Jack knew the Sons of England marched to church twice a year, taking each of the three churches in turn. So did the Foresters. Those were occasions of no small importance, but were not to be compared to the Orangeman's Parade. Only the Orangemen had a proud banner with a figure of King Billy embroidered in gold and crimson. Only the Orangemen wore large, embroidered fronts covered with imposing figures and signs. In the Orange Parade each man wore an orange badge and a uniform cap with a gold band. Some of the men carried staffs bedecked with orange-yellow ribbons, poles that had been hewed out of solid pine many years earlier by the present grand master of the lodge, before there had been even one saw mill in the whole of Muskoka District.

To Jack, Orangeman's Day, was second only to Christmas. His father had said the Twelfth stood for freedom and the right to go to the church next door. Jack should never forget it.

His mother disturbed Jack's focus on the land of gold and sepia.

"Isn't the sunset beautiful tonight, so peaceful?" Mrs. Beasley was looking westward through the wavy glass of the french doors... Jack did not respond.

After a pause his mother moved closer, reaching for his hand, "Is this my little boy?"

"Yes Mummy, it's me," responded Jack dutifully.

She helped him up from the rug. Together they stood close to the window watching the golden clouds turn to brown and then to slate and twilight.

"It's time my boy was in bed," she said at last.

༺ღ༻

Next morning, Jack was awake and out of bed in the gray of dawn. The air was cool. He trembled as he hurried into his clothes. He could hear the men on the road going up to the Orange Hall. Jack's father Thomas was away with Jack's brother, Thomas, on a two-week fishing holiday at Slide Lake. His oldest brother, Alfred, was working on a job in Gravenhurst, but Jack knew that one of his brothers, Clarence, had left the house already and was at the Orange Hall to be part of the day's festivities.

Once downstairs, Jack headed to the kitchen to join the women of the family: his mother, his older sister Hannah and his baby sister, Sarah. He hurried through a breakfast of blueberries and milk. His mother handed him some of her freshly baked bread, thickly spread with fresh-churned butter and homemade strawberry jam. He took it gratefully and scooted out the back door. Mrs. Beasley followed him with her eyes as

Jack ran along the board walk to the pump. From there he picked his way carefully across the wet grass, disappearing amongst the rows of corn and pole beans. She followed his progress by the waving of green leaves, then waited for his head to appear as he clambered onto the roadside fence.

From this perch on the fencepost at the far corner of their lot, Jack could view the whole parade. He knew that it was the doctor who always rode in front and that it was old Crier who played the drum. Old Crier had played it every Twelfth for years.

The blacksmith carried the flag and Mr. McTavish played the fife. Most of the men were from the village, but there were one or two shanty boys come in from back in the bark woods or the hemlock ridges, happy to be part of the day's outing. After the parade to the village wharf, the steamer would take the men somewhere all day, returning in the dark, to march by starlight, albeit less smartly, back to the Orange Hall.

When Jack heard the weird trill of the fife followed by the bang, whang, whang of the drum, his heart leapt. The parade was coming straight toward him. The fife told the long-drawn hidden mystery of all that lay behind the rites and symbols of the occasion. Leading the parade the village doctor no longer rode his quiet dappled mare; he was a plumed and shining knight astride a noble steed. McTavish and the rest likewise were transformed into a stalwart throng of mighty defenders of the faith.

There on the banner was King Billy, flapping bravely above the marchers, a low cloud of dust rising from their pounding feet. The Drum God, itself at the end of the parade, boomed forth, boisterous, bombastic, defiant! Left, right, left, right, the Orangemen strode in front of Jack, then down the road past the blacksmith shop. It was a magic parade that gave Jack a link which he craved, an access to the past of which he felt an inseparable piece.

When the last marcher had disappeared down the hill, the fife and drum sounds faded in the distance. Jack listened for the toot of the steamer. Then, thoughtfully, he picked his way back to the house. Instinctively Jack knew he had nothing to say to his mother. She wouldn't understand the cult of the Drum God.

At Lynnehurst Matthew Brown also had risen early that day. He figured the fish would be biting and was headed toward his row boat with Alan and Mary in tow.

They heard drumming and raucous voices as the steamer came their

Lynnehurst

way, so they went to the big wharf.

"Is the boat coming in today?" asked Mary.

"I don't think so," Buppa replied, "but it's the Glorious Twelfth. Let's wave."

"The Twelfth?... What's that, Buppa?"

"Orangemen's Day," explained Alan.

"What's Orangemen's Day?"

"There are several answers to that question," said Buppa, "It is part of our history, but right now, I think it's a day for those hard working men to feel glorious. They will be regarded as heroes all day. I hope they enjoy it for they won't be home 'til after sunset. Tomorrow, each will go his own way again and become a hard working husband, father, brother or a lonely bachelor."

"Do they all really work hard, Buppa? Do you mean like Mr. Webster and Uncle John?"

"Yes, like that. People who live in Muskoka all year round don't last long if they become lazy. It takes work just to eat and keep warm all winter."

"We don't get cold in New Orleans."

"People down there don't know the meaning of that word. Even a Toronto winter is less severe than here. As long as your Buppa has a few dollars for coal, he can keep pretty snug in Toronto."

The steamer passed out of their sight.

Mary was trailing her grandfather and her brother Alan back to Buppa's boathouse, thinking as she went. She knew she didn't like very hot days but she wondered what real cold would feel like. Her cousin Willie had shown her his foot that got frozen last New Year's. He said it hurt badly at the time and still felt tingly.

"Buppa," she said loudly.

By this time Buppa and Alan had the boat floating in the water beside the dock.

"Yes, Mary?" Buppa motioned to Mary to get into the steering seat while he held the gunwales steady. Alan got in the bow unaided.

"When I grow up, I think I'll live in Toronto."

"Why Toronto?"

"It won't be too cold there. And as soon as the winter cold leaves Lynnehurst, I'll come here every spring, early, like you do."

"That's a good idea. I'll come with you and if I'm dead by then, you'll know I'm here in spirit."

Dumpy and the First Season of Summer

When Doris Amelia Drayton was a small child, she divided the year into two equal halves, summer and winter. As she grew in knowledge, she understood that even those years when she and her Mother left New Orleans in May, ahead of the others, and lengthened their stay at Lynnehurst to the end of September, that only added up to four months, as opposed to eight winter months. However, she stuck to her original theory by explaining that there was twice as much living in the months allotted to summer. Mary Lynne laughed at her for this grotesque logic but Buppa Brown said she was quite right.

Within summer, there were seasonal changes that stirred distinctly different feelings within Dumpy and dictated different activities. Blackfly season came first.

Old Reverend Mr. Withers preached that there was something good in everything.

Dumpy believed that God created blackflies to protect the delicate spring flowers from destructive people. She loved the trillium that carpeted the woodlands all around Lynnehurst.

Blackfly season was her time with Buppa Brown. Dumpy helped Buppa start his vegetable patch. Uncle John let the Browns fence off a small area half way up the slope which, being a hayfield or cow pasture by turns, had the necessary sunlight that Lynnehurst, itself, lacked. To till the soil, they had to dress suitably. Dumpy wore Alan's old trousers over her long stockings and tied the legs close around her ankles.

Arms and neck had to be covered as well but she resisted any proposal of head gear. The bug hat, with its fine mesh netting over the face, suffocated her. Rather, she trusted citronella to repel the little biters. Buppa didn't wear the bug hat either. He said he was too tough and old to interest insects anymore.

With garden tools in hand, forth they went together, child and man, both resembling scarecrows. Early in the spring chill of the morning with seemingly never a nasty fly in sight, their thoughts and conversation were fertile with anticipation.

"Have you got enough marigolds, Buppa, to put around the edge?"

"Yes, child."

"Will the chives be there still?"

"We'll see."

"I'll pull all the weeds!"

"Let me loosen the soil first."

"Here's the rhubarb. I nearly stepped on it."

"Yes, and there's a bunch over there that's almost big enough for picking. Your mother will be happy. "

"I can tell where the beets were last year. Are you going to use the same place?"

"Don't tell. It's a secret. I'm putting in a row of gladiolas this year."

"Yes, Buppa. I won't tell anyone. Can I put Mother's mignonette in?"

"Caw, Caw, Caw," chorused the crows, whose tree was positioned at the edge of the woodlot and half way between them and the park-like area around the house.

"Listen to those fellows," cried Buppa, "They think they own the place."

"Maybe they think we're talking too much about flowers and not enough about vegetables."

"Very likely."

Straightening his back and shaking a fist skyward, Matthew Brown then called out in his best school room tones, "You'll have to plant your own corn this year. I'll not do it for you."

"Caw, caw, Caw... Caw, caw, Caw!"

"Oh, Buppa, they understand you. I know they do."

"Very likely."

The crows took turns swooping from branch to branch. The more daring ones circled high in the blue above the pale green maples, their flight patterns punctuated with several caws from their stationary compatriots.

Matthew paused and glanced upward again. In a less antagonistic mood, he reflected, "perhaps they're exulting in the increased strength of the sun. The sun's invasion and mixture with spring air is intoxicating to all species."

Man and maid continued their work, the warmth becoming oppressive under heavy clothing. About half way through the soil turning process and a tenth of the weed pulling, their enthusiasm diminished. Clouds of blackflies rose up in open rebellion from earthy hideouts. Many found gaps in Dumpy's cloth fortifications. She felt their bites at ankles, wrists and around the waist as well as in the vulnerable neck and hair line areas. She emitted little noises to distract herself from the urge to scratch and kept bravely tugging at weeds, all the while loving the earthy smell mixed with a sweet-sour blend of plant fragrances. It was good to be close to the ground and to be with Buppa and the crows.

As he dug or rested on his shovel, Professor Brown taught his granddaughter both agriculture and botany. It didn't sound like teaching. He was just chatting about his friends the flowers, or their cousins, the herbs and the vegetables.

Buppa always seemed to know when Dumpy had had enough. At just the right moment, he stopped his flow of knowledge and regarded Dumpy.

"Look child, the narcissus and daffodils yonder want some picking."

Dumpy's eyes followed his gesture to a long row of yellow blossoms and their creamy star-shaped companions over at the edge of the woods.

"It's a longer line than last year," she exclaimed.

"Yes, I dug them all up after you left and divided them. When I replanted, the line was twice as long with bulbs left over. I've started a new clump on that flat, grassy place down behind the steamer wharf where the Indians used to camp."

"Can I go look?"

"Later. Right now, why don't you pick some of those daffys and take them to your mother."

Picking flowers was an easy job. Dumpy did not need any persuading. And by the time Matthew Brown returned to the house, the flowers were adorning the dinner table. Dumpy had changed into lighter clothing and her bites had been soothed by soap and water. Liza Brown Drayton was a great believer in the healing properties of soap and water.

Garden work, like housework, is never done but Buppa called a halt to it after a few days. He yearned for his row boat and his fishing rod.

"If we go far enough from shore, the blackflies can't reach us," he explained to Dumpy, who was getting ready to join him, no invitation being necessary.

"Buppa dear, I don't think you should take the child. The water is still icy cold. You know the ice went out late this year."

"We don't plan to swim."

"But still, you might upset the boat and she is so delicate."

"Nonsense, it's impossible to upset my boat!"

"Very well, then, but do sit still, Doris dear, and do exactly everything Buppa tells you."

It was unnecessary to instruct Dumpy. She was not a wiggler like her sister and it was in her nature to be obedient to sensible orders. She and Buppa trotted happily off to the sturdy old boat house that Webster's men had made years earlier out of the extra load of lumber.

Buppa wouldn't let Dumpy help him push the boat into the water but she watched as he carefully balanced it on the keel and lifted the bow end before shoving.

She knew he did not want to scrape the clapboard pine sides. The keel and the keelson were made of white oak designed to withstand years of use. Dumpy never got strong enough to push the Big Row Boat but later on in her life she would apply the same principles when setting out in her lightweight canoe.

Once launched, Buppa handled the oars and the rod too. Dumpy concentrated on sitting still. She also helped him with the bait. They both enjoyed the serenity of this particular morning. Buppa told stories of the good-old-days or they kept comfortable silence.

Towards noon a breeze developed. Dumpy watched Hunchback but said nothing when a sailboat came forth. Old Mr. Webster never missed a chance for a sail. His retirement years were divided between his son, Frank, at the lake and his married daughter in Toronto, with Frank getting the larger half of his father's time.

Eventually Matthew caught sight of the *Dragonfly* and gave his usual grunt of disapproval.

"They shouldn't let that old man out in that boat alone. Something might happen."

As for Knowles Webster, he had seen the Brown rowboat a full ten minutes earlier and had just finished muttering his own litany of disapproval, later to be voiced to Frank.

"What kind of people are those Draytons! They shouldn't let old Mr. Brown go out in that boat alone... Well, he had that young one with him, but what could she do? I've seen him out there many times all by himself. It's just not right. He's too old! You ought to say something to them, Frank... you ought."

Frank, knowing that Matthew Brown was only one year older than Knowles, usually held his peace at these outbursts, frequently letting them go on until his father's fury had spent itself. He knew it was the quickest way back to a state of good humour.

As for Knowles and Matthew, the two elderly men never expressed the slightest disapproval to each other and they were, in fact, the best of friends.

On this particular morning, when the *Dragonfly* caught up with Matthew's rowboat, Matthew greeted his friend serenely with, "Nice morning, Mr. Webster."

"Couldn't be better! Catch anything?"

The sailboat was quickly out of earshot but Matthew replied by holding up a string of six beautiful trout, one of which was to find its way to the Webster kitchen before tea time.

Matthew then turned his bow towards Drayton Beach. They were soon there and easily pulled the boat up on shore, well out of wave's reach.

"We'll just go invite Aunt Sally and your cousins for tea this evening; it's about time we had a visit."

Beginning in June, one of the John Drayton cousins, usually Willie or Susan, came to Lynnehurst early each morning with some milk and, perhaps, eggs or butter.

In May, they were still in school, often staying overnight at the Beasleys rather than taking the extra three-mile walk home. Willie and Susan were close to Alan in age.

Carolyn was the same age as Mary Lynne. There was no double first cousin Dumpy's age. Aunt Sally had lost two babies at, or shortly after, birth. Bob, Regina, and May were like a second family and too young to become playmates for Dumpy.

When they got past the baby and toddler stage, Dumpy found that she enjoyed looking after these younger cousins, which meant reading to whichever one would listen, or inventing little games for them.

Dumpy was thinking of these little cousins as she and her grandfather directed their feet toward the steep, woodsy path that led south and uphill to the John Drayton home set well back from the lake. They didn't go too close to the old Drayton homestead.

Although she couldn't remember her Drayton grandparents, Dumpy did not like to think about the empty place. She would be glad when either Uncle Philip or Uncle Peter would arrive in July with their lively families and awaken the old log walls.

Their visit in Aunt Sally's large, warm kitchen was brief. Regina was wailing because of something Bob had done with the Noah's Ark animals that they had been playing with on the floor. A savory stew was bubbling away on the stove, its beefy scent sending forth a message that dinner was ready. Through the window, Dumpy could see Uncle John coming in from the fields with a tired look of anticipation about him. She wondered if he could smell the stew out in the field.

Aunt Sally said it would be a good day to come for tea. Carolyn would be staying with the Beasleys but Willie and Susan would come home soon. School was finished for the year. She would ask the children to collect violet leaves if they could find enough tender ones. There was plenty of parsley, chives and, maybe, some lambs quarter. Aunt Sally promised to make a salad for tea. Matthew and Dumpy greeted John Drayton when he came in through the door, said their good-byes all around and hurried down the path.

Dumpy was glad that Buppa made no suggestion of visiting the senior Drayton home. She knew that her mother loved the old garden and that a daffodil plucked from Old Drayton Farm would bring a smile from Liza, but after all, there were lots of daffodils at Lynnehurst now.

"May I help you row?"

"That's a good idea. We're a bit late for dinner. Your mother will be worried."

Liza was not worried. She had seen where the rowboat had headed and guessed the rest, including the invitation to eat fish.

She greeted Buppa and Dumpy with, "Are they coming this evening or tomorrow?"

"This evening for tea. Sally will make a wild leaf salad."

"It will be all of them except Carolyn," added Dumpy.

"Good. I'll make a macaroni and cheese to go with the fish. The children will like that."

"Can we have a cottage pudding with chocolate sauce?"

"We'll see."

This meal of trout was becoming an annual event. In May or June, the John Draytons could count on at least one special tea and evening with the Charlie Draytons.

After the meal was over and cleared away, there would be singing around the piano.

Then Liza would play the Sir Roger de Coverly. Everyone else would dance. The dinner table was shoved aside; ladies and girls lined up against one dining room wall facing men and boys lined up opposite. After one or two sets dancing, the younger ones got sleepy and were put on a bed or sofa and covered up. Then Buppa would freshen the flames in the fireplace, add a 'keeper' log and settle back for story telling. They shared highlights of their winter lives with each other, especially anything humorous. New Orleans, Toronto and Muskoka came together under the roof at Lynnehurst.

Reluctantly, near midnight, Aunt Sally, seeing the look in her husband's eye, would break up the party and start the walk home. The smallest children got carried.

Sometimes one child would stay all night. John Drayton loved these family get-togethers as much as anyone but he knew the cows would need him early in the morning. Perhaps tomorrow, with the help of a breeze and some mosquito netting, he could steal time after dinner for a nap in the hammock on his porch. Or, perhaps he would never catch up on the loss of sleep.

Strawberries

As the "first" season of Lynnehurst summer progressed, blackflies gave way to mosquitoes which, in turn, heralded the strawberries.

One morning, Liza would announce, "it's time to inspect Aunt Sally's strawberry patch."

"Hurrah!" would be Dumpy's response, "That means the others are coming soon."

"Yes, but we don't know which day... tomorrow or Thursday... depending on how long they stay in Toronto."

Dumpy ran to get her berry basket and to find some citronella. Aunt Belle said she would go too. Buppa went with them but strawberry picking was not his forte. He would repair that outdoor bench he had made his daughter some years before. One of the legs could do with a bit of bracing. Perhaps Sally would reward him with a cup of tea in her warm kitchen afterwards. Grandmother Brown walked as far as Buppa's vegetable garden. Liza was with her mother to steady her and prevent any falls. Both Mother and Grandmother promised to husk any berries that came back to Lynnehurst.

At Drayton New Farm the berries were, indeed, ready. Susan and Carolyn were already picking. Dumpy and Aunt Belle joined them. Sally was in the house, rounding up and cleaning jars. She hoped to make jam before the week was out.

Robert and Regina were "helping" by hiding the Noah's Ark animals in the huge jam kettle. Baby May was napping on the kitchen settee. Matthew elected to have his tea right away. His joints were feeling a bit stiff this morning, he explained, as he settled himself next to May on the settee. Perhaps the tea would limber him. Sally pulled the kettle forward on the wood stove, at the same time, giving her father an anxious glance. It was not like him to want to pamper himself.

Out in the large berry patch, Aunt Belle was chatting constantly, sometimes giving the children instructions that they felt they did not need, sometimes telling them stories relating to her various friends in Toronto and sometimes, pausing to sample a berry or two. Dumpy never ate a single berry until the picking was completed. It was her policy regarding all types of berries. In this, she was following Buppa's philosophy of berry picking. She agreed with him that one taste only created a desire for more which, in the end, defeated the whole purpose of picking.

"There's the chipmunk again," declared Susan, nodding her head to indicate which direction.

"Why don't you chase him away?" Aunt Belle asked.

"We did, at first, but he keeps coming back so we decided to pick the ripe berries as fast as we could before he found them."

"Besides, he's so cunning and sweet to watch," added Carolyn.

Dumpy watched the little fellow as he sat on his haunches and nibbled daintily.

She decided to count how many berries she could pick in the length of time it took Mr. Chip to eat a whole berry. Her record was ten but by then, the chipmunk was slowing down. In the beginning, she could only manage six or seven. At length, he scampered off with a full tummy and left the children to their work.

After an hour and a half, Aunt Belle declared they had picked enough.

"Leave some for tomorrow," she said.

The children did not argue the point, but gathered their baskets and headed for the house. Aunt Belle had picked only the biggest and best. She wanted every one for the guests expected at Lynnehurst. Dumpy, who had plucked every size and shape so long as the berry was ripe, had a much larger amount. She decided to leave some for Aunt Sally's jam.

That very afternoon, Dumpy was in the hammock reading *The Cuckoo Clock* and swatting the occasional mosquito. What wind there had been was now almost nonexistent, leaving the lake's surface a quiet, pale blue under an overcast, grey-blue sky.

A loud, long *toot* split the silence.

"They're here today!" Two little thuds of Dumpy's feet on the porch floor accompanied her words. Almost immediately, four pairs of feet were pounding the earth between the house and the steamer wharf.

It was several minutes before the *Medora* reached the Brown's Landing wharf. Buppa, Aunt Belle, Liza and Dumpy were soon joined by Susan and Caroline.

They could see Mary Lynne waving frantically from the deck.

"That must be Ruthie Mae Lee beside her."

"There's father and Alan."

"Who are all those other people following them down to the lower deck?"

"It looks like... yes, I think it's Philip," Aunt Belle had always been partial to her brother-in-law, Philip Drayton.

Once on the dock, Charles Robert Drayton, President of C. R. Drayton and Co., took several minutes to embrace and hold Mrs. C. R. Drayton. There was so much commotion and chatter amongst all he others that no one seemed to notice this unseemly display of affection in public. Then, quickly, Liza regained her role as hostess.

"Ruthie Mae, welcome to Lynnehurst. Have you had a good trip?"

"Yes, thank you, Mrs. Drayton, but everything is so different from the way I pictured it. I can't believe what I see."

"I was about your age when I first visited Old Drayton Farm. I think it was the beginning of life for me."

"That's when she met Mr. Charles, you know," added Belle, who, at age twenty-nine, was still trying to decide which was the most interesting young man in the world.

"I fell in love with the place first," added Liza, somewhat irritated by her sister's remark.

"Come," cried Mary Lynne, grabbing Ruthie by the arm, "You are to have the other cot in my room. Let me show you."

Liza decided that her beef and barley soup could be expanded to accommodate the Philip Draytons, too. They protested. She insisted.

"Old Drayton Place hasn't even been aired yet. No one was expecting you so soon."

"I realize that," apologized Philip, "Ann was worried about it but Charlie and your children infected me with a strong desire to get here as soon as possible. With Charlie's help, we'll row over there now in the two boats. At least we can get it all ready for sleeping. The children can run to brother John for fresh eggs and some milk for our breakfast. I have to go back to the city in a few days but can come again with more supplies."

"Don't forget, Liza, the trip from Toronto is only half a day now. The train and steamer are fast," added Charles.

"That's true," Liza's mind shifted to immediate concerns. While Charlie helped his brother, she could make a large batch of tea biscuits. Perhaps Mary Lynne and Ruthie Mae could run over to the farm to see if there was any extra cream to be had. Thank goodness, Nora Webster had already started to come by the day to help at Lynnehurst. There were plenty of strawberries. Some accompanying short bread could be easily made.

True to form, Liza fed them all to repletion. Before light faded from sky, everyone was under each appropriate roof, either in bed or preparing so to be.

As she sat on her side of the bed that Buppa had made for Lynnehurst his first year there, Liza sighed a great sigh of contentment. She was brushing her long tresses of hair and enjoying the loose flowing feel of her cotton night gown.

"It is good to be in Lynnehurst," she said to Charlie, "It is more than good when you are here too."

Crazy Week

THE THIRD SEASON OF SUMMER WAS "BUSY SEASON." It came upon them one morning with the rising of the sun. Busy season would reach a midsummer crescendo which they affectionately called "Crazy Week", a time that enveloped every cottage, hotel and Inn. Even the farmers and winter people were swept up into it's frenzy.

Winter folk supplied food and services. They also participated in some of the frolic.

At Lynnehurst, Mary Lynne heralded the swift change of pace.

"Ruthie Mae should go to Needles Point. Let's have a picnic."

Glancing skywards, Liza replied, "If the weather holds, we could go tomorrow."

"Why don't you and Ruthie take Dumpy over to see Henrietta today," suggested Charlie, "Then you can invite all the Chadwicks too."

"Can we take the Big Rowboat, Daddy? You could push it in for us here. I could tie it at their place and it would be protected on the shore side of their dock."

"Very well. But tie it at both ends so it won't drift on those rocks by the shore."

"Ask them for a fowl too, please... and anything else they may have," added Liza, "Aunt Sally's pullets aren't big enough yet."

"I'd come with you," said Alan, "but mother needs some ice brought in from the ice house and then Daddy and I want to cut that tree that came down over the road."

"Why? We can climb over it."

"Yes, but the horses can't and Uncle John needs to be able to haul loads to and from the steamer wharf. While I'm over that way, I can pass the word on about the picnic to the 'Johns' and they can tell the 'Philips.'"

"I hope they don't bring that Jack Beasley with them like they did last year."

"Mary Lynne! That is not very kind of you," declared Liza, in a firm tone of voice.

Mary Lynne squirmed in her seat. It was dreadful to earn her mother's disapproval. She would have preferred to be spanked.

"I just mean, he doesn't know how to have fun and he stares at me so much, I feel uncomfortable."

Arrangements and rearrangements went on throughout breakfast but soon after, three young girls were trailing Charlie down to the boat house. He saw them off and stood to watch for awhile. There wasn't much wind. The boat glided along smoothly enough, considering that Ruthie's stroke was a bit uneven. Charlie reckoned that her unaccustomed arms would give out about half way there. It would be all right. Mary Lynne seemed made of steel.

Despite a winter away from boats, Mary was in good form. Coming back, the west wind would be strong enough to bring them, whether they were tired of rowing or not. Dumpy could steer with the rudder. Charlie smiled to himself as he thought of the stiff muscles the girls would have tomorrow. He watched his young people until they were out of sight, beyond Point Caroline.

"What they need is a sailboat," he said to himself. Why should I delay any longer? This is the year."

When Frank Webster came over to see if any work needed doing, he was immediately enlisted for the tree and wood cutting project, but the talk was mainly of sailboats and boathouses.

"Let's get Alfred Beasley to help. He's the best dock and boathouse man I know," suggested Frank. "He'll know the place to put it, anyway."

"I think we should ask my father-in-law, too," Charlie paused, remembering that he might have touched on a sensitive topic.

"Yes," there was a shadow of a smile across Frank's face and then he went on with, "you'll want a breakwater for summer mooring as well as a large boathouse."

Turning to Alan he added, "how are you at hauling stones?"

"Sounds like a good diversion to me. I also want to work on making a tennis court this summer. Father has already ordered a roller to flatten the earth after I clear a space."

"Oh? Where is that going to be?"

"Out beyond Dumpy's gym trees and a bit to the right."

"Are you going to train the crows to play?"

Mr. Brown's crows were the bane of Frank Webster's existence. He felt they were a more stubborn lot than anyone else's crows. Certainly, there were more of them at Lynnehurst. Frank had been known to fire his rifle at crows. Once he actually hit one. The other crows had filled the air with raucous lamentations and then settled back on their tree, seemingly, in complete control of the universe.

"That's a good idea," replied Alan, "We'll have two teams... the crows and the chipmunks. I'll ask Miss Ruthie to train them. She takes lessons from her brother, Kinnard, who is an excellent player. I hope to get Kinnard Lee up here next summer."

"I should think working on a cross cut saw would be good exercise for your tennis arm."

"Swimming helps too. Anyone interested? We're almost through the heavy cutting."

"Come now, we've only half begun," said Charlie, "We need to split some and fill the wheelbarrow. "

"You two go along if you want. I don't swim, so I can finish this," said Frank.

"We'll do more," insisted Charles, "We need to work up a decent sweat to make the swim worthwhile."

"Horses sweat, men perspire and ladies get all in a glow," chanted Alan.

"I must be related to the horses then," said Frank, pausing to indulge in a good laugh.

When it finally came time to swim, Liza and Buppa joined Charles and Alan.

Liza was a strong swimmer. She liked to head straight out using a breast stroke. Her husband always told her it was just as wet nearer the shore. This was a ritual with them. After several strokes, Liza rolled over and floated on her back to enjoy some sky gazing. This morning, the sky was a study in shades of grey. Liza wondered when grey stopped being itself and began being blue.

A gull glided overhead and circled. Liza remembered her childhood and all the romance this place had held for her. As she had earlier feared, some of that romance was gone but she didn't mind. The landing, Little Bluff and Lynnehurst had become home, a good, wonderful home.

At length, Liza swam to shore and climbed out on a rock. It was not the big, flat rock they had used in the early days. That one was now under the steamer wharf.

As she sat on the warm rock to dry off, Liza continued to think.

"Charles," she said suddenly, "we need a bath house. I find this bathing costume cumbersome. If we had one of those places which are half dock with a small changing hut and half fence around some water, I wouldn't have to wear it. And if we took our baths at the lake, it would save carrying water."

"Your wish is my command. Choose your spot and I'll speak to Alfred Beasley about it."

"Why Alfred?"

"Frank says Alfred is the authority on these matters."

"I think you ought to consult Buppa."

"Yes dear."

The girls did not return in time for dinner. No one worried. Obviously, they were having a good time. Mrs. Chadwick must have invited them to her family table.

When they did not appear at tea time, even Buppa Brown was concerned.

"This is the first time I've ever wished for a telephone in this place."

"I've been thinking about that too, Mr. Brown. I promise you, someday Lynnehurst will have a phone, but I don't know if Chadwick Manor ever will."

While the two men were talking, the Lynnehurst row boat appeared around Point Caroline, a Chadwick canoe in tow. Aunt Belle was the first to notice. She had taken her crochet work and stationed herself on the front porch to serve as look out reporter.

Belle's announcement of the sighted boat promoted an immediate exodus to the wharf. The saga concerning the girls' delay was soon revealed.

Mary Lynne had hurt her ankle while jumping from the hay mow in Chadwick's barn. While Ruthie Mae stayed with Mary, Dumpy and Henny Chadwick had run to fetch Henny's brother, Roderick, who came in haste and gallantly carried the injured girl to Chadwick Hall.

Mr. Chadwick's knowledge of injured animals had come in handy. He and Roderick examined Mary Lynne's ankle. Mrs Chadwick sent Hilda, Henny's older sister, to find some material with which they bound the ankle as best they could. Then rest, the great cure of many ills, was prescribed. Ruthie loyally stayed with her comrade, who was now confined to Chadwick's stately parlour. Heavy drapes over all the windows and dark oak panelling made the room oppressively dark, a stark contrast to the sunshine outside.

Dumpy and Henny escaped with Roderick, promising to help him with the second planting of lettuce, if he would take them off to the bog for "exploring and explaining." They were sure no one knew as much as Roderick about all the strange plants that grew in Chadwick Bog. It was an enchanting place to be... a different world with its sour peat smell and uncultivated, open expanse. They loved to make squishy sounds walking on the floating moss. Roderick said the place enthralled him because people had never cultivated or destroyed it in any way.

In due time, the budding botanists and the injured had joined forces again. Some sustenance had been provided, but no dinner. Unlike most of the neighbours, the Chadwicks dined in the evening. When the visitors attempted to disembark for Lynnehurst, Mary Lynne's courage failed. When she braced her feet for rowing, a gush of pain sprang upward through leg and body which, in turn, led to faintness.

Ruthie did not feel equal to rowing. Once more Roderick came to the rescue. It was slow going for him with a canoe tied astern.

When all the above had been explained to the anxious waiters at Brown's Landing, Mary, fearing she had over-emphasized her suffering, quickly added, "I'll be able to go to the picnic tomorrow. I just won't be able to do any rowing."

"Mrs. Chadwick is coming too," added Dumpy, "Hilda persuaded her because grandmother is going. Hilda can help Roderick with the rowing."

Roderick had no need to speak. The young females were so proficient at explaining everything. When he was thanked properly, he made his departure, promising to participate fully on the morrow.

Matthew stood on the dock watching Roderick's departure.

"How well I remember when that young man was born. It seems like yesterday."

"I remember too," added Charlie as he held his hands up for inspection.

"I should think you would. If you hadn't been there to help Mr. Chadwick row down the lake to fetch that lady doctor, I don't believe Mrs. Chadwick would be alive today."

"True enough. Her first doctor didn't know what he was doing. She would have bled to death after that quack bungled the baby's delivery."

"He left the area fast enough when that story was told a few times."

They were still talking about Roderick's birth when they returned to the house.

"I never thought women should be doctors," commented Polly, "but I have to admit that lady knew what to do, Praise God."

"And she never complained about having her vacation interrupted either," added Matthew.

"That was a cold September, I remember," said Charlie, "After we got back to Chadwick's, my fingers remained bent like this," As he spoke, Charlie's hands reassumed a cupped position for holding oars, "It was hours before I could move them."

※

The next day dawned bright and clear. By late morning, a fleet of rowboats and two canoes landed three Drayton households, the Chadwick family, one Webster and two Beasleys on the shore of Needles Point. All craft were safely pulled up on accommodating logs above the sloping rock surface of the point. Food hampers, including such delights as tinned sardines, devilled eggs, homemade breads, some early baby carrots, bottles of ginger beer, and rock cakes were unloaded and carried to the picnic table that Buppa Brown had first created and which had been roughly repaired over the years with available driftwood. Dumpy loved the gray surface of the table, now weathered to a comfortable smoothness.

The next job was to make Mrs. Chadwick and Grandmother Brown comfortable. Seated on cushions and with backrests from the boats against two tall pine trees, the inactive ladies looked snug. Mrs. Chadwick had brought a book to read, Grandmother Brown, her knitting scraps and a crochet hook.

Dumpy always remembered Grandmother with an afghan in progress.

The able-bodied headed for the woods to change into bathing suits. Women and children were assigned one direction and the men, the opposite direction. Soon all swimmers were in the water except Mary and Ruthie. Carefully, Mary Lynne took off her bandage and in a sitting position inched down the rock slope toward the lake until she was completely in, all the while urging Ruthie to get right in.

"The water feels cold at first but you soon warm up. It's the most wonderful water in the whole world."

Her southern friend was not so sure, "The Gulf Coast is warmer."

"But you feel sticky after being in salt water. This water makes you feel absolutely great. If I ever die, I hope someone puts me in the lake to revive me."

There were no appointed life guards or any buddy system at those early swimming parties. Most mothers and some fathers kept a look out for their own children. Liza kept an eye on everyone. The Beasley children did not seem to care for swimming as much as their summer friends. Jack, who was not being a pest as Mary Lynne had feared, was soon off by himself carving his name into a smooth driftwood log. Sarah Beasley was staying close to Carolyn Drayton. Dumpy and Henrietta joined the smaller children in the shallow water with the sandy bottom, for a game of froggie-in-the-middle. Those who felt chilly got out to dry off lying on the warm rock slope.

Eventually, everyone was out, dried and reclothed.

There was not enough room for everyone at the picnic table. Dumpy, Henrietta, William and Jack took their enamel picnic plates, well laden, and sat together on a shady area of rock. Mary, Ruthie Mae, Carolyn Drayton and Sarah Beasley found another spot nearby.

After a leisurely meal, Liza lifted a large black pot of boiling water off the campfire for washing up. Tin cutlery, enamel mugs and plates were soaped and rinsed as carefully as the silverware and porcelain would have been at home. The young girls helped dry every item with a linen tea towel.

The boys helped put the fire out, with water brought from the lake, in other black pots. The wire loop handles, being similar to bucket handles, made these pots convenient for the purpose. Buppa Brown, acting as fire chief, made them douse the flames completely and then add three more potfuls of water 'just to make sure'.

Children were taught early, the dangers of fire.

"I remember the year Prowse Point burned," remarked Uncle Philip, "They figured, afterwards, that a fellow in a canoe had camped there and had not put his fire out properly. The fire went underground and smouldered along some roots."

"I remember that too, That's why we always put our picnic fires on bare rock," added his brother, Charles, "Sometimes I still dream about Prowse Point. I see the flames shooting up and finding new places to catch hold. Our little buckets of water seemed almost useless."

"Yes," replied Philip, "That is when I learned how small and helpless we human beings are."

"It made me realize that an ounce of prevention is worth a pound of cure," added Charles, "Remember how mother used to say that over and over?"

Roderick got restless when the Draytons and Browns began to reminisce. He started off toward the woods to explore. Dumpy, Henrietta and William plus Jack went with him. William checked out the blueberry patch first and had an argument with Dumpy as to whether they were called huckleberries or blueberries.

"Whatever you call them, there's going to be a good crop this year. Look at all those little tight, green ones," proclaimed Roderick, who was used to having the final say.

"If they're this good here, they'll be even better on the other side of the woods, on top of Altar Rock. Lets come back in two weeks."

"Prowse Point would be better. "

"Yes, but it's too far away."

They went as far as the stream that runs below Altar Rock. Roderick showed Dumpy some trailing cedar on the ground. They even found a lady slipper in the marshy part. Roderick gave lectures on everything they saw. He found Dumpy his best listener.

"That Doris Drayton," he declared to his mother later, "is very intelligent for someone so young."

On the way back, they picked wintergreen leaves to chew. Meanwhile, the group that remained at the picnic site had divided itself into two. The adults were in various states of repose under the pine trees. Grandmother Brown was sufficiently asleep as to be snoring. Only Aunt Belle remained erect in a sitting position. She was knitting a pot holder, with half an ear cocked to listen to the younger folk who were clustered around Ruthie Mae. Any awkwardness that Ruthie earlier had felt in her new surroundings had vanished. She was holding the attention of an admiring circle of children. Whenever she paused in her talking, one or the other would ask questions to get her going again, just for the pleasure of hearing her southern drawl.

At length, Charlie Drayton, eyeing the rising west wind, declared it was time to head home. All were reluctant to respond... even the adults who understood the wisdom of his suggestion. Unwillingly, the ladies went about picking up cushions, baskets and spare wraps. The men lifted the boats into the water and helped the women and children into each assigned craft. The canoes were the first to embark but the last to reach home. Charlie Drayton rowed slowly, keeping within range of the canoes, in case the paddlers should require assistance.

"Tomorrow," he declared to himself, "I'll order that dingy that old Knowles recommended."

Crazy week, itself, defies description. It makes one dizzy even to think about it. There were picnics galore, an all-day canoe trip up the river, dances and singing in the long evenings. The lake water was at its best and warmest. Swimming took place at least twice a day. Some indulged in midnight dips as well. The steamer kept bringing and taking away, but mainly, it brought people. The Philip Draytons left Old Drayton Farm. The Peter Draytons arrived to replace them. Aunt Tilda Armstrong and family came, filling Lynnehurst beyond its capacity. The Montreal Browns arrived and stayed in a Webster cottage. Mary Lynne revelled in every minute of it, but Dumpy felt pulled apart. She wanted to enjoy each cousin thoroughly. There was no time.

One event of Crazy Week that Dumpy did enjoy completely was the annual Church Bazaar. She loved the large supply of sweets that mother always bought at the Bake Table. She never really outgrew her delight in the mysteries of the fish pond and she liked helping Mrs. Jacob at the flower table. There was a profusion of Jacob sweet peas, mother's mignonette, nasturtiums and phlox of every colour. Mrs. Jacob showed Dumpy how to arrange little bouquets and to price them for selling. By keeping her ears open, Dumpy could learn a year's worth of news as winter and summer Church goers greeted one another and chatted. She liked to observe the various children present, learn the names of those she knew less well and note how much some had grown and changed. She speculated about what each would become when they finally reached adult status. Henrietta Chadwick shared these delights with Dumpy, just as she shared the duties at the flower table.

The highlight of the social season was the 'Ball' that followed the Bazaar.

Dumpy didn't mind that she was still too young to attend. Instead, she enjoyed the boat ride back to Lynnehurst with her parents. They took Henny with them to stay overnight as a special treat. This nighttime boat ride allowed the little girls to experience stars, moonlight and the soft, velvety feeling of summer night air. As they neared Lynnehurst wharf, there was always a mellow, off-shore breeze that glided out from the low lying woods behind Buppa's boat-house to envelop them with its special ambrosia. This sensation, more than any other, meant home to Dumpy. It said, "you are here, you belong."

Charlie and Liza were content to go home before the night was over. They let the ever-resilient Belle act as chaperone for Mary Lynne and Ruthie. The Chadwicks or Armstrongs would bring them home later. Mary Lynne was really too young for the dance but she had begged and been allowed to go. Roderick did the propers in his stiff, non-rhythmic manner, with both Lynne and Ruthie. The Beasley boys sat around the edge, staring at everyone. Their schoolmaster father had not seen fit to instruct them in dancing and ballroom tactics. However, their bachelor uncle, Ted, had a gracious upbringing back in London. Even in his advanced years, Ted Beasley was clearly the best male dancer in the room. Furthermore, he enjoyed himself, making a point to dance with every available lady, including Ruthie and Lynne. The music, provided by members of the Raeburn and Beasley families on two violins and a piano, was lively and sprightly, contributing greatly to the atmosphere of conviviality, all of which went to Mary Lynne's head. Both she and her southern guest were thrilled.

It was while dancing at the Bazaar Ball that Aunt Belle finally met the man of her choice. George Whitby was a friend of Uncle Harold Brown. The Browns had brought him from Montreal to Muskoka for a much needed holiday. Whitby had spent the last ten years of his life caring for his ailing mother. Then her death had left him alone. He was thirty-nine years old but looked more like forty-nine. The strain of constant responsibility had taken a toll on his health. Belle's heart went out to George immediately. She longed to use her share of Brown family mothering ability on him.

For a start, she used her sense of humour and fun to get him to relax and laugh. He responded with courtesy and for the rest of the summer gave Belle his complete attention. The following winter, the

Lynnehurst

Whitby jewellery business in Montreal prospered as its owner's happiness increased.

Belle spent most of that winter visiting her brother Harold and his family in Montreal.

Ritardand

AFTER CRAZY WEEK, LIFE WOUND DOWN GRADUALLY to the final season of summer. Ruthie was the first to leave, travelling with southern friends who had been staying at the hotel. Later the Montreal Browns and George Whitby left from the Websters.

Another day the morning steamer called at Brown's Landing to collect the Peter Draytons, the Armstrongs and Aunt Belle Brown. The two remaining Brown sisters, Sally and Liza, assisted by various members of their families, were in charge of farewells. Matthew Brown stayed in the background; departure time was becoming increasingly sad for him.

Good weather lasted a while, but early mornings were quite chilly. Dumpy shared her sister's bedroom now, presumably a warm room, but early in the morning, there was nothing warm about it. Mary and Dumpy both snuggled deep under the bed covers, not wanting to make the leap into each new day. By the time they were dressed and down to breakfast, the day would be warm enough and so would they. In the meantime, the floor was cold. So was the water for washing their faces. Night gowns, warm from body heat, had to be exchanged for clothing that felt cold and clammy.

The girls would encourage each other several times before finally jumping out of bed like two buterflies bursting from cocoons with a, "one, two, three, Go!."

"I beat you."

"No you didn't. I was up first."

"My feet hit the floor first. I heard them."

The very worst day of late summer came near the end of August or early in September when father and Alan left for New Orleans. The whole family forced themselves up early, reluctantly ate a little breakfast and then trailed down, luggage in hand, to the steamer wharf to wait for the early morning boat. Often, there was fog. One such year, the mist was so thick that they could not see Hunchback or even Old Drayton Farm. Point Caroline had, likewise, disappeared. They were entirely closed in.

Mary Lynne was uncomfortable. Always wanting to be in control of her life, she was frustrated by not being able to see anything. Fogs should not be allowed.

"The steamer should be here by now. Perhaps it's not coming," blurted Mary.

No one answered her. They simply stood there, each with their own thoughts. Even Charles was speechless. An unreasonable knot of fear was building in his throat. *Would anything happen to Liza while he was away? Would anything prevent him from returning to Lynnehurst if he left now?* It was silly to think like this. He must say something cheerful and reassuring. Nothing he thought of felt convincing so he remained silent.

Dumpy, on the other hand, loved the peacefulness and the mysterious intimacy of the place and people. To her, Brown's Landing had become a world apart, suspended in time. She could not explain her feelings but treasured the memory of them in her heart all her life.

As for Liza, she was contained within herself in prayer. She upheld all travellers, especially her husband and son and, as well, all those who served them along the way, mentioning first, Captain Fraser and his weather-beaten crew and ending with a favourite train porter whose shiny black-brown face was ever a welcome sight. She visualized, in detail, the steamer and train journey to Toronto and the later train trip south through Chicago to New Orleans.

Suddenly, a loud, hollow whistle pierced the silence. Hardly had it finished when the fog seemed to part like gossamer curtains being pulled aside. There, hulking over them, just a few yards away, was the black and white bow of the steamer. The Captain's bell clanged. Someone shouted. The boat slowed, halted, backed, and turned to make the neatest landing any of them had ever seen.

When the ropes were secured to bollards and the gang plank in position, Captain Fraser came to the railing and leaned over.

"That was a close one, my friends! Why were you all so quiet? Usually I can hear you from further out."

"You've made a good point, Sir," replied Charles. I'll have a bell installed as soon as feasible. In the meantime, I'll instruct the family to sing and shout on foggy days."

※

Once the painful departures were over, life settled to a new pace. Afternoon swims ceased. Morning swims became late morning events. Dumpy and Mary Lynne learned that if they kept swimming every day, they would not notice the increasing cold of the water. Liza's enjoyment of swimming was not quelled by the coolness of the water either. All three of them revelled in the post swim sun bath. Weathered wharf planks absorbed sun warmth to a delightful degree. Often, they used the new bath house in order to have a real soaping and bath. Here, after a vigorous rub down, they could remain unrestricted by clothes to luxuriate in total freedom and sunshine.

"No wonder the Egyptians used to worship a sun god," remarked Mary Lynne on one such occasion.

September fell both in the last season of summer and in the first part of autumn. On the trees, a blush of russets and yellows grew daily, blurring the greens on far shores. Near at hand, a few maple saplings on rocky ground already had vivid red leaves. The new freshness of air made Dumpy glad to take on outdoor chores such as carrying kindling into the kitchen from the generous pile that Alan and father had left outside.

Sometimes Dumpy and Mary Lynne took the Little Row Boat around the shore to collect small drift wood to augment the kindling supply. Often, Mary Lynne helped Mr. Webster cut logs. She was as good as any lad on the end of a cross-cut saw, he declared. However, he wouldn't let her split the log chunks into firewood, believing that an axe was a tool for men only. Dumpy couldn't handle the heavy wood at all. Instead, she and Buppa might pick wild blackberries or walk to New Drayton Farm on errands.

On rainy days, Buppa stuck to his books. The women would gather to discuss recipes and then perform gastronomic experiments in the kitchen. The cast iron, woodburning stove, endured in mid-summer out of necessity, was now a welcome companion. It was definitely food time. Never was the eating so good as in September. Everything seemed to ripen at once, squashes and corn topping the list, to say nothing of apples. When Uncle John killed a lamb to sell, always a quarter together with the liver, found its way to Lynnehurst. Dumpy gathered mint from the ditch near Buppa's vegetable garden. Back in the house, she carefully chopped the mint leaves into thin slices. Then, into a custard cup they went to be mashed together with vinegar and sugar. The best lamb must have the freshest and the best mint sauce.

Imagine, if you will, a cold and rainy day. Outside, wet droplets fall on rocks, earth, roots, wooden steps and porch, making roots and wood slippery, turning earth to a black, soggy carpet. Lynnehurst's porch has been abandoned, the hammocks and two wicker rockers brought in. The windows facing the lake and west wind are shut. Probably, most of the other windows are closed also. Inside, Buppa has laid and started a fire in the dining-room fireplace. The table is set with a centrepiece of red maple leaves in the green wedgwood vase. Steaming potatoes arrive, adorned with chopped parsley and melting butter, followed by platters of baked squashes. Dumpy puts her mint sauce near Buppa's place and Liza brings the lamb roast. Muskoka lamb has never been equalled anywhere in the world then or since. Liza returns to put a 'keeper' stick in the wood stove and check the welfare of two blackberry and apple pies slowly baking in her oven. Now she is back, bringing a loaf of her homemade wholewheat bread with her. Buppa is put in charge of cutting the bread. Liza takes her place near the roast. Grace is said with everyone standing and heads bowed. Chairs shuffle. The roast is cut, plates are filled. The wondrous eating can begin. There is silence as the first mouthfuls are savoured. Then lively conversation resumes. This noon time dinner is not rushed. There is no need to spoil the full leisure and pleasure of it.

The fullness of time, thinks Mary Lynne, *This is it, and it will continue right here in Lynnehurst every September.* She glances across the table at her sister.

Dumpy's eyes are focused on the hearth fire behind Mary. Inside Dumpy's head, the story fairies are at work. Buppa and Liza are fully occupied, reminding each other of earlier times in Muskoka. The past, the present, the future and the imaginary are all gathered together in this room.

Indian Summer

IN THE FALL OF 1908, Doris Amelia Drayton learned the meaning of the word adolescence. She and her mother remained unusually late at Lynnehurst that year.

With the help of Mrs. Webster and Aunt Sally, they were nursing Buppa, who expressed a wish to die at Lynnehurst and be buried in the graveyard beside their church. Dumpy's role was to read his favourite books to him or to talk, if he wished.

He seldom stirred from his bed in the old north room, but seemed to lie there suspended between life and death.

Often, when there was a wind stirring, the top branches of a young birch tree would flap against the window pane, drawing Buppa's attention to them and to the top of Little Bluff beyond. The Bluff's gray rock summit summoned his memories. Polly had died in this very room two summers previous. She had been a burden to them all in her declining years, but he missed her desperately. He looked forward to their reunion. He could leave all the miserable experiences behind and take all the joy with him. Surely, that was what was meant by heaven. It would be a Lynnehurst, but a more glorious Lynnehurst, full of beauty, truth and love.

Sometimes Buppa slept. Then Dumpy could read to herself. She kept Miss Alcott's *Rose in Bloom* nearby for that purpose. If anything unusual happened, she could call her mother who was napping in the next room.

Something very unusual did happen. It happened to Dumpy, not to Buppa. At first, she did not believe her feelings and then, filled with dismay, she went, in agony, to find her mother.

Dumpy felt thrusts of pain in her tummy followed by a numbing sensation in her head, as if a thousand minuscule needles had enveloped her in darkness coupled with a sinking sensation. As the world was blotted out, mother's arms were there.

There was some dragging and lifting and something else, but Dumpy could not concentrate on what. She had, in fact, fainted... just as many of her romantic heroines did in novels. There was nothing romantic about this experience.

After a while, Dumpy became conscious that she was in her mother's bed with a warm 'pig' at her feet and a hot water bottle near her middle. Raindrops were beating against the window panes, distorting a view of trees that were thrashing in the wind to rid themselves of every remaining leaf. There was relief and weakness all over her body. The pains in her abdomen were now one dull but bearable discomfort.

"How do you feel? "

"What happened? Is Buppa all right?"

"Yes dear, Buppa is still dozing. Aunt Sally had to go home but Susan is coming over. It is Saturday."

Liza looked out the window and then back at her daughter's ashen grey face, "Doris dear, I am so sorry. I should have told you this might happen. I completely forgot that you are growing up. I have just been too busy thinking about your grandfather to notice changes in you."

"What kind of sickness do I have?'

"It is not sickness... It's part of nature's plan to change you into a woman. You know there are days when Mary Lynne doesn't go swimming and isn't interested in doing much?"

"Yes."

"It will be like that with you once a month."

Then Liza attempted to explain the physical mysteries connected with female functions. Dumpy, who was usually keen to hear anything scientific, responded with silence. Inside herself, there was emotional confusion. Life had generally been beautiful in her eyes. Now she was a prisoner of Life. Were all the beauties camouflaging ugly, underlying facts?

Dumpy thought back over the summer. It had held the usual happiness for her, but, also, there had been some awkward episodes like the berry-picking expedition to Prowse Point. She had asked Roderick to give her a piggyback ride for part of the hike. It did not feel right as in earlier years so she had dismounted fairly quickly, thinking that she must weigh too much to fit properly anymore. Roderick, himself, seemed different. Later that same berry trip, she had paused from stripping blue clusters of ripe berries off a low bush, only to notice Roderick gazing at her. She felt a rush of blood to her face. Did he see her blush? Was that one of life's tricks? Was it connected with growing up? She did not ask her mother, or anyone, any of these questions. They simply had stirred in her mind for several days.

For Dumpy, the next two days were depressing. Liza encouraged her to rest and keep warm. She managed to resume her share of bedside vigils. Buppa seemed only to moan and stir himself uneasily under the bed clothes. He was hardly eating anything now.

Rose in Bloom held her attention only for short periods. The rains continued, keeping her entirely within doors. As she could see from Lynnehurst windows, most of the leaves were down, making a carpet of withering colours and leaving a wider canopy of sky above to provide the only drama in her life as it changed from stormy charcoal to quiet, pale grey and back, again, with each new gusting rain. Clouds were embankments of dullness rather than the free forming white shapes of summer.

On the third morning, sunrise revealed a sky full of misty light. Warmth caressed the silent woods and open fields alike. Sunlight entered Lynnehurst through the east windows, making the fire in the dining-room fireplace redundant and warming Dumpy's upstairs bedroom with a mellow dream-like quality. Dumpy lingered in bed a few minutes, listening to the new silence outside.

It was no dream. She could hear the usual kitchen noises directly below as her mother stirred the big new stove into action. *Clank* went the door to the fire box followed by two taps of the poker before Liza hung it beside the chimney.

Dumpy waited to hear the scrape of the kettle being brought forward. She didn't wait for the porridge-making sounds but rose sedately to perform her morning ablutions, trying all the while, to think of herself as a woman.

Was anyone in with Buppa? Perhaps she should go and check.

The north room did not receive morning light but, even so, Buppa seemed aware of the changes outside. He was wide awake.

"Indian Summer," he announced.

"Indian Summer?"

"Yes, the Indians use this time to harvest their crops for winter."

"Harvest?" exclaimed Dumpy. "Uncle John did that in August and

September."

"Uncle John is not an Indian. He will be storing his root crops now. Tell him to hurry. He should finish ploughing his fallow field ready for spring use."

"Buppa, the trees are so bare and grey, but I don't feel sad today; why?"

She felt warmth rush to her face. Did he see her blush?

"Look more closely, little one. The trees are not bare. There are knobs and in those knobs are the embryo blossoms, tiny like seeds. Each embryo flower is as complete as it will be in May. Like me, it must wait for new life."

"You?"

"I am in tune with nature. We die at the same time but it is a death that leads to new life. Read about it in the Bible and read about it in nature."

Buppa didn't die for another five days but it was the last coherent conversation of Matthew Brown's life on this earth.

Dumpy continued to take her turn with Buppa but she also found time for the out-of-doors. Her favourite places were strangely different, comfortable, with warmth and the new openness of Indian Summer. At her jungle gym, she realized that she hadn't used it lately. Some of the climbing bars were decayed.

"Buppa won't be able to repair them," she told herself. "But it won't matter... I won't need them anymore. "

She climbed the narrow trail to the top of Little Bluff, book in hand. Not many pages were turned. Dumpy was absorbed by the world around her. The land embracing Lynnehurst was so familiar and yet, so different, with the rocks and earthy contours unveiled to light and space. The trees stood silent, a battalion of grey sentinels. With her eyes, she began to trace the course of a nearby root system through patches of ground and over bare rock spaces. No wonder birch saplings and small pines never got big on Little Bluff.

Not a ripple disturbed the glass-smooth lake. The distant shore was silent and still, with a mystic greyness akin to the pale growth of spring.

The next day, Dumpy was seized with a longing to explore the lake. What could be better than a canoe in weather like this. She paddled as far as the south shore, hugging the shore line and inventing stories about each little place she passed.

Forgetting about her new status as woman, she let herself become an

Indian maiden who had lost the rest of the tribe, or a fairy child come to find hidden flowers and to free them from enchantment. Then, taking advantage of the lake's smooth surface, she ventured forth on a mission to discover the exact middle of the lake. At length, unable to decide where the real middle should be, she let the canoe rest to savour the stillness. A pair of loons popped up quite close by. They studied her with a steady gaze. She was quite enchanted.

"Why are you still here?" she asked. "Can't you go south like others?"

They continued to look. Then, suddenly, silently, they dove into the depths. She heard them a few minutes later, calling their special call from a distance.

Dumpy wondered about the loon's world below the level surface. Was it calm in the depths or were there strange currents swirling around? And what was life like for a bass or for a lake trout?

Hunger and common sense eventually overcame her. She pointed the bow straight in to Brown's Landing. Skirting around the big wharf, the big new boathouse and the sailboat pier, she was soon at Buppa's old boathouse. However, she was late for dinner, late for her turn with Buppa and, worst of all, too late to say good-bye to her favourite person.

"No, no, NO! " she screamed when her mother told her the news.

Liza's arms reached out to comfort her daughter. Dumpy was beyond comforting, so overwhelming was her grief. She pushed her mother away.

"I wasn't with him, I wasn't with him," she kept repeating.

"Doris, you mustn't cry. Buppa's time had come. He is better off where he is. No more suffering."

"I know. I know, but I wasn't with him. It was my turn and I wasn't there. Oh Buppa! Buppa! Buppa!"

Dumpy fled to the north room. Her sobs could be heard throughout Lynnehurst.

Fortunately, Indian Summer held on long enough for them to arrange the funeral, the burial and the closing of Lynnehurst. The steamers were still running.

Matilda and Belle arrived in time for the funeral and now were part of a little group waiting at Brown's Landing for the southbound steamer that November morning. The Brown 'girls' were glad to be together at this time but they were unusually quiet.

Sally broke the silence with, "It's like him to go at a convenient time. He realized the steamers won't be running much longer this season."

"Yes," answered Liza, "I thought of that. Also, we would have run out of split wood and it would have been difficult to keep Lynnehurst warm if we stayed much longer."

"I'm glad Belle and I could get here," added Tilda, "He always said we girls should stick together."

"That's not going to be easy," said Belle. "I'm in Montreal. You're in Toronto. Liza's in New Orleans and Sally is stuck here on the farm."

"True, but we all have Muskoka in the summer and we can write letters in the winter."

"But I didn't marry into the Drayton family and now that Buppa's gone, I don't belong here anymore," Belle's voice was unusually plaintive.

"You will always belong at Lynnehurst as long as I live," Liza assured her.

"It hasn't been difficult for me," added Tilda. "Lynnehurst is not big enough for all my family to visit at once but there always is a house nearby to visit or to rent. The Websters have quite a few cottages now and sometimes old Drayton Farm is available. For that matter, the hotel is near enough."

"You have no idea how I long to see you all return in the summer," said Sally.

"And I look forward to your letters in the winter. They make me feel part of your lives. Forgive me if I don't always answer, but I'm so busy just keeping everyone fed and clean during the day and we don' t like to burn our kerosene for long in the evenings. John reads but I always have mending to do. Sometimes John reads aloud to me. If there are old letters around, we read them again and again to remind ourselves of all your news. The children are interested too."

All this time Dumpy said nothing; she was listening. When the steamer arrived, she hugged Aunt Sally and watched as Uncle John and Mr. Webster brought the trunks, by wheelbarrow, over the dock to the gang plank for the steamer crew to store on board. By the time the steamboat pulled away, Dumpy, her mother, and two aunts were waving from its upper deck. How lonely the three remaining adults looked as they stood silently together in the middle of the big wharf, all eyes toward the four travellers.

"I must remember to write to Aunt Sally," Dumpy told herself.

As the boat rounded Point Caroline, Dumpy saw Mr. Webster, in his rowboat, heading for Hunchback. She knew Aunt Sally and Uncle John would be trudging up the road to New Drayton Farm. Lynnehurst, with its windows covered in shutters and boards, looked to be already in its winter sleep. She had never before seen Lynnehurst so completely closed.

Liza's New Stove

By A. Tournay. Reproduced with permission.

Opera Lovers

SIX YEARS AFTER THE DEATH OF MATTHEW BROWN nineteen-year-old Dumpy was standing in the downstairs vestibule of Charles Drayton's New Orleans home talking with a young man named Julian de Poncier. Julian faced the spacious hallway from which a stairway and carved bannister seemed to glide gracefully upward. Behind him, a bevelled glass insert in the front door duplicated his shapely figure and framed his masculine reflection with an etched design, entwining leaves in frosted glass. Julian and Dumpy were engaged in a serious conversation which, as usual, fell just short of solving all the world's problems. Next they indulged in nonsensical badinage, to which they often resorted when their intellects ran dry.

After a good chuckle over their own nonsense, Dumpy put her mind to their plans for the evening.

"Alan is eating downtown. He had late business, so will probably meet us at the opera house. Mary Lynne can't go because of her sprained ankle. She never saves herself at all but must practice her precious basketball until the last ounce of energy has been sapped or some segment of her anatomy injured."

"Why basketball?" interjected Julian, "Nobody plays that here. Does she want to introduce the game? Or is she planning to return to her northern boarding school as a teacher?"

"Personally," replied Dumpy, "I don't think she'll do either. Anyway, she's given her ticket to our friend, Geraldine Blandford. Geraldine is upstairs now, consoling Mary."

Julian took Dumpy's cloak from the rack and held it ready for her to wear.

"Blandford? Father has a friend at the club... Michael Blandford."

"Yes, it's the same family. Mr. Michael is her uncle."

Before she turned her shoulders to receive the proffered wrap, a reflection in the etched glass of the vestibule door caught Dumpy's eye. At the same time, she saw Julian's face undergo a complete transfiguration. Even his favourite opera had never produced such a look. His eyes were alive with delight. Geraldine Blandford was descending the stairs.

Dumpy gallantly made the introductions, then retrieved her cloak from the floor where Julian had unconsciously dropped it.

"Mr. de Poncier, I feel I know you already. The Draytons have spoken of you so often," Geraldine spoke with a cultured southern drawl.

"Please," stammered Julian, "in these modern times, I'm sure we can use Christian names without being guilty of impropriety. You are a friend of the Draytons. So am I. They all call me Julian. Your first name is such a lovely one; I hope you will let me use it."

"Certainly."

From that moment on, it was 'Geraldine' and 'Julian'.

A raucous noise drew their attention to something outside.

"That sounds like the horn of an automobile," Julian predicted as he went off to investigate... "Alan! What on earth!!"

"My little surprise for the evening," announced Alan Drayton, stepping out of the shiny new vehicle, "I've bought a Hupmobile."

The young ladies, now out of the house, exclaimed surprise as they gathered round the new machine. The wind screen, a straight erect piece of glass, divided the black metal hood from the passenger area. The seats were covered in quilted maroon leather. What drew everyone's attention most, was the ornate horn in the shape of a snake with a big rubber air bulb. Alan squeezed the bulb two or three times to demonstrate. Across the street neighbors came to their windows staring in amazement.

Geraldine had never been in an automobile before. She obviously was nervous.

Alan offered her the front seat and assured her there was no cause for alarm. Benefitting from expert instruction during the last hour and a half, he felt himself to be in perfect control of his new vehicle.

Julian thought Geraldine might feel safer in the back seat. He could sit with her for extra protection.

Alan countered with, "She can see better from the front."

"In the sailboat, father says whoever holds the tiller gives the orders," commented Dumpy, "That wheel is your tiller, Alan. We will sit where you tell us."

"Yes, of course," said Geraldine, relieved that she would not have to choose. It was Dumpy who was assigned to Julian's protection in the rear seat, but there was little joy in it for her. Julian made no effort at conversation during the entire trip.

In the front seat, Geraldine was telling Alan about her trip to Paris the previous year.

"Did you know, Alan, that our old French Opera House is a reproduction of the Opera Comique of Paris?... a Gallier design, only I think ours is slightly smaller."

Alan acknowledged her remarks but kept his concentration on the street and on handling his Hupmobile.

"Our tickets are for the Grand Opera House tonight," put in Dumpy, "but I do love the old building. Whether or not the Gallier design was chosen on purpose or whether it was an accident, I don't know, but the French Opera House is gracefully suited to its surroundings."

"I agree, and aren't we fortunate in New Orleans to have so much opportunity to hear opera?" replied Geraldine, "I do love operatic singing!"

Rigoletto was the opera that night. It was a favourite with New Orleans audiences. The Drayton young people were as enthralled as everyone else.

"What lovely music," said Geraldine afterwards. "It just lifts one up out of the everyday world."

"I wish I could sing like that," said Julian.

"I feel the same," responded Geraldine. My longing for that much beauty is like hunger."

"You have a lovely voice," said Alan. "Why don't you train for opera?"

"So many of the opera stories are sad. I would be crying all the time."

"Yes, I think you would," added Dumpy. "However, the plots are ridiculous; I seldom accept them as real. I see them as mere art form to furnish a frame on which to hang the various emotional outpourings or expressions of philosophical ideas."

"Music needs emotion or it would be as dull as everyday prose," added Julian.

"On the other hand, we would go insane if we experienced deep tenderness, passion, grief and sorrow every day, all day."

"I didn't want the music to stop."

"Yes, but if it didn't ever stop, how would you feel?"

"That's an interesting thought."

The next day, Geraldine went over to visit Mary Lynne and Dumpy. The three girls were gathered in Mary Lynne's room. Winter sunlight had found its way in past green gingham curtains to lighten up the whitewashed walls. Dumpy was arranging yellow chrysanthemums that Julian had sent to cheer the invalid.

"Have you heard from your mother and Mr. Charles?" asked Geraldine.

"Yes, a long letter arrived in the early mail this morning. They've nearly finished the business part of their trip. Mother is looking forward to sight seeing in Italy. Then they sail for home near the end of March."

"Father had a strange experience with one of his clients. Herr Herman has been dealing with us so long that he is like a family friend, but he told father that Germany will have to go to war with Britain. Father was shocked and said, 'You know I'm a British subject because I was born in Canada. Would you want to fight me?' Herr Herman replied that, of course, they were friends. Still, it was his opinion that Germany would and should declare war on England."

"Several of Father's clients ordered extra supplies and asked for the earliest possible delivery dates," added Mary Lynne, "It looks like Europe expects war."

"Very strange," commented Geraldine, "but, of course, it wouldn't affect us in America."

"Let's be more cheerful," said Mary Lynne. "It's a beautiful day. Do tell me, Geraldine, how you enjoyed last night?"

"The opera was beautiful, both the music and the costumes. Guilda had the most beautiful blue velvet gown. The Duke was in scarlet and blue. Rigoletto was a bit dull in black and yellow."

"And how did you like my friend, Julian de Poncier?"

Dumpy felt a tightness in her throat. It was one thing to have Julian become enchanted with Geraldine; that was entirely understandable, but to hear Mary Lynne use the possessive pronoun was too much. It was wrong and positively deceitful, unkind...

"Mary, I'm so glad you've identified him as your friend," continued Geraldine.

"I had the idea that he was Dumpy's special friend. I see now that it is, as he says... a family friendship. That relieves my mind greatly because, my dearest friends, I must speak straight from the heart. I felt an instant attraction to Julian. He remained on my mind all night. Only time will tell, but, so often, one's first impressions are correct. I sincerely hope mine are."

Dumpy went quickly to the window.

"What is it?" asked Geraldine.

"I thought I heard Mammy calling. She's so blind these days. Sometimes she locks herself in that cabin of hers and can't get out, but I don't think so now. Perhaps it was a mocking bird."

Mary, oblivious to her sister's ruse, expressed delight in Geraldine's confidences. Her generous, outgoing nature was truly happy at the prospect of a serious friendship developing between two such nice people.

"I think he was attracted to me too, but maybe it's just wishful thinking on my part."

"No, you're quite right. I know him pretty well." Dumpy's voice was controlled and deliberate. "He was totally infatuated with you at first sight."

"Do you really think so? Please don't tease me."

"If Dumpy says so, it's true," interjected Mary. "Dumpy doesn't tease in that tone of voice. I think we should have an evening dinner party, don't you?"

"You angel! What could I do to help?"

"You can help us with the guest list. For starters, can you think of a nice young lady to suggest for Alan's benefit? Both you and Ruthie Mae seem to be out of the running."

"What about Miriam Herbert?" suggested Dumpy, who could not resist the joys of party planning.

"Or Florence Aubelin," added Geraldine. "I would suggest my sister Audrey but I don't think Alan likes her. We don't like the man Audrey sees so much of these days. Perhaps it's unkind of me. He didn't have a happy childhood and doesn't have very good manners. I shouldn't judge him, but I do wish Audrey had a nice man like Alan for a friend."

"Geraldine, does your mother have any flowers in her conservatory?" asked Dumpy.

"One or two blooms. Would you like me to bring something for a table centrepiece?"

"Yes please, we only have greenery but we can concoct something and add candles."

"Sounds elegant," said Mary Lynne, "I'll be able to hobble around soon and can help Mammy in the kitchen. I'll make mother's famous coconut cream or would you rather, a Canadian trifle?"

"Mammy will do her hot biscuits."

"It's enough to make a growing girl hungry. What's for lunch?"

Lunch was a standard Drayton family noon dinner of roast beef, potatoes and vegetables. While eating, the girls continued their discussion of Julian.

"He's from one of Louisiana's oldest families. His grandfather's plantation is at Pencierville, up near Baton Rouge."

"Yes, it may become his someday but I'm afraid it won't be much of a legacy. His father's older sister lives there alone. Claudius, the only remaining negro servant, is as old as she. She looks after him as much as he does her. Claudius' mother was one of the de Poncier slaves who refused to leave when emancipation came. He has known no other home."

"Aunt Challa is valiantly ignoring the changes in southern society as well as the decay of their once, lovely family home. They say she was quite a belle in her youth but never goes anywhere now."

"Julian looks after his aunt's money which means, he often sends her some of his own because he cannot bear to see her suffer."

"She was upset when her brother married into a nouveau riche family instead of someone of good old New Orleans French descent. All her thinking centres on the past."

"I don't think Julian will ever be like that. He is proud of his de Poncier ancestry and ideals such as family honour and gallantry."

"Yes, but his form of gallantry is good manners and gracious customs, not the ridiculous stuff like fighting duels to protect names. And he makes it his business to keep abreast of the times."

"There are some de Ponders near where the Herberts live. They have two grown children who aren't quite right. Are they any relation?"

"Yes, they're distant cousins. It's a case of inbreeding for several generations because they refused to marry out of their exclusive Creole circle. I think that may be one reason Julian's father rebelled from that particular family tradition."

༄

There was lively conversation as well as good food at the young Drayton's dinner party, followed by a musical evening. The musical talents of Ruthie Mae Lee and her brother, Kennard, were an asset to the gathering. Kennard and Dumpy took turns at the piano to accompany singing.

There was much group singing of popular songs, hymns and airs from operas. Ruthie and Julian sang duets. Geraldine was persuaded to sing *My Wild Irish Rose*.

Afterwards, Julian sang solo *The Holy City*, which turned out to be an unplanned finale. His rich, mellow voice stirred his friend's emotions. There was silence before anyone could put words into a spoken compliment. The young people just chatted for the rest of the evening. Florence Aubelin had been unable to come but Miriam Herbert proved to be a good choice for Alan's attention. Miriam, their minister's daughter, was a conscientious person and a good listener. Her intelligence, like her father's, was orderly and reliable but had none of the brilliant qualities for which her mother's people were known. Neither she nor Alan were performers. They could join the group singing. Otherwise, they were audience as was Mary Lynne who sat with them, her offending foot propped unceremoniously on a large cushion-covered foot stool.

The Lees and Miriam did not notice the development of emotional bonding between Julian and Geraldine because Ruthie's future plans took much of their attention. The previous summer, both Ruthie and Kennard had spent 'Crazy Week' and most of August at Lynnehurst where they met the Russell family, Whitby relatives, who were renting two of the Webster cottages. Then, at Christmas, young Christopher Russell had visited New Orleans. He and Ruthie became engaged. Ruthie could think of little else. The June wedding would be in New Orleans. After a Niagara Falls honeymoon, Ruthie and Christopher would live in Montreal where Christopher had a job in his cousin's jewellery business.

"How do you think you'll like living in Canada?" asked Miriam.

"I like Canada quite well. After all, I have visited the Draytons in Muskoka several times and I spent one Christmas in Toronto. The cold and snow there didn't bother me. Canadians keep their houses warm in winter."

"But Montreal is much colder than Toronto," warned Alan.

"I wonder if you'll get along with the French Canadians," added Mary Lynne.

"New Orleans is a French city too," insisted Ruthie, "I know some French already and I love New Orleans, so why not Montreal!"

Both Mary Lynne and Dumpy felt that Montreal must be dramatically different from New Orleans, but they kept their thoughts to themselves.

"When I get settled, you must all come and visit," continued Ruthie. Everyone agreed to that.

Make Hay

Dumpy resented having to remain in the South for the wedding. She would miss the first season at Lynnehurst. Even without Buppa, early spring in Canada was her time to be keenly alive.

"Don't worry about the vegetables," said Mary Lynne in an effort to console her sister, "Willie will do the digging and planting for us."

"Tu a raison, but I'll miss the crows and the loveliness of budding trees and spring blooms. Think of all those daffodils and narcissus running along Uncle John's fence. I divided them last year. The line will be three times as long. It goes right from the wood lot below the crow tree, all the way to our road."

"The trouble with us is that we're spoiled. We get two springs every year. You 'll just have to console yourself by remembering that down here it was a lovely April for azaleas and dogwood."

For a moment, Dumpy's face lit up as she remembered their short trip into the Tennessee Mountains.

"Ah, the dogwood and redwood at Sewanee," she murmured as if uttering a fervent prayer.

Considering her sister sufficiently consoled, Mary Lynne plunged into wedding talk with full gusto. It was un-thinkable that they should absent themselves from such a momentous Lee family celebration. Mary was to be maid-of-honour. She enjoyed the excitement of making plans and she attended several pre-nuptial parties.

"It should be you, Dumps, instead of me. Although I love the parties it's a real strain finding something different to wear each time. But you love clothes. If father says I can buy something new, you must come help me choose. After I've tried on one or two dresses, I'm bored, so buy whatever the saleslady likes."

"That's all too true! It's too bad Miss Gismunda is ill. She always knows what to make for us."

"Dear Gissyl."

"Tailored look for Mary Lynne," chanted Dumpy.

"Frills and lace for Doris," responded Mary Lynne.

"You'd think we were reciting the psalms!" In spite of herself, Dumpy was laughing and getting into the festive spirit.

❦

Regarding the Lee-Whitby wedding, Charles and Liza Drayton were of like mind with their younger daughter. The social exigency, caused by their association with the Lee family, coupled with their concern for the Whitbys, put a strain on their natural urges to travel north before a humid Louisiana summer set in. Consequently, they purchased train tickets for the day after the June nuptials. They would be on the same train that would carry the Niagara-bound honeymoon couple.

"It's not proper," declared Charles, "to hover near the newlyweds, but, Liza, you and the girls must not stay a day longer in this heat. We can be in a separate car. I will ask the porter to arrange that we dine at a different hour from the honeymoon couple."

"Poor Alan," sighed Liza. "I wish he were coming with us."

"Yes, I know, but someone has to keep an eye on business. He says he doesn't mind and I think there is a young lady who will help him forget any discomforture he might feel."

"Yes, indeed." Liza's voice reflected a blend of motherly pain as well as felicitude, "It's good that he has the Hupmobile. They can drive over to the Gulf some weekends to visit the Lucans. The breezes there are sweet."

"The Russells were anxious to return to Canada also, so boarded the same train as the Draytons. The two families had a lovely two day visit en route to Toronto, where Mr. and Mrs. Russell and their two younger sons continued on to Montreal, promising to visit Muskoka in August. The bride and groom were glimpsed only as they changed trains in Chicago. Their fellow travellers pretended not to notice them in the slightest.

That July, Liza thought that every relative and every friend who was at all mobile, came to visit Lynnehurst. It was as if people knew something was hanging over their lives. They wanted to take holiday time while it was still available.

Muskoka rang with joyous sounds of picnickers. Hotels were full. In the evenings, hotels opened their doors to locals and cottagers, as well as resident guests, for dances and entertainments. Neither Mary Lynne nor Doris Drayton lacked for dancing partners. There were also bonfires on Needles Point with lots of singing, nonsensical songs being the favourites. Every breezy day, the lake's surface supported sailboats full of happy, laughing crews. Every visible moon shone down on canoe loads of young people and some who were not so young, either going somewhere or just drifting.

At Lynnehurst, Liza had two Webster girls to help in the kitchen. The Montreal cousins couldn't book hotel space for more than three weeks so Uncle Harold, Aunt Elsie, little Matilda and Harold Junior squeezed into Lynnehurst for one extra week. During July and part of August, Liza's 'family' was never less than ten in number for dinner.

Laundry day became serious business with sheets to be washed after every departing set of house guests. Charles instituted a custom Lynnehurst dwellers were to observe for several years. Every Monday, the family including all guests were loaded into canoes, rowboats and, if necessary, the sailboat, together with a large supply of picnic foods and ginger root beer. They would spend the day at South Shore Lookout to give the domestic staff uninterrupted time with suds, tubs and scrub boards.

Dumpy had several good times with Henrietta. Two or three times, they sailed down to Point Prowse to pick berries, taking an assortment of Lynnehurst guests with them. One sunny day, they took Dumpy's cousins, Robert, Regina and May, along with the two Webster boys, on a long canoe trip down the lake, through the river into the next lake, returning via the portage at Slide Lake.

"I'm so tired," exclaimed Henny at the end of that canoe excursion, "but let's do it again next year."

"I'm heavy with fatigue too ... such a good tiredness," agreed Dumpy, "We'll sleep tonight!"

As for the younger ones, they hardly had any tea before falling into bed. The Websters let James flop on his bed without undressing. Emily Webster covered him tenderly with an old quilt. In Chadwick Bay, Roderick had his hands full with most of the farm responsibilities. Stnce the fateful letter from his father's cousin in England, the Chadwicks were no longer wealthy. They had to relinquish hired hands. Miss Hilda virtually became maid of all work. Mrs. Chadwick's poor health prevented her from doing much besides her beautiful embroidery. If she did any mending of personal garments, it was in her own bedroom, secretly. Not even family members saw her do it. Mother Chadwick's hands could not be soiled, so Henrietta dirtied her lovely piano hands with vegetable paring and weed pulling.

"It doesn't bother Henny," declared her mother, "she has inherited her father's tough skin."

Mr. Chadwick said nothing about his wife's sense of justice, but when some of their fine furniture had to be sold, he refused to let the piano go. July went. August began.

The steamers still carried holiday seekers to and fro. Newspapers with declaration of war headlines arrived on the same steamer as the Whitbys and the Russells. The Russells could talk of nothing else. They said Prime Minister Borden had abruptly left The Royal Muskoka Hotel to return to Ottawa. Stanley Russell was determined to become a soldier. It was only a matter of time.

The Beasley family also was affected by the news headlines. The drums of war were calling Jack, their youngest son, to abandon his plans for graduate studies.

Always a scholar, Jack had done well at university but at a cost to the whole family.

His mother had scrimped and made many little sacrifices just when life could have become easier for her. She was devastated by her son's military aspirations.

"You are the only one in the family to have received so much education, even more than your father. Such a waste!" she declared with more vehemence than anyone had heard from her before.

Mr. Beasley, who had coached his youngest through the secondary school years, was of like mind.

"You are not gun fodder. You're a scholar. This young country needs people like you at home."

Alfred Beasley, whose prosperous building business had provided the well paid summer jobs that covered most of Jack's University expenses, took a different view.

He lectured Jack on the futility of war, but added that if he were younger, or without a family to support, he himself would enlist in defence of the Empire.

Mary Lynne Drayton was a witness to these conversations. She had become a constant visitor in the Beasley home. Every summer, she worked on Church Bazaar preparations with Mrs. Beasley, Hannah and Sarah. Over the years, she had overcome her childhood dislike of Jack. She had even played her part in encouraging his educational aspirations. She didn't know which way to advise him now, but she listened and shared his thoughts. Surprisingly enough, she found it a wonderful tribute that he should confide in her so completely.

Despite the war news, or perhaps spurred on by it, Dumpy and Henny organized a haying party to help Roderick Chadwick. Mary Lynne readily agreed to join them, as did Stanley and Basil Russell. Jack Beasley and Tom Armstrong took time off to help. Uncle John said Robert could join in as well.

The appointed week dawned clear and warm... perfect for haying. They had not been working very long on the first day when Mr. Chadwick noticed that pitching hay was too much for the delicate looking Doris.

"Please, Doris my dear, would you be kind enough to go to the house for some water. We'll be needing it in a little while."

Gratefully, Dumpy leaned her pitch fork against the wagon and picked her way between stubbles back to the house. They were working some distance from the Chadwick home. From this angle Doris noticed that the big house looked even more like an English Manor than it did from the lake. There was something incongruous about the towering walls intruding into rough cut fields and untamed woodlands. The log out-buildings nestling amidst lilac bushes were more at home in the rustic Muskoka setting. Chadwick Manor stood in contrast like some ancient obelisk in a barren battlefield.

Little breezes from the lake brought welcome refreshment to Dumpy's otherwise long, hot walk back to the house. She had opportunity to give full reign to her imagination. She fantasised about her dear Henrietta being a lost princess enslaved by a fearful monster named 'Poverty'. Poverty had locked his beautiful captive in a castle far from civilization. During the day, the friendly fairies transported her outside where she could talk to the birds and small animals. She could pick the loveliest of wild flowers and be warmed by the sunlight or refreshed by jewelled raindrops... all gifts from the good Queen Mother of the fairies. Alas, at night the Tyrant rattled his chains, calling her once more to be a prisoner within his dim, dark and damp walls.

"Never was a rescuing Prince Charming more wanted than here for

Princess Henny," thought Dumpy.

Once the house was reached, Mrs. Chadwick stirred herself to the extent of insisting on making weak lemonade, using some of the precious fruit the Draytons had given her earlier.

"This is a special occasion," she explained, "Roderick works so incessantly. I tell him to save some of his energy but he won't listen." She paused, then added quickly, "I am sure you are all working hard too."

Mrs. Chadwick stopped herself before uttering any complaints or alluding to Chadwick family misfortune. That would be beneath her dignity. Gentility and character must be preserved at all cost. Furthermore, it was difficult for her to express gratitude. That would be close to grovelling, which she detested in anyone.

"Here, my dear, can you carry this jug carefully?"

"Wouldn't a pail be easier?"

"Yes, child, of course. You are such a practical person. There are two tin mugs in the back shed. Perhaps you could take those as well... and a dipper," she added, remembering what the hired men had used.

The whole haying operation took several days. Some of the guest labourers dropped out before the job was done. Roderick worked at a fantastic pace. Nothing seemed too much for him. He was embarrassed that his family could not supply the usual hearty meals associated with work parties. Sensing his feelings, his guests not only brought their own picnic dinners with them ('to save time'), but in the afternoon, countered with apologies of their own.

"We hate to leave while the sun's still shining, but we want to sail back before the wind dies down," Or, "Mother has company for tea this evening, so we must get back."

Sometimes Roderick would remain in the fields or the barn to finish a task.

Other times he would follow them to the dock and stand for several minutes, watching the departing boat or boats.

The reward for these haying efforts was to be an expedition to the Chadwick's Bog. It was September before time could be found. The number of participants dwindled to three, Roderick, Henny and Dumpy. They were the ones who best appreciated the bog anyway. Mary Lynne would have enjoyed an outing of any sort but she felt called to spend more time with the Beasleys. Jack had still not made up his mind. He was enrolled at Toronto University working toward a master's degree in English Literature. Should he stick with his academic career no matter what, go for a term and then enlist if the war were still on, or leave his studies and enlist right away?

Mary and he talked these matters over during long walks or on evening outings in the Beasley family canoe. Mrs. Beasley and her daughters seemed to like to have Mary around the house during the day. They chatted comfortably on a wide range of topics, sharing domestic wisdom. Mary perfected her bread-making skills and learned how to make scones.

While the other haying helpers were scattered elsewhere and Mary Lynne was busy with the Beasleys, the three stalwart bog lovers set out, undismayed by the smallness of their expedition. All were equipped with biscuits and cheese, and high spirits. Henny took a basket for picking wild cranberries. Roderick had a book of poetry. Once there, they tramped the squishy bog to their hearts content. They checked on the welfare of pitcher plants and half filled Henny's basket with berries.

Then they trekked back to firm ground and rested on a pile of dry logs in a nearby open space, with a good view of the whole marshy expanse and its surrounding woodlands. They munched on biscuits and cheese and savoured the wonder of their wide wilderness. Roderick read aloud from his book. Then a comfortable silence fell upon them. Silence was a friend to those three. They often shared it in deep contentment. It was like that now.

Abruptly, Roderick broke the silence with 'I'm going to enlist!"
"What?"
"Roderick!"
"Why? How will your folks manage without you?"
"I've thought it all through. "I'll be an officer, of course. That will allow me to send money home to them. They can re-hire Will Jacobs."
"Can Will do as much as you do?"
"I don't know, but this'll give me a chance to see something of the world."
"Oh, Roderick." Henny couldn't find words to express her state of shock.
"Maybe I can make a career out of the military. I don't see much prospect here except hard work and poverty."
"Roderick, I'm so sorry." Dumpy could think of nothing more to say. She was seeing that he had more options in his world than did his sister. He misinterpreted her look of concern.

During most of this discourse, Henrietta had maintained a deathly silence; then, rising to suggest the homeward trek, she asked, "When are you going to tell mother and father?"

"I don't know."

They trailed back to Chadwick Manor in silence... an uncomfortable silence.

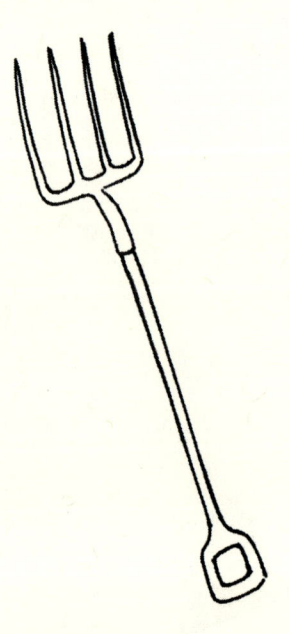

Blame The Blandfords

A few days after Roderick's explosive decision, Dumpy received more disturbing news. This came by steamer one morning, bound in a fat envelope bearing American postage and addressed in a familiar handwriting.

"My apologies, Miss Drayton," the purser explained, "I don't know how this got mislaid when we left the rest of the mail yesterday."

Dumpy held the letter at arm's length as if it were a hurtful weapon she did not wish to bring nearer.

Just then Alice and Jack Armstrong ran up to Dumpy, begging for one last story before their family left that day. Tom (Junior) stood aloof, being too old for stories, but Dumpy noticed he was within earshot.

"Did I ever tell you about the fairies that were stowaways on a steamer?"

"Tell us, Tell us!"

"Jack, stop jumping. Honestly, you are a real Jack-in-the-Box. I think we'll have to call you Boxie."

"Tell us the story!"

"There isn't time. Perhaps you can find those stowaways on the boat."

"Come children," called Aunt Tilda, "It's time to board."

"Say good-bye to Doris, but hurry," added Uncle Tom.

"Good-bye."

"Good-bye."

After the hubbub of farewells and departures, those remaining stood waving until the *Medora* rounded Point Caroline, the echoes of her whistle simmering into silence. Aunt Sally, who had brought her brood to see their cousins off, now hustled them off the wharf and onto the road. Mary Lynne and Liza glanced at Dumpy.

Curbing their curiosity, they went without comment back to Lynnehurst. Charles was already in New Orleans. Dumpy had Brown's Landing Wharf to herself.

Dumpy settled on one of Buppa's old benches and stared at the lake before opening her letter. The lake was so calm this morning. Some of the trees on the Drayton-Webster shore were beginning to turn, sending yellow and red reflections to the lake's mirror surface. The closer reflections were larger and more awe-inspiring.

There was no boat or canoe in sight to cause ripples. Dumpy broke the seal and opened Julian's letter.

She read carefully, every lengthy paragraph and much 'between the lines' as well, following in her heart, the feelings Julian and Geraldine must be experiencing.

It seems that all had gone smoothly at first. The Blandfords had welcomed Julian into their midst, piling extravagant praise upon him at every opportunity. The blind infatuation between Geraldine and Julian blossomed into friendship which, in turn, deepened into uncamouflaged love. The more the young lovers came to know and understand one another, the stronger their love became.

Then, when the Senior Blandfords suddenly realized that de Poncier wealth was greatly reduced from the glories of earlier times, their attitudes changed drastically.

Nor did they wish to relinquish the daughter who was willingly useful to them in so many ways. Their home life without Geraldine would be bleak. In the midst of realizing all this, they received a grievous shock. Audrey Blandford eloped with her villainous beau, Maurice Beaumont, whose gambling debts were already causing them such dismay. To make a long story short, both Caddo and Stella Blandford positively refused to grant permission for the youthful Geraldine to marry within the foreseeable future.

They worked on her feelings by citing exaggerated gossip concerning "one branch of the de Ponciers."

"You wouldn't want to bring idiot children into our family, Geraldine!" cautioned Mrs. Blandford.

"Think about it very carefully," urged her father. "We are only considering what is good for you, darling Geraldine."

"Umph!" exclaimed Dumpy when she read that sentence. Her heart ached at the injustice.

"When did Mr. Blandford ever consider anyone's good other than his own!"

The Blandfords had asked their daughter to stop seeing Julian altogether.

Geraldine, torn by natural affection and sense of family duties on the one hand and by her complete love for Julian on the other, had asked Julian to be patient.

"Patient!" she groaned, "Nothing of the sort. Julian should ride in on a white charger and carry her off. Those selfish people. Don't they know what they are doing to our Geraldine?"

Dumpy slapped Julian's letter down onto the bench.

She regarded the lake once more. It was still there, spread out before her, calm and serene. Was there a divine message here?

"Blessed Assurance," she commented, "You are undamaged by our passions and human follies. How I envy you."

Obviously Julian was worn out with the wrangling and emotional torture. What helpful language could she use in her reply?

Eventually she returned to Lynnehurst to consult her mother and sister.

They were made privy to the letter and concurred completely with her view of the situation. They good-naturedly agreed to return to New Orleans earlier than they had planned.

That night she wrote to Julian endorsing his misgivings about the motives of Mr. and Mrs. Blandford. She counselled him to persevere.

Mary had wanted to stay for the fall colours which Jack Beasley had predicted would be particularly brilliant. However, she put that consideration out of her mind.

"Geraldine needs us," agreed Liza, "Her parents wouldn't dare refuse her friendship with us."

"Our house could be a haven for her," added Mary Lynne.

"Perhaps I can talk to Mrs. Blandford," suggested Liza, "She's not a bad woman; I can allay her fears."

"I'm not so sure," put in Mary Lynne, "but you can try."

"We can at least talk to Geraldine," said Dumpy, "and assure her that to deny Julian would be a greater fault than leaving home. Can't we quote the Bible on that one? The Blandfords are great Bible quoters themselves, but sometimes I think they don't really understand it."

Once the reply letter had been written to Julian and plans were underway for closing Lynnehurst, Dumpy managed to have some peace of mind. One night, as she lay abed regarding the rough beams on the ceiling of the north room, she thought of Buppa, who had died in this very room. She remembered her anguish at the time and how the painful feelings healed with the passing years. His death had not destroyed the happy childhood memories of her grandfather; they still lived inside her. She murmured a short prayer of thanksgiving for her family.

"Geraldine is being victimized by her own family. My friend Henny is a prisoner in her home. But even if I never marry, I'll be happy enough and entirely free. Thank you, God, for arranging my birth. I love the places where I live. I love the family you gave me... Mother, Father, Alan, Mary Lynne... There's my larger family too, everyone belonging to Lynnehurst and Brown's Landing. Thank you."

Changes

NORA WEBSTER LEFT THEM WHEN SCHOOL STARTED AGAIN but Elsie decided she had enough education. She would stay to help close Lynnehurst.

"Your father has promised to make us a mouse-proof cupboard someday," announced Liza, as she and Mary Lynne were wrapping wool blankets in moth balls for storage in an old trunk.

"I hope he makes it big enough to stack all our mattresses inside too," added Dumpy, who was helping Elsie lift a mattress from one of Buppa's homemade wooden beds onto the 'new' iron bed. The metal bedstead was pulled to the centre of the room every winter and piled high with mattresses. They had discovered that mice couldn't climb its cold, hard, slippery legs.

"Elsie, tell your father that Mr. John is bringing Willie with him this year to drain the water pump and board up the windows. Your folks have enough to do at your place closing those cottages and extra rooms."

"That's good of you. I'll tell him, but I think he always enjoys his time here. Of course, it was easier in the years when Alfred Beasley came with him. Alfred always took great pride in Lynnehurst... said it was his first building job."

"Here's the groundsheet," interrupted Dumpy, "I think it's big enough to cover most of the mattresses... top ones at least."

"Yes," continued Elsie without pausing in her work, "Dad says he used to see Alfred as a lad, rowing all the way here each spring and fall, just to look, so he started asking him to help. Now look at Alfred!"

"Indeed. He's always busy these days. People know he's an excellent builder."

"Says he learned from Dad, but Dad says Alfred knows more. It just seems to come natural to him."

"I saw the designs he drew for the Walkers. He could call himself an architect too," added Dumpy.

Liza's mind was still on Frank Webster, "I think your father lost heart in Lynnehurst after that last crow episode. He didn't say much, but I know he doesn't like to think about it."

"Yes, for all his gruffness, he really is tenderhearted inside."

"I heard a crow yesterday," remarked Mary.

"There are a few, but they no longer conduct their crow parliaments in our tree," answered Liza.

Dumpy, pausing in her work, looked out the east windows and sighed. She could just see a corner of the new vegetable garden near the place where Buppa had first started a garden. For a few seconds, she was a little girl again on an early spring morning. Then she returned to the job at hand, but she was silent.

A few days and several conversations later, the four women pronounced their job done. Liza said she wanted to have her last swim at Old Drayton Farm just for old times sake. Her daughters and Sally's family joined her, knowing the shallow water would be warmer than deeper water elsewhere. The C. R. Drayton's ate their last meals and slept their last night with Aunt Sally and Uncle John at New Drayton Farm.

Mary Lynne was with her mother and sister on the steamer and train as far as Toronto. It had been decided that she should spend the winter with the Armstrongs.

Aunt Matilda and the young cousins welcomed the idea enthusiastically. Though it was explained that Mary was having a change of scenery and giving Aunt Tilda a hand with the children, everyone knew there were other reasons.

One of those reasons was Mary Lynne Drayton's long-time yearning to attend university. She had heard that women were being admitted more often now. Despite her lack of Canadian Matriculation, it was arranged through enrolment in St. Hilda's College that she could take a few courses at Trinity College. Some University of Toronto students had gone to war already, leaving their collegiate spaces behind them. Charlie Drayton's powers of persuasion, and his money, convinced the authorities to make special arrangements. Mary was not to live in residence or be considered a candidate for a degree. She didn't mind. Was it a strong thirst for knowledge or a large case of feminine curiosity that motivated her? Whichever, she now blissfully contemplated a winter in Toronto. Jack Beasley met them at Union Station, promising to see about a cab and to deliver Mary safely to the Armstrongs. He had come earlier to settle in at Trinity College and now was completely at Mary's disposal.

"I was surprised when I got your letter," he said later, "but it certainly cheered me up to know you would be here too."

In deference to his parents, he had decided on compromise. He would pursue his studies for one term.

"If the war is over by Christmas, I'll stay, but, Mary, I have a feeling it won't be anywhere near over. Mother and Dad know my intention. I pray they'll be proud of me in time."

"Jack, no matter what happens, I promise always to be their friend."

"Thank you."

಄

Two days later, in New Orleans, Charles Robert Drayton met his beloved wife and youngest offspring with news that Julian de Poncier would join them for tea. Charles also warned them that Mammy had gone to great effort to clean house for them.

"I don't need to remind you that her eyes aren't what they used to be, but she struggled valiantly through all three floors and even made a Spanish Cream before exhaustion forced her to retire to her quarters.

"Cleaning never was her strong point; in fact, she hated it. Why didn't you get someone else to do it?" asked Liza.

"She wouldn't let me. She didn't want no strangers touching Miz. Liza's things!" He mimicked Mammy's drawl, heaving his shoulders and marshalling his eyes in perfect Mammy-like indignation.

"Oh dear! Whatever are we going to do?"

"Do? You're going out to her cabin to tell her everything looks just perfect and she's not to worry herself. Dumpy can finish getting the tea together."

"Of course. But the poor loyal soul needs someone to look after her as well as to do her work in the house. How can we hire anyone if she's going to object?"

"Ask her to find someone she knows to come, live with her and help out a bit in the house," suggested Dumpy.

"Well said, sagacious child."

The word "child" was a term of endearment from the lips of Charles. It was not offensive in the slightest to his grown-up daughter.

Weary as they were, the two travellers did their best to comfort and encourage Mammy, and later, Julian.

Dumpy managed to produce an excellent collation of salad, ham and hot, creamy macaroni with cheese. She was grateful for the Spanish Cream. Desserts were essential for her father and brother but, neither she nor her mother enjoyed making them. After the meal, Charles and Alan volunteered to clear and clean up.

"Julian, you go in the living-room with the ladies and visit a bit more. They haven't had the pleasure of your company for a long time," suggested Charles.

"On the contrary, it is I who have been deprived, but I shan't keep them long. They're tired after the trip and will want to retire early."

Sometime later, Liza joined the kitchen crew while Doris accompanied Julian to the door.

"Dear Doris," Julian began, as they stood in the vestibule, "I've always thought you and your mother the gentlest of women. Tonight, I detect a ferocious spirit in your support of my cause."

He turned his head slightly, appearing to be deep in thought. Then, turning to look straight at Doris, he continued: "At one time, I rather thought it would be you that I might marry. You're a true friend. We could have made a satisfactory team, but... Geraldine. You know how I feel about Geraldine."

"Yes, I do. Julian, I believe that friendship is the best basis for marriage, but, it must be even better if the romantic feelings are there as well."

"Feelings, ah yes, there are many wonderful feelings, but, quite apart from my feelings is the realization that Geraldine is so unprotected. Doris, she needs me. The world, including her own relatives, could so easily take undue advantage of her. You, on the other hand, are so practical, so perceptive of the world as it really is that, married or not, you'll be able to look after yourself. I hope you understand. There is no one in this world I admire more than you, but..."

"Julian," her eyes met his, "I understand."

Julian squeezed her hand, then quickly exited through the long glass door. He was gone down the front steps. Dumpy stood looking after him. She thought of their night at the opera, seemingly long ago.

"Did I love Julian?" she asked herself, "Or did I just enjoy his company? Perhaps I'll find another opera lover someday."

❦

In the morning, Mammy did not appear. Dumpy went out to call her. There was no response. The door to her small cabin would not budge. Dumpy's heart sank. Somewhere, a mockingbird was singing. Sunshine filled all available places in the Drayton back yard as Dumpy let her eyes roam over the familiar scene. In one corner, was the swinging tree, a meagre shade beneath it. Nearby was the place where their sand box had been and where no grass grew, even yet. On the other side of the yard, there was a pile of firewood, Mammy's wicker chair, and a few yellow chrysanthemums struggling to remain cheerful. Dumpy's gaze shifted to the board walk between cabin and kitchen. It's well worn planks told of many a trip to and fro.

That boardwalk has been the highway of Mammy's life, thought Dumpy, *It's been, to her, what the railroad to Toronto has been for us. Mammy's 'highway' terminated at the back porch. Those wooden steps must have been a challenge to someone with rheumatism*, Dumpy's thoughts continued... *thank goodness Alan made that railing for her.*

All these scenes and thoughts passed instantly through Dumpy's mind. It was one of those moments in life when time seemed to stand still for Doris Amelia Drayton. With heavy feelings, she made her way back to the house. Later Alan climbed in through the cabin window to discover what his sister had suspected.

"Were you terribly upset, Alan?" asked Liza. She was good to you when you were a little boy. I think you were fond of her too."

"She has a lovely smile on her face," replied Alan, "If this is sadness, it is also peace."

"I feel that too," said Liza, "All she wanted last night was another pillow to raise her head and shoulders a bit. When I tucked the big soft one from my bed behind her, she thanked me with that smile. I thought, then, it might also be a farewell smile."

Charles sighed deeply, heaved his shoulders, then did the necessaries.

A few days later, in Toronto, Mary Lynne clutched a letter from New Orleans, cried her eyes out, and beat her fists fruitlessly on Aunt Matilda's dressing table.

So ended the life of a woman who started life as a slave and lived it as a servant: Gone were all her memories, memories of the old plantation at Poncierville and memories of the frenzied excitement of Emancipation Day, when hundreds of black arms waved kerchiefs and flags high in the air or hoisted little black children onto black shoulders to see over bigger black bodies.

Mammy's death did not get mentioned on a printed page anywhere nor is there a grave marker to say where she lies, but she left behind five white people who would never forget that one black woman. The memory of her, was passed down for generations with other Drayton family treasures.

The following week, Mrs. and Miss Drayton paid a social call on Mrs. and Miss Blandford. When the conversation had settled to congenial chatter, Liza suddenly broke the mood by inviting Geraldine to come for a visit.

"I'm doing some sewing. Geraldine, you have such good taste, I would appreciate having your opinion," then, turning to Mrs. Blandford, she added, "without Mary, the house seems empty. I know Doris would enjoy some young company."

"Thank you. I'd love to come," Geraldine glanced uneasily at her mother, picked up the tray of coffee cups and disappeared.

"Now Liza," began Stella, "I'm not sure I should allow it. Geraldine has been so strange lately. The truth is that she's fancied herself in love. We've forbidden her to see the young man. You know about Audrey. I have my fears."

Mrs. Blandford nodded her head knowingly in Liza's direction and rolled her eyes towards Dumpy. Dumpy understood the intended hint but did not budge.

"Geraldine will be perfectly safe with us," continued Liza, "A change of scenery will do her good. We'll bring her back before Sunday."

Again, Stella looked towards Dumpy and back at Liza, "There are many things I'd like to discuss with you."

"Please feel free to talk. Anything you have to say to me can be said in front of Doris. The years have passed, Stella. Our girls are not children anymore."

"Well then, I warned you. It's this de Poncier fellow," Turning to Dumpy, Mrs. Blandford added, "I always thought he was your friend. I trusted that he was a gentleman."

"He is a gentleman."

"Perhaps he's genteel, but the family is strange. You know those de Ponciers near the Herberts. I don't need to spell it out. Then there is that insane Challa up on the plantation. There is a reason they don't let her visit New Orleans."

"Stella, someone has misled you. Those simple de Ponciers are not closely connected to our de Ponciers. As for Challa, she's perfectly sane. I think it's sad that she prefers to stay at home now that she's elderly, but that's not a sign of insanity."

"Well," Stella's voice had less assurance in it now. "People say she used to be such a beauty but became ugly because... well, it's a punishment... she's ashamed... they say she has a nigger lover."

Here, the good woman buried her face in her hands as if the thought was too horrible; even the uttering of it was pollution to them all.

Liza was silent a moment, grieving over the power of prejudice.

Dumpy simply burst out laughing, "Mrs. Blandford. I've visited Wisteria house at Poncierville. Aunt Challa is sentimental. She lives in the past but she's quite sensible. As for a negro lover, please banish the thought as vile gossip. 'Uncle Claudius' is an old family servant. He lives alone in one of the old slave cabins. She lives alone in the big house. Sometimes he sits on the back steps to listen while she plays the piano. Sometimes he sits there and plays his banjo. There's nothing improper."

"Stella," began Liza in a low, steady voice, "Miss de Poncier remembers happier days when she was a beautiful young woman, a belle, with many admirers.

"There must have been wonderful parties in the ballroom at Wisteria House and in other plantation homes before the war. Perhaps she lost a beau in the war. Do you blame her for living in the past? It's sad to think of her like that, unable to face the changes. I wonder how you or I would be if we'd lived through the same circumstances."

"Perhaps you're right, but... still, I don't like to let Geraldine out of my sight."

"Stella, have you ever had any cause to distrust us?" Liza's grey-blue eyes were gazing straight into those of her friend. There was prayer behind those eyes.

Mrs. Blandford paused. She knew that Mr. Blandford owed much of his success in the business world to the recommendations he had received from Charlie Drayton. Her heart melted.

"Very well, Geraldine may go. You are kind, as always."

"Thank you," uttered Dumpy, quite spontaneously.

"I should thank you," replied Mrs. Blandford, the good-natured part of her once more gaining control.

Aftermath

IN HER EFFORT TO FORGET THE REALITY OF THE 1914 - 1918 WAR, Mary Lynne Drayton destroyed most of Jack Beasley's wartime correspondence. She kept only his last letter from the trenches as sufficient commentary on his experience of war.

My Dear Mary,

Fighting a war is not the glorious encounter with danger that I imagined as a boy. So much is a matter of waiting, enduring and hoping to survive. I live in a wet ditch. That's what a trench is, a big ditch sufficiently deep that when we stand we can see enough to aim our rifles. When we exchange fire with the enemy, the noise is deafening.
However, most of the time, we are not firing. The waiting is tedious. We try to avoid the rats which crawl or swim around our boots looking for our rations. If we kill one, three more appear. If I try to snooze at night, leaning against the muddy trench wall, I fear a rat will crawl over me in search of a biscuit in one of my pockets.
I keep telling myself that someday it will all end. I'll be with you in Muskoka.
    Love,
        Jack

If Jack had been in the Battle of the Somme, his letter would have contained more gruesome details or it never would have been written. As it was, Jack Beasley was lucky to receive a crippling leg wound which took him out of action in November, 1915. After several hospital shifts and a turn at recruiting back in Canada, he finished out the war with a forestry division in France. The German prisoners of war assigned to duties under Jack's supervision were happy enough to be out of the fighting action too. These prisoners worked well in the woods, enjoying a degree of camaraderie with their captors.

Mary Lynne spent the war years dividing her time between university courses and knitting for the Red Cross. She, Aunt Tilda and Alice Armstrong had many knitting bees together. By the end of four years, Mary also had as many course credits as her university colleagues who received degrees. Had she been fully enrolled, she would have been given the prize in Ancient History. In later years, she often bragged about this non-prize; the young man who actually got the prize forgot the honour within ten years.

During Jack's six months of recruiting back in the Muskoka area, he was in and out of Toronto. He and Mary Lynne became engaged. Mary was at Toronto's Union Station when Jack returned from France as part of the General Demobilization. They were married that April in New Orleans.

Roderick Chadwick returned from the war without any serious damage to his body but he was a changed person. Vimy Ridge had turned him into a Canadian rather than a colonial Englishman. His time in England introduced him to a maiden aunt who was so impressed with her brother's son that she made him her chief heir. Now Roderick was only too glad to return to life as a farmer in Chadwick Bay. Seeing the world no longer held any charm for him; neither did he have the slightest desire for a life with the military. Furthermore, every time he was on or near a farm in England or on the continent he had put his powers of observation to work. Now, loaded with fresh ideas, he was eager to promote them in Muskoka. As soon as he could find a convenient time, he would propose to Doris. Together, they would build a glorious Chadwick Kingdom in Muskoka. Roderick bought a lovely diamond ring in Toronto en route home.

Stanley Whitby died at Somme. Melvin Jacobs lost his left leg. When Christie Street Hospital in Toronto finally finished patching him together, Melvin returned home to become the telephone operator in the village. With the help of his wooden leg and a cane, Melvin was able to stand in front of the altar to exchange marriage vows with Nora Webster.

Dumpy spent all the war years between New Orleans and Lynnehurst. She felt a partial guilt that her life was virtually untouched while others experienced deprivation or tragedy or both. Once the Americans entered the conflict, some of her New Orleans acquaintances enlisted but none were killed.

At Lynnehurst, Dumpy didn't mind the reduced number of visitors. She rather enjoyed having time to savour the natural world around the lake or deep in the woods.

She could wander freely on her own with nothing to fear . On rainy days and in the evenings, there was more time to indulge in reading. Unlike her sister, she saw little point in university. One could educate oneself through books. Henrietta was of a similar disposition. They shared everything from novels to serious books on scientific subjects found on the Chadwick or Lynnehurst bookshelves. Many and varied were their discussions carried on while Dumpy helped with Henny's gardening chores or on berry-picking expeditions.

Dumpy also spent more time with her Aunt Sally. She grew to understand why her mother was so fond of this cheerful, intelligent person. New Drayton Farmhouse seemed empty with no small children about. With Will away, Robert took over many of the farm functions. Susan was married and living in Victoria. Carolyn had a job in Toronto. Regina and May were old enough to be quite helpful to their mother but they still liked inventing stories with Dumpy or sailing in the Lynnehurst dingy.

Almost daily, the two families swam together, either at Lynnehurst or down on Old Farm Beach. Together, they picked strawberries in June, raspberries in July, blackberries in August and September. Some Julys, Regina and May went with Dumpy and Henny on the long huckleberry treks. If Aunt Belle was around, she too joined them.

Once 1920 arrived, the effects of the war seemed to fade. Times were prosperous. Summer visitors again invaded Muskoka. Charles Drayton decided to enlarge Lynnehurst. He hired Alfred Beasley to draw plans for a larger kitchen, the addition of an office with telephone and a library extending eastward to an open sun porch. Over all this, there were to be more bedrooms and a screened sleeping porch.

Half of Aunt Belle's old bedroom was to become the much-coveted 'mouse room'.

The floor space was to be just larger than the largest double bed mattress. Walls, ceiling and floor were to be lined in sheet metal. Even a stray beaver would be unable to gnaw its way through this fortified cupboard.

For starters, Alfred built a launch house between Buppa's old boathouse and the steamer wharf. He also enlarged the "new" boathouse on shore behind the sailboat pier.

In June of 1921, a brand new Ditchburn motor launch arrived to occupy the launch house and the additions to Lynnehurst were begun.

Dumpy quickly learned how to drive Daisy Belle, as the new boat was christened. Daisy Belle made regular visits to Chadwick Bay. On one such occasion, a walk to the Bog was planned for 'the three musketeers' as Henny, Dumpy and Roderick now were called. At the last minute, Henny couldn't go. She had to clear and clean her room for the new school teacher who would arrive the next day. It would take time to re-establish her modest wardrobe and personal belongings in the small bedroom down the hall at the back of Chadwick Manor... an area once reserved for servants.

"I thought when Mr. Beasley retired, he offered to board the new teacher and assist her," protested Dumpy.

"Yes, she started out there but said Sarah Elizabeth's old room was too small and that she would prefer to be out in the country. She likes to take long walks," explained Henny.

"She certainly will have a long walk from here to the school."

"Indeed."

"Can I help you?"

"No, you go along. Roderick has been looking forward to this."

Sensing that Henny preferred to work alone, Dumpy was soon trotting off with Roderick. She looked forward to seeing the bog which they had not visited for some time. Once there, but before they crossed over to the floating moss, Roderick halted right beside the pile of logs where he had disclosed his departure plans in 1914. He attached poetic importance to this particular spot.

"My dear Doris," he began, "you may have wondered why I took so long to speak to you. I wanted to make sure the farm was in good shape. Our prospects are good now. Poultry are selling well. Cottagers will want fresh vegetables from Henny's garden. Since the supply boats stopped servicing this part of the lake I make deliveries to cottagers twice a week in our D.P. We hire a man full time again. I'll soon be able to hire a maid. I couldn't tell you this earlier because of Father's death. How could we celebrate our happiness until the grieving period ended?"

"What do you mean?" she faltered. Dumpy sensed in the back of her mind that something unusual was happening. She realized but did not want to know.

"Here it is!" he announced triumphantly, producing a diamond for her inspection. I am now well able to look after you. You can choose the date and place for our wedding. It would be easier if it were in Canada rather than Louisiana."

Her mind spun in somersaults. It required every ounce of strength she could muster to restrain herself. Surprise, shock and anger vied for control.

"Roderick," she confessed, with her eyes fixed on the glistening ring. "I didn't realize you felt this way. We've always been good friends. I hope we always shall be, but, I cannot marry you."

It was his turn to experience shock. "But Doris, I thought... I mean, you always... is there someone else?"

Poor Dumpy wished she could tell a lie. It would have been so easy to invent a romantic interest in a man in far away New Orleans. With Julian safely married to Geraldine, she could conjure up no possible suitor.

"I don't think I want to get married... at least, that's the way I feel now."

"You need time?... I can wait... How much time do you need?"

"Roderick, it's no use. I don't want to marry you. I like you the same way I like my uncles. I respect you, but I don't feel the kind of love for you that a woman should have for a husband. It would be wrong to marry you unless I have that kind of love."

"Your uncles!... Your feelings!..." Stifling an impulse to fling the ring into the bog, he jammed it into his pocket. Clenching his fists for a few seconds, he paced back and forth, completely at a loss for words.

Neither knew what to say or do next. Literature in their homes described what civilized people do and say when a proposal of marriage is accepted. They had read nothing on the proprieties of rejection.

Dumpy hoped Roderick would not recall the rejection episode in Pride and Prejudice. In Jane Austen's novel Mr. Darcy later became acceptable; Dumpy knew Roderick would never be. She didn't want to raise his hopes.

"I'm sorry, Roderick; it never occurred to me that you would think of me this way. Does Henny know?"

"She may have guessed. I spoke to no one of my intentions... what shall we do now? If we go back to the house right away, someone may ask why."

"That's true. I don't think I want to face any questions either. Perhaps we should proceed as usual to inspect pitcher plants and pick wild cranberries. That'll give us both time to compose our thoughts."

They followed her suggestion but the place did not hold it's usual charm for them. The muted, earthy colours were as lovely as ever, the bird songs as sweet.

But, instead of spelling freedom, the wide open expanse oppressed them with a message of boredom. The stagnant water stank. The sun's warmth irritated. They did not stay very long.

On the trail back, Dumpy's mind was working on strategy.

"Roderick, I'll go straight to the boat. If anyone inquires, you can explain that I don't feel well. I want to go home right away."

"Doris," He hesitated.

"Yes."

"I hope we're still friends."

"Of course."

"I wish there were something I could do for you."

"There is."

"What is it?"

"Please put a telephone in Chadwick Manor. It would make life so much easier for your mother and the girls."

"Yes, Doris. I'll do that."

"Roderick, I don't think I'll mention this to Henny unless she asks me something outright or unless I learn that you have spoken to her."

"Thank you. I don't think I want to speak about it to anyone."

༄

As it happened, no embarrassing questions were asked. When Roderick got back to the house, his women folk were all in a dither. Miss Ethel Thorne, the new teacher, had evidently been in a hurry to take up her new quarters. Instead of arriving the next morning, she'd hired Seth Talbot to transport herself and her worldly goods to Chadwick Bay that very afternoon. Seth had long ago exchanged his horses and wagon for a sturdy Ford pickup. However, the back roads were little improved since early days. Miss Thorne arrived much shaken and in need of a bath. Being new to the area, she did not realize that travel by boat was the usual choice for lake dwellers.

Miss Thorne realized her second mistake when she came down for tea. The dining-room table was resplendent with white linen, silver service and Spode bone china. The savory stew which Hilda and her mother had hastily stretched with last minute additions from Henny's garden was now ensconced in a large soup tureen near the teapot at Mrs. Chadwick's end of the table. A loaf of homemade bread, still warm from the oven, was emitting a wonderful odour from the other end of the table where it sat upon a silver-rimmed circular board. There was home churned butter, fruit jam, a jug of milk and a glass bowl of blackberries. Ethel's timidity, when faced with the formal niceties of a Chadwick meal, was soon overcome by her pangs of hunger. She carefully sat herself in the chair indicated, trying to adjust herself properly as Roderick moved it closer to the table.

"Miss Thorne, would you care for some stew?" Mrs. Chadwick's icy politeness cloaked the instant dislike Ethel had inspired. Hilda and Henny noticed something was amiss but Roderick was too engrossed in his own unhappiness to notice anyone else.

Ethel's next action was to congeal Mrs. Chadwick's poor first impression into permanent disapproval. Propelled by hunger and unchecked by any instruction in good manners, Ethel simply accepted the offered plate of stew with an eager grunt and, grabbing a spoon, she began shovelling in the food as fast as she could. Her head was bent over the plate to position the mouth as close to it as possible.

No one else had been served yet.

A formidable person at the best of times, Mrs. Chadwick could, when displeased, stiffen herself with dignity to a silent intensity that could quell a room full of normal people. There was that kind of silence now. Roderick remained immune.

Hilda and Henny froze. Ethel felt it, paused and looked up.

"Uninstuit!" was the only word Mrs. Chadwick uttered.

Ethel did not understand French. There had been no such thing as a French governess in her background, but she did understand the language of eyes. Her own fearful ones were locked in a stare with those of her hostess.

In a few seconds, Mrs. Chadwick relinquished her victim and continued to preside over the meal. Miss Thorne was served other items of food but no one made any effort throughout the meal to converse with her.

Ethel was left to study the situation around her. Being an exceptionally clever woman, she did not often make mistakes. She knew her lack of culture was a strike against her. That was why she elected to leave the Beasleys before it became obvious.

It was now painfully clear that her choice of a backwoods home was based on a very false assumption. These Chadwicks were even more cultured than the homey Beasleys.

Could she find an excuse to bolt and run again or should she make the best of a bad situation?

Perhaps she could learn manners by watching these people. Roderick was the one she watched the most carefully. He was clearly unhappy. She knew what to do about that. Men were usually easy targets for her schemes. She might as well give up on the women.

Ethel's early life had been beset with every kind of misfortune and human vice imaginable. She had had two choices: give up and sink to the lowest level available until extinction finished her off, or use her wits to claw her way to the top of the heap in order to survive. She had chosen the latter. With much effort, she had procured some schooling and had decided to become a teacher. Teachers were always needed somewhere. Being quick to learn, she could easily keep ahead of her students. She drilled them well. Most of them succeeded at tests. Discipline was no problem. For these reasons, her last two school boards had rated her highly.

Roderick was truly unaware of Ethel's gauche behaviour and of the discomfort she produced in his mother and sisters. In the days that followed, he took pleasure in the flattery offered and in all the requests for further knowledge. Ethel had him reading favourite poems and books to her almost every evening. Not only did she enjoy the sound of his voice, he enjoyed it also.

Ethel's attention restored Roderick's personal happiness before another week had passed. So fast was the recovery that his sisters and mother never really noticed anything wrong. Later, Henrietta thought she had noticed a shadow of something on his face that fateful afternoon. She asked herself what she could have done if she'd paid better attention, an unanswerable, haunting question.

More Changes

ETHEL THORNE SPENT THE WINTER OF 1921 IN MUSKOKA pursuing her own interests at Chadwick Manor. Charles, Liza and Doris Drayton spent that winter, as usual, in New Orleans. Let us join Charles in his office at C.R. Drayton & Son one day the following spring. He is asking himself if this is the time to fulfil his dream of retiring home to Canada? Liza would enjoy living closer to her sisters and to Mary Lynne.

However, she would miss being near her only son, Alan. Alan had married Miriam Herbert six years previously and was now the father of a son, Seigfried, and a baby daughter, Elizabeth.

Alan was taking hold, more and more, in C.R. Drayton but there was more responsibility than one person could handle. Forey Saunders, the senior accountant, who knew the business well, wanted to retire in a few years. All but one of the senior positions in the firm were filled by men of Charles' generation. The exception, warehouse manager Tom O'Neil, liked to give orders. He could keep the darkies in line but Charles always suspected that black Sam had more brains and kept better track of everything in the storage areas. Certainly, it was Sam, acting with his customary, slow motion, who had been sensible enough to extinguish a back room fire before serious damage had occurred. On the same occasion, Tom had run hither and thither shouting contradictory orders, generally creating panic. Clearly Tom would never be a partner in the firm.

"It would be fun to promote Sam," said Charles to himself with a mischievous smile, "Alas, someone might notice that he can't read or write."

Another wry smile danced briefly over his handsome Drayton face.

"Something has amused you?" inquired Forey Saunders as he entered the office with a handful of papers.

The President's office at C.R. Drayton & Co. consisted of a large roll-top desk in one corner of the Second Floor Cutting Room. The office extended as far as a wall of elbow-high wooden filing drawers over which the President could view activities on the entire floor. Atop the President's desk a mass of wooden pigeon holes were labelled neatly, A to Z. Above, a green shielded light bulb hung from the ceiling, its meagre light amplified by rows of large windows. More large windows lined the two outer walls of the Cutting Room. A wide oak table bearing a few cardboard file holders, defined the office's rear limits.

"Amusing?" returned Charles. "Maybe, maybe not. The fact is..." he looked over the files to be sure they were alone today, "The fact is, I want to retire someday, but Alan needs a partner. I believe you would like to retire also?"

"Someday. Yes, I would," replied Forey, "Alan needs a young partner with energy as well as brains. This business is building fantastically fast. Have a look at these figures."

Charles received the papers gratefully, taking a minute to glance over them.

"It's about what I thought... Forey, I have a feeling this won't continue. The bubble will burst. I've counselled Alan not to expand the business. We'll just enjoy the extra while it comes, even if we have to put up with a little crowding."

"That's wise. I'm thinking the same way. I worry about all the young families who have mortgages on big homes these days. If anything happens to this prosperity, they'll lose everything... Say, Charles!"

"Yes?"

"I have an idea. My nephew in Massachusetts is looking for fresh fields to conquer. His mother's people, the Ames family, are wealthy business people. He's received an excellent education and I think he has the makings of a good businessman. Why don't I invite him to visit?"

"It wouldn't do any harm, Forey."

That Sunday, Charles shared his thoughts about the business with Liza and Doris. After a light lunch the three of them took a stroll along the levee. There wasn't much boat traffic to watch, but it was pleasant to feel a warm March sun and to look for signs of spring.

"When we move back to Canada, would you rather live in Toronto or at Lynnehurst?"

"Oh Charles! Do you think we could manage the wintertime in Muskoka?"

"John and Sally do."

"I've always wanted to have a Christmas at Lynnehurst, but if we lived in Toronto, we would be near Mary Lynne and Jack."

"If we move, we won't be near Alan's little ones," Charles reminded her.

"We can always visit New Orleans."

"If Miriam will allow it, Seigfried and Elizabeth could spend extra time with us at Lynnehurst."

Dumpy said nothing. New Orleans had always been home. Moving to Canada would be a major change. But the more she turned the matter over in her mind, the more she realized that the larger half of her soul was Canadian. There was little to hold her to the South.

"Doris, dear, you're very quiet. What are you thinking?"

"I'm thinking that if I were to leave New Orleans, there would be a sad hole in my heart... but I could live with that... if you told me I would never see Muskoka again, I'd be completely devastated."

"You could come South for Opera Season. Alan and Miriam would make room for you. You have friends here who'd do the same."

"What about our house?" asked Liza, "Does Alan want it?"

"No, I asked him about that one time. He says it's too large. These days houses don't need high ceilings; they can be cooled with electric fans. Besides, he likes living nearer to Lake Pontchartrain."

"Charles, how soon do you think you can retire?"

"It's pretty much a pipe dream at the moment. I'll need to find a partner for Alan. So keep this under your hat, Liza. We don't want to start rumours."

"Of course. Have you thought of anyone yet?"

"No, not yet. Julian's prospects are excellent where he is. It would be a mistake for him to make a change. There are other young men of business in town. I must make an effort to become familiar with more of them."

"What about Kennard?"

"Alan suggested him, but I don't think he's the one."

Dumpy remained silent. The future loomed large and vacant before her. At twenty-six, she could be considered a confirmed spinster. No doubt Roderick's was her first and last proposal. Many of her southern friends could not understand why both she and her sister had declined their father's offer of "Coming Out" in New Orleans in favour of a foreign trip.

"You prefer to travel?" Florence Aubelin had declared, aghast. "You're throwing away your chance to have a marvellous time and to catch a husband. You'll regret it!"

Dumpy had not regretted. She had never received the alternative, either. War intervened, making travel difficult. Now, money had gone into improvements at Lynnehurst. She was happy about that. If there was no money for a trip, she could live without it.

Her father's voice interrupted her reverie: "Doris, you must have your Caribbean cruise before we leave the South, or would you rather go west to see California?"

"I don't need either, really. Besides, think of all the cruises I can take in Daisy Belle."

"You shall have as many Daisy Belle excursions as you wish, but I promised you a trip. A Drayton never goes back on a promise!"

"If you really have the money, I'd love to see the West Indies."

"You and your mother can go. Find someone younger to go, as well, to make it more fun. Could Julian spare Geraldine for a month?"

"Or there's Florence. She still grieves that her folks couldn't afford a debut for her."

"Even better! She'll fall for the purser on board."

"Indeed; she loves a uniform."

❦

In April, long before the cruise could be planned, something much nicer came into Dumpy's world. C. R. Drayton and Co. took on a new assistant accountant, Mr. Raymond Saunders. His Uncle Forey and Aunt Marie Saunders decided to host an informal musical evening so that Raymond could become acquainted with people in New Orleans. Another reason to celebrate at this time was Mme. Renee Du Bouvier's birthday. Madame, recovering from a lengthy illness, had been unable to go anywhere or to have soirees. Several friends noticed that she was becoming depressed.

However, Forey enticed her with the promise of a ride to and fro in his new Ford sedan. He was away, fetching her, when the Draytons presented themselves a few minutes early at the Saunders residence.

Bella-Rose let them in, explaining that her Mistress was still upstairs.

"Jes cum on in anyways. Y'all folks is at home here anytime, I reckon."

"Thank you, Bella."

"Look thar, that Mr. Raymond is so bizzie wid hiss piany, he done took no notice. Shore nuf, dees Yankees have no manners."

Charlie chuckled. Liza's face broke into a warm-hearted smile.

Dumpy stood mesmerized. She could not take her eyes off the figure at the piano. The ears fairly flapped, so large and straight did they stand out from his head.

A slightly crooked Roman nose extended towards the piano. Then she noticed the hands.

"What absolutely wonderful hands!" thought Dumpy, "They could do anything their owner chose to command."

Right now, those hands were making more music than Dumpy had ever heard the Saunders' piano produce before.

At last, the hands stopped moving. Raymond became aware of his audience.

"My goodness, Mr. Drayton. I didn't realize! This must be your wife and..."

"Doris," She was looking directly at his face as she spoke. His eyes! Had she ever seen such beautiful intelligence in a pair of eyes before. They were dark hazel, different from her father's.

"Do come in and sit down. Aunt Marie will be down directly and Uncle Forey won't be long."

"Do you like opera?" Doris blurted the question.

"I know very little about opera, but I'm willing to learn."

He evidently was finding something interesting about Doris' eyes, too. Doris felt confused.

This is silly, she told herself, *I'm not an adolescent.*

Aloud, she remarked, "you've missed Opera Season here, but it will come again."

"Which is your favourite?"

"I have several favourites; perhaps Rigoletto for the music."

"The only one I've seen is Martha. Do you know the aria, 'Ah So Pure?'" Turning to her parents, Dumpy asked, "Was that one that Kennard used to sing?"

"It's in this book," persisted Raymond, "I'll play it for you. I think you'll recognize it."

Doris instinctively followed Raymond to the piano. They both sang, their unprofessional, but tuneful, voices caught up in the romantic melody. At the end, Liza and Charlie clapped. Dumpy burst out laughing.

"What's so amusing?"

"You must excuse my imagination and my sense of humour. I just had a mental picture of some obese tenor warbling those lyrics to a soprano of Wagnerian dimensions, wearing layers of clothing and theatrical make up to cover her wrinkles."

"Doris, dear!" Liza's voice was gently suggesting more propriety in conversation.

"Don't worry, Mrs. Drayton, I don't have any relatives or friends who are obese tenors and I have never even met a Wagnerian soprano. Further, I am delighted that a southern girl can speak freely and openly. I prefer honest converse. I thought southern belles spoke only polite mush or flattery."

"We aren't really southerners," explained Charles, "We're from Muskoka, Canada. Be careful, we may have wild, primitive streaks in us." His eyes twinkled as he spoke.

"Now Charles," put in Liza, "don't blame Canada. It's the Welsh in you."

They were interrupted by the arrival at the same time of Forey with Mme. Du Bouvier, through the front door, and Marie Saunders, down the stairs. A great fuss was made over Mme. Renee. Marie piloted Madame to a comfortable chair and Forey placed a foot stool for her legs. Raymond was introduced.

"Ah, so you are the son of the black sheep," pronounced Renee, as she sent her appraising eyes up and down Raymond, "Black sheep?"

"Bien sur, garcon! Any southerner who goes beyond the Mason Dixon line to live, is considered to have gone astray. Certainment, your father is the mouton noir of la famille Saunders, n'est pas'?" She turned to Charles for confirmation.

"Indeed, Renee, as always, you are perfectly correct. But please tell me what do you call a Canadian who finds his way south of the Mason Dixon line?"

"Mon Dieu, Charlie, we are in polite society. I cannot speak."

Turning back to Raymond, Madame demanded information, "Are you married?"

"No, Madam. There is no woman who would wish to inflict these ears and this nose upon another generation."

"Pauvre garcon. I do not believe it. More likely, you have come here to escape the pursuit of those interested in your riches. I have heard that you are related to the Ames family."

"You are an amazing woman. The relationship exists, but you must inform any pursuers that I do not stand to inherit Ames money. I must make my own way in this world. I have come to you wealthy southerners with my hat in my hand," He made a sweeping gesture towards her with an up-turned hand.

Raymond was obviously enjoying the good-humoured camaraderie of his uncle's friends.

Next to arrive were the de Ponciers. The room filled quickly. Music and conversation mingled as in the days of Madame Renee's soirees. Renee herself was much restored in spirits.

"Doris, ma petite, I must scold you. You came to my door with custards and jellies but you never came inside."

"But Madame, your nurses would not permit it."

"Fools, don't they realize that a brief look at a nice young face is as good as any medicine."

"Oui, Madame, I will remember that."

Raymond was standing a little apart with Julian. He was intrigued to see the previously free and independent Doris now as docile and meek as any child.

"That is an interesting young woman," he commented to Julian in a low voice.

"Do you know her very well?"

"The Draytons are my closest friends. They are the kind of people you can count on always. As a matter of fact, before I met Geraldine, I thought of marrying. Doris, or, as we call her, Dumpy..."

"You don't need to explain. Your wife is unusually beautiful. And what a glorious singing voice she has."

"Yes, and Geraldine is as lovely a person as she looks."

Bella-Rose brought in a large cake loaded with birthday candles.

"Bella, why so many candles!?"

"Lars, Miz Renee, de lites is fo good looks. Anyways, in 'nother twenty years, y' all be braggin 'bout yor years."

"Come everyone, we have to sing for our supper."

"Happy Birthday to you, Happy Birthday to you..."

Raymond Saunder's arrangement with Charles Drayton was for a trial period of four months. This was to give him time to understand the workings of the business and to learn whether he could tolerate a warm climate. Before accepting the position, Raymond had explained, there also was an opportunity in California that he wished to investigate.

Charles was pleased with Raymond's skills and work habits. As an extra inducement, he offered a vacation in Muskoka. Thus it was that early the following August, Raymond Saunders found himself disembarking from a Muskoka steamer at Brown's Landing. The whole Drayton family and several Brown cousins were on the wharf to greet him, including Mary Lynne and Jack Beasley with Ted, their first-born.

That summer there were several young people around. Phillip Drayton's new place on the north side of Old Drayton Farm was full to the rafters with family and friends. The Armstrongs were established at Old Drayton Farm, which they had purchased from Peter who found it impracticable to visit from Victoria. Aunt Belle Whitby was with them. Tom Armstrong was articling with a law firm in Toronto but was able to have two weeks with them. Alice Armstrong, now a willowy and lovely young woman, was there all summer, as was the irrepressible Boxie who, at nineteen, considered himself completely arrived at manhood. At the farm, Will Drayton usually was busy but his brother, Robert, took time off, as did Regina and May, whenever anyone planned a picnic or a sailing expedition. They frequently joined their cousins for swims or starlight canoe drifting. Staying in two Webster cottages were Uncle Harold Brown, Aunt Elsie, Harold Jr. and 'little Tilda', who had thoroughly outgrown her title. They also had rented the Webster sailboat, the Dragonfly. Ruthie Mae and Christopher Russell, with tiny son, Timothy, were at the hotel, as were several Russell cousins from Montreal.

Raymond fit right in. He and Boxie instigated swimming races and canoe stunts. Raymond sang romantic ballads for the benefit of Regina and May. He was an excellent berry picker, but most of his time was spent in the Lynnehurst sailboat.

Being used to ocean-going yachts, he was fascinated by the toy-like quality of the Lynnehurst dingy.

"It's an entirely different technique," he explained to Dumpy, Alice and Boxie one day when they had turned the tiller over to him.

"Do you find it easier than the larger vessels?"

"Not really. It's just that everything seems much closer, including the water."

"Don't worry. We've never upset."

"There's always a first time."

Jack Beasley was often part of the sailboat crew. As English teacher in a private school, he had two months off in the summer which he divided between Lynnehurst and his parents' home in the village. Mary Lynne seemed anchored to baby Ted who was proving to be a fussy child. Many an afternoon, Mary spent in the old wicker rocker on the front verandah, rocking her little one into relative peace. In the evening, she seldom could detach herself long enough to join the others out on the lake. However, she did enjoy hearing their voices float across the water, muted and transmuted by the evening air, into a symphonic blend of song, talk, and laughter.

"I'm a mother now. My youth is over," she remarked to Liza who was sharing the verandah and the soft summer air with her one night.

"Mercy me! Don't sound so dismal," replied Liza, "It's not all that bad being a mother. You'll have good times again."

"Do you think my little Edward will ever settle?"

"All things pass in time."

Liza paused, remembering that her sister Annie had been as fretful an infant as this Edward. When she spoke again, it was with a different thought.

"I must admit, he's more troublesome than I remember any of my babies being. You demanded more attention than the others but not like Ted. As for Doris, I almost ignored her. If she fussed in the evening, your father used to read aloud to her, whatever book he was reading to himself. That always made her quiet again."

"Perhaps that's why she's such an avid reader now."

"Perhaps so."

The night before Raymond left for the west, Lynnehurst was packed with young and old, all gathered in fancy dress costumes to dance the Sir Roger de Coverly. For a full hour Liza played the piano accompaniment while the young people performed on the now greatly enlarged verandah. Liza then played for another, smaller set.

Everyone seemed to enjoy themselves immensely, the excitement of their exertions elevating their spirits to a glorious level. Even Mary Lynne's feelings were ignited by the flames of fun. As for baby Ted, his wails upstairs were drowned out by the merry din below stairs.

Dumpy danced one set with Raymond and the other with Boxie. She looked more like sweet sixteen than twenty-six in the blue and white Dutch costume that her parents had years earlier brought back from Holland. The rosy glow to her cheeks was a picturesque contrast to the porcelain whiteness of her fair complexion. Atop her blond wavy hair, a white cambric hat, with its turned up edges, echoed the perkiness of the dimples at the edges of her smiles. Rather than wearing her Dutch wooden shoes she chose a pair of white dancing slippers to keep her nimble.

"It still happens to me," thought Dumpy, "the company, the music, the rhythm and the night air... a heady mixture."

Hot chocolate and rock cakes were next on the agenda, after which Aunt Tilda began collecting her brood to shoo them homeward.

"Another day tomorrow," she declared.

It takes a long time to empty a house of that many people. Aunt Belle kept finding one more thing to say to whoever was nearest her. The truth was, no one really wanted to break the spell of congeniality.

"Come Belle, you are worse than the young people," complained Aunt Tilda.

No one resented Aunt Tilda for her sensible efforts. They just didn't feel like moving. However. when at last quiet reigned over Lynnehurst. every Lynnehurst bed held a sleeping body.

The next morning, Raymond Saunders left on the early steamer.

Prospects

Later in the season, the steamer that bore Mary Lynne, Jack and baby Ted southward to Gravenhurst and to the Toronto train, also brought a letter for Dumpy from Raymond. It described his journey west and, enthusiastically, thanked Dumpy for her part in making his Muskoka holiday wonderful. It was the happiest vacation he had ever had and he would never forget it. She waited a tactful week or so, then wrote an answering epistle which, in turn, was rewarded by a second letter from him, telling his first impressions of California. Again, she answered. There was no third letter from Raymond.

The Draytons returned to New Orleans for the winter. At Christmas, Dumpy's name was included on the greeting card Raymond sent to her parents. Forey Saunders told them that Raymond liked his business prospects in California. He feared his nephew would decide in favour of the west rather than New Orleans. This proved to be a true prophecy.

Dumpy didn't need Mr. Saunder's prophecy. Her own instincts told her that California was big enough to contain at least one interesting spinster. Perhaps the boss out there had a daughter. Perhaps she was musical. Perhaps she had beautiful eyes.

Perhaps she had the kind of seaworthy sailing yacht he loved. Perhaps she had no objection to a large nose or bat-size ears. Perhaps...

Dumpy, she told herself sternly, *you don't need a husband. You are capable of looking after yourself.* And herself replied, ironically, *two cheers for me.*

Her father, detecting a certain bitter lassitude in his daughter, reminded her of his earlier offer.

"Dumpy, it's time we made plans for that cruise I promised. Or would you rather see the West?"

"It had better be the Caribbean cruise," she replied, "The West may have some wonders to behold but there is nothing out there that beckons me."

Her father understood. She knew he understood.

"As a matter of fact," he continued, "I have talked to Florence Aubelin. She is delighted by the prospect of going with you."

It did not take long to arrange. In a few weeks, Liza, Dumpy and Florence were happily situated aboard the Lady Magnolia, bound for "fifteen exotic West Indian Ports." They laughed at the antics of the coloured children on the receding dock as the boat left New Orleans. The little black figures were scampering after bits of streamers and confetti that friends had tried to throw to the departing passengers. Remaining at the railing, the three women enjoyed their first glimpse of open water with its dashing waves and refreshing breezes. White and grey gulls circled overhead.

"Not unlike the steamers in Muskoka," thought Dumpy.

Their cruise had all the necessary components: food, comfort, people, entertainment, scenic views on a grand scale and uninhibited leisure.

Doris quickly scanned the ship's library. Her first choice was a slender volume entitled Chita, by Lafcadio Hearn. So vivid was his description of the terrible tidal wave that Dumpy always felt it had been part of her cruise. However, their entire trip was smooth, unmarred by any turbulence.

The purser on the Lady Magnolia was handsome indeed in his smart white uniform. It was not the purser however, who attracted and won the attention of Miss Florence. On the homeward leg of their voyage, Dumpy received from Florence, a confidence regarding her conditional engagement to a Texas widower named Benny Howard.

"Dumpy, I thought he noticed you at first," admitted Florence, "but you didn't give him any encouragement."

"Mr. Howard is a kind gentleman, Florence. I wish you every happiness, and 'tho there is a nursemaid, I do not envy you your responsibilities with those five children."

Dumpy did not voice aloud, her misgivings about any gentleman who sired five offspring in as many years. Spinsterhood seemed to her a joyous state compared to union with such an ardent progenitor.

"Really? I thought you liked children. You frequently talk about your little cousins."

"Quite so, but I am not totally responsible for them. I enjoy their company and I watch them develop over the years. Some one else does the work."

"Dumpy Drayton! I can't believe this. There is not a lazy bone in your body. Are you quite sure you don't envy me? I feel as if I trespassed on your chances. Your father, after all, is paying for this trip. He gave it to you instead of a debut."

"Florence, please don't feel badly on my account. I do not envy you in the slightest. You're a brave girl. Enjoy your happiness, unmarred by any concerns about me... But, tell me, what do you mean by conditional engagement?"

"Benny feels I should visit Galveston to meet the children before I commit myself. I could stay with his sister. He suggested you come too, as chaperone. He has thought about all the proprieties."

"That was considerate of him," replied Dumpy.

Florence is one year older than I, but I'm considered old enough to be a chaperone; oh, dear me, mused Dumpy to herself.

"Will you come with me?" persisted Florence, "You are smart. I'd appreciate your judgement as well as your company."

"Yes, I'd like to. I've heard so much about Galveston."

"Benny says the children love to go to the beach. We could all go. You like picnics and swimming."

Dumpy brightened at the thought, but she did not point out to Florence that what one does in ocean waves is not true swimming. One needed a clear, clean, deep lake for a real swim.

The Galveston trip duly took place and so did the Aubelin-Howard engagement.

A radiant Florence was eternally grateful to Dumpy for her part in promoting the union. Afterwards, Dumpy was given two snapshots of herself, Florence and the homely Howard brood, semi-submerged in Gulf waters, all wearing the ridiculous swimming attire of the period. Future generations got a giggle out of the picture in Dumpy's album. Dumpy offered a prayer of thanksgiving each time she saw that picture.

Back in New Orleans, Drayton business and family plans were progressing rapidly. Alan's choice of a potential partner was working out well. On the strength of this, Liza was sorting and disposing of unnecessary household items, preparatory to packing. Charles wrote Alfred Beasley about improvements to make Lynnehurst suitable for winter occupancy. He also wrote Mary Lynne and Jack about the possibility of renting an apartment near them in Toronto.

Stimulated by her travel experiences and happy to have some real work into which she could invest her energies, Dumpy plunged with gusto into packing and decision-making. She soon reduced her personal possessions to manageable proportions. Her personal library was reduced by giving the entire juvenile collection to Miriam and Alan for Siegfried and Elizabeth.

Mattie, the new hired helper, didn't want to live in Mammy's cabin. She came by the day to prepare meals. Like Mammy, she didn't like cleaning, but was helpful enough, carrying boxes to and fro and running up and down stairs with questions and messages between Liza, Charles and Dumpy as they worked in separate areas.

"It's amazing," declared Liza one day.

"What is?"

"I was thinking of all those years we took to accumulate, furnish and embellish this place. Each year, we added something. Now, in a few weeks, we've un-wound our efforts almost completely."

Charles looked around, "Yes, it's not our home anymore, just a place."

"An empty shell," commented Dumpy.

☙

Early in June, when the three Draytons boarded the train for Chicago, accompanied by more than the usual number of trunks, several friends came to see them off. Geraldine and Julian presented a box of pralines and some flowers to enjoy on the journey.

"Don't forget. We're coming up one of these years to see Jack's school perform its annual play or operetta."

"A visit to Lynnehurst is required from you, as well. Please remember!"

"Don't forget your southern friends," added Forey, who, with Marie's help, was supporting Renee Dubouvier. Renee's eyes were wet. For once, she had nothing to say.

"We'll never forget friends and good times together. Come and see us in the summer. You're all welcome at Lynnehurst!"

"Good bye... Good bye... Goodbye!"

The long train pulled away from extended arms and fluttering handkerchiefs.

Home and Native Land

THEY SHOULD HAVE BEEN EXHAUSTED, but Charles, Liza and Dumpy were too excited to think of tiredness when they arrived in Toronto. There were people to see, arrangements to be made and a turbulent toddler, Ted, to love and to soothe. Mary Lynne looked drained. Jack seemed constrained. He suggested that his wife and babe could visit Lynnehurst early this year. He would follow after the school term was over and all his marking finished.

"How was the school play?"

Jack's face brightened, "It was excellent! We have some talented students here. The lead role called for some singing. We cast a first form lad, whose voice hasn't changed yet, as our singing heroine. She, I mean, he was beautiful. Unbelievable."

"We will be able to be in Toronto for next year's production," promised Charles, "In the meantime, we are determined to spend Christmas at Lynnehurst. Will you join us?"

"Seth won't drive his truck down your hill in winter. Would Uncle John bring the horses out to meet the train?"

"We'll see!"

By the time they boarded the Muskoka Express, Liza admitted the existence of tired legs. Closing her eyes she slumped gratefully into the nearest seat. Charles and Dumpy were still alert and eager to see every passing scene, as if for the first time.

"Doris, I suppose you cannot feel this homecoming as strongly as I do. This is the most wonderful day of my life. Everything I did in the south was for this purpose, to earn the right to come home. Now I can start living!"

"I think you have done a great deal of living already."

"Yes, child, I have. We have all had fortunate lives, but the past pales in comparison to now."

As the train chugged along, Dumpy remained calm until the topography changed from green and brown farmland to grey, rocky shield with wild woodlands.

Then something stirred her blood. Her thought quickened. She remembered her mother's stories of that first discovery trip with Buppa so many years ago.

"How many changes have occurred since then?" Dumpy wondered, "How many future generations of Browns will make this trek?" Aloud, she said "Father, I suppose one of these days people will come to Muskoka by automobile. There are good roads already."

"Cars will never replace the trains and steamers. Certainly not for me. Alan may drive that contraption of his to get here if he likes, but I'll never learn to drive. It isn't safe and it isn't comfortable."

When they boarded the steamer at Gravenhurst, Liza, feeling considerably freshened, joined Charles and Dumpy at the deck rail to look, listen and savour. The smooth, clean air was scented with tangy essence of pine and hemlock trees which were still dominant on shores all around, despite earlier lumbering activities or subsequent development of farms and cottages.

Noticing the cloudy sky, the few other passengers on board that day had elected to remain in the forward lounge. In contrast, the three homecoming Draytons felt privileged to have the deck all to themselves. It was their space, a world of grey waves and wooded shores reaching to a distant horizon under a canopy of grey-cast sky.

"This is what the Irish call a lovely, soft day; God be praised," remarked Charles, "A suitable welcome!"

Liza and Dumpy let his remark pass; then Dumpy said, "I feel I own every mile of this route."

"That's strange," replied Charles, "I was just trying to decide which one of these empty points of land I should buy. We could build a small hotel, a family business venture. But no, we have enough. Let the pristine beauty remain."

"It belongs to God," added Liza. "He put it here to inspire our worship... Charles, if we feel stirred now by this small experience of God's Glory, what will we feel when we come to His Kingdom, fully?"

Charles put his arm around her, "I hope I'll be with you when you get there."

Dumpy let her parents enjoy their sacred closeness for a few minutes, then interrupted: "Father, I think you should buy a point or island somewhere down here. There are not that many left vacant. Every spring, we see at least one new cottage. It would be a way to preserve the natural beauty. We could use it for camping trips, but it would also be an act of charity. Everyone in Muskoka benefits when Nature is preserved."

"Once again, I must say, 'oh wise and sagacious child,' I'll find out what land's available."

"Charles, why did you struggle to find a good business partner for Alan. Doris could have done it."

"By Jove, I never thought of that. Dumpy, forgive me. I had it in mind that you are an academic like your Buppa, perhaps a naturalist. Also, you could be a writer. Goodness knows, you've read enough books. There ought to be at least one you could write. Now I see that you have an understanding of human nature and the ability to make decisions that would be useful in business. Would you like to have been Alan's partner?"

"I thought about that, Father. On my cruise, I realized that if Mr. Benny Howard could be successful in business, so could I. I didn't say anything because in searching my heart, I knew Lynnehurst and Canada were calling me northward. Besides, Alan might not enjoy having baby sister at the decision-making level."

"True indeed," commented Liza.

"Well, don't give up on the idea of a business career. Why don't you go to Shaws in Toronto and learn typing, shorthand and accounting? Many a lady secretary is far more to a business than a clerical servant. I know one woman who became the real brains of her firm. When her so-called boss refused to raise her salary above the generally accepted level for secretaries, she threatened to resign. He gave in immediately. Think about it."

The steamer reached Port Carling. In the soft rain that now fell Charles, Liza and Dumpy held their possession of the deck. Dumpy wanted to watch the lock man at work. Cranky Stan had been replaced by a war veteran. Old Mac was still around.

Dumpy looked for him. There he was! She waved.

He waved back, "there aren't any children today. You better come ashore and help!"

She grinned broadly, "Maybe next time. My arthritis is bad today."

"Ah shucks! I can't do it without you," He sauntered over to sit on a wooden bench nearby.

Dumpy realized that Old Mac must be retired, but still liked to be part of the excitement when a steamer was locking through. She wondered how long the highway of his life had been. Perhaps he lived in one of those frame houses she could see on the hill behind the docks. She pictured him trudging from it, along the short block of main street, down the steps to dockside. That would be longer than Mammy's track, yet just as restrictive. Both Mammy and Old Mac were happy people, seemingly, completely content with their lots in life. She wondered how content she could be if her life's tether were shortened.

At Port Sandfield, no one got off. Dumpy stood gazing at the spot where Prospect House once had stood. It seemed only yesterday, she had admired it's huge bulk with the little cupola on top and the leisurely crowds of summer guests swarming over lawns and docks.

Once again, Charles exhibited his ability to respond to her thoughts. She heard him say, "it was a busy place for thirty years or more. Then, in a few hours, there was nothing left except the cupola, lying somewhere in the woods to rest and rot."

Dumpy and Liza had seen the fire's glow from Lynnehurst that October day.

"Was that 1915?" asked Liza.

"No, it was 1916. I remember distinctly, October 16, 1916. I'll never forget," said Dumpy.

After a pause, she added, "let's take a camping trip past here this summer. I want to explore the woods and find that cupola."

"Let's take two camping trips this summer; one, just the three of us and one, later with guests, after mosquito season is over," added Charles.

It didn't seem very long before they were craning their necks to catch sight of Needles Point. Dumpy glanced towards Chadwick Bay, but turned her back quickly.

She felt a pang of guilt. Poor Roderick. His chances for finding a suitable wife were not much better than Henny's for finding a congenial partner. She tried to thrust the thought from her.

"One does not marry for charitable reasons," she repeated to herself firmly, "I could never have hidden my unhappiness, which, in turn, would have made him miserable. Married love is not charity. Eros, alone, is not enough either. Someone should invent a new word for the right kind of married love. It must be a blend of friendship, eros and Christian agape. Many married couples have less, but I could never have less than what my parents have shown me.

"There's Point Caroline."

All three of them held their breath until the Point was rounded.

"It's still there," whispered Liza. "Thank you, Lord."

"Yes, it is still there, my dear. Lynnehurst is properly built. We have taken every precaution. It's not likely to catch fire but don't stop saying your prayers."

Aunt Sally and Uncle John were both on the dock to greet them. So were Robert, Regina and May. A little way behind them stood Elsie Webster, holding a small boy by the hand. She waited 'till the family greetings were over before coming forward to explain.

"This is Joshua, Tommy's boy. His mother's in the family way again and not very well. I brought him along to help."

"How do you do," said Liza, bending with hand outstretched towards the child.

"I heard about you last summer. I'm glad to meet you."

Joshua rejected the gesture and hid behind his aunt's skirts.

"Please take no notice. He 'makes strange' with everyone. Mother says his Uncle James was the same."

The two year old lad was given a light basket to carry as he and the women moved up the path toward Lynnehurst, leaving the men to wrestle with the trunks.

Since they had only one trunk dolly they made several trips before everything was safely delivered at the house.

The women managed to exchange news without interrupting their immediate unpacking. Regina sounded thrilled as she spoke of her plan to live in Toronto next September. There was room with Carolyn. She expected to work at Eaton's and was currently making a suitable black business outfit.

"Dumpy, you must come over tomorrow to see it."

"Yes Dumpy, you can help pin the hem line."

"I hate hems," added May.

"That is true. She complains that I don't stand still."

"Elsie, how about a cup of tea all round on the front porch?" asked Liza, "The men will want some too."

"Yes, I'll bring the kettle forward. We have fresh tea because the Michie order came yesterday. But, wouldn't you prefer the screened porch out back? The mosquitoes are still bad."

"I suppose so." Liza cloaked her disappointment, managing to add cheerfully, "there will be many days ahead when we can look at the lake."

"The woods and the field are beautiful too," put in Dumpy.

"This summer, I'm going to build a screen porch south of the dining-room. It could be an extension to the southern part of our present verandah. We'll turn one window into a door for access. Then we can have tea out there," declared Charles.

"Charles, that would be lovely," cried Liza in delight. "The larger verandah will be better for dancing parties, too. We can have one set there and another in the dining room. The piano will be heard through the open door and the window beside the fireplace."

While her parents were talking about a larger verandah, Dumpy was learning from her cousins that Roderick had married the new school teacher. What a relief. Her feelings of guilt vanished. However, a few days later when the three Draytons made their congratulatory call, a cloud of doubt replaced Dumpy's former burden. Ethel did not seem to be right for Roderick... *some indefinable lack of refinement*, thought Dumpy.

Mrs. Chadwick, Hilda and Henny were gracious, as usual, but Dumpy sensed that they were not at ease.

Henny wanted to go to the garden to pick some early lettuce for tea. Dumpy went with her.

"What do you think of Ethel?" Henny queried.

"She's not what I expected, but then, I don't know what my expectations would be for Roderick. Does she like poetry?"

"I don't know. She seemed to, before they were married."

"Is he happy?"

"I don't know. I heard a very strange conversation one night when I was having trouble sleeping."

"Oh?"

"1 had a headache. I was walking up and down the hall in my bedsocks. Maybe I didn't hear correctly."

"What did you think you heard?"

"I... well... he sounded quite angry."

"Angry?"

"He said, 'Now, my lady, the law is on my side'!"

"Strange."

"Maybe I didn't hear correctly. I dare not ask."

"Of course not."

"There, I think this will be enough lettuce. Shall we go back to the house?"

"Henny, there are several weeds here that want plucking. The air is lovely. Let's stay in the garden a bit longer."

They worked silently, then tried to relive some of their earlier joys by giving voice to happy, girlhood memories associated with the garden.

※

Dumpy made a point of including Henny in Lynnehurst activities that summer. Henny enjoyed especially the long camping trip to the Georgian Bay. Hilda and Mrs. Chadwick sometimes were pried loose to take part in picnics. Roderick seemed unable to free himself for any frivolities. Ethel, by observing Chadwick manners, had refined herself considerably over the past two years. Her new confidence and her curiosity led her to accept an invitation to tea at Lynnehurst. However, she was not interested in swimming, picnics or boating of any sort. In fact, she feared the water.

The Draytons learned not to invite her.

Ted and Joshua

Ethel was not the only one who had an aversion to the lake. When Mary Lynne arrived with little Ted, she took him down to the dock every swim time, but if she tried to dip him in the water, he shrieked in terror.

"Don't try anymore," suggested Liza, "He's too young to learn to swim and you'll just teach him to hate it."

"But you said you started us this young."

"People are different. I remember that all three of you loved the water right from the start. He doesn't. Maybe there is something he feels that we don't understand."

"I'll ask Jack. He loves boats, but he doesn't enjoy swimming the way the rest of us do. He tells me many people in the village can't swim at all and are afraid to work near deep water. It seems such a shame to me when they are here more than we are. If I lived here all year and even if I worked six days a week, I would go swimming every Sunday until ice formed. I just don't understand."

When Jack Beasley joined his family at Lynnehurst, he spent much time in the sailboat. One day, when the wind was light, he took Ted with him as well as Mary and Dumpy. Ted was unhappy about sailboats.

"He's too young. Don't force him," Liza kept chiding them.

The only joy Ted seemed to have was the sand box, out under Buppa's crab apple tree. He was intelligent enough not to put any sand in his mouth, but would sit, watching it fall through his fingers or he would make little sand hills and pat them down firmly. Joshua, who frequently joined Ted at the sand box, delighted in stepping on Ted's hills. Unlike Ted, Joshua had to be restrained from eating sand. Ted would merely gaze in wonderment, but never attempted to emulate or complain when his sand hills got smashed.

"It's strange," noticed Mary Lynne. "He complains about everything else, even yells when there's no reason."

Liza decided to change the subject, "Dumpy and I will look after the boys. Why don't you sail into the village with Jack. He's promised to get me some fresh meat at the butchers. You can even stay for tea with his folks if they want you to."

"Thank you. That would be lovely."

Joshua did not come over in the Webster rowboat every day with Elsie. Some days, he stayed with his grandmother. After a month or so, he returned to his own mother. Liza missed him.

"I have a feeling we'll see more of that young man over the years," Liza said as she waved good-bye and blew kisses to Joshua on his last visit to Lynnehurst that summer. In the few weeks he was with them, she had won him over completely. The shyness vanished totally. It was mutual. Liza was completely captivated by Joshua.

Christmas

That year the Draytons remained at Lynnehurst after everyone else had left. Fall had its share of bright, crisp days as well as a full quota of wet, chilly ones. Charles, Liza and Dumpy loved them all. Their September swims were the best of the season. Dumpy savoured sun baths in the bath house too. With enthusiastic pioneer spirits, they stripped their vegetable garden, dividing the produce between the root cellar of New Drayton Farm and the pantry at Lynnehurst. Bunches of garlic, parsley and herbs soon hung in festoons from the hemlock rafters of the pantry.

Dumpy helped Elsie and Liza cook and preserve for the winter. They made wonderful pies out of their own apples and wild blackberries, to say nothing of the roasts of lamb and well-seasoned baked squashes that began appearing on the Lynnehurst dinner table. They regretted the lack of visitors to enjoy this bounty.

Farm cousins did come for tea and the Lynnehurst Draytons sometimes had tea at the farm.

Liza and Sally talked recipes daily. even while swimming. Liza helped Sally with projects in the farm kitchen while Dumpy helped May pick apples. The girls told themselves that they did not envy Regina at all. Still, they fantasized about what sort of adventures she might be having in the city.

"Regina thinks Toronto's glamorous."

"She did look smart in that new black outfit she made. It went well with the trim hat she ordered from Eaton's catalogue."

"Remember her on the steamer wharf? Did anyone ever feel so chic?"

In the farm house, the mothers were expressing their dreams and concerns for their young people.

"Toronto isn't like it was in our day," sighed Sally, "We knew everyone and felt quite safe everywhere."

"Regina probably feels safe too. With all the cousins there to keep an eye out for her you don't need to worry. Matilda will have her over often."

"You're right, I suppose, but she was positively giddy before she left. I worry that she'll do something silly."

"Worry never did anyone any good."

"True."

They glanced at each other and changed the subject. That night, both women remembered Regina in their prayers.

༄

Charles missed his father-in-law. Whenever there was something to be done with the boats or at the wharf, he did not have Matthew's knack with repair jobs.

Also, he missed his son-in-law. Jack had the Beasley family creative insight with boats, buildings or anything made of wood. Charles found himself wasting time fretting and figuring. However, he loved to swing an axe. Splitting firewood had been his hobby every summer. This hobby was becoming serious employment as winter approached. The larger chunks, he was stacking in the cellar for the furnace. Stove wood and kindling was stored in the shed or under a porch.

From time to time Charles and his two ladies sailed or went in the Daisy Belle to visit Chadwick Bay, the Websters or the Beasleys. Sometimes they hiked to Southshore to enjoy the vistas of colour on shores further south. Frequently, they rowed or paddled to old Drayton Farm just to look around or to pick crab apples off the ancient trees there. Dumpy took early morning paddles in her personal canoe, a gift from the family on her twenty-first birthday. The evenings generally found the three Draytons around the open fire, reading privately or aloud to each other. Liza kept knitting and mending within reach. Dumpy started a needlepoint wall hanging depicting a lake scene.

It was incredible how much wood they burned daily. Robert helped his Uncle with wood cutting but Charles knew that Robert was thinking of leaving the farm for work in Toronto.

"I don't like to take you away from your folks too often," declared

Charles one day when he and his nephew were hauling the Daisy Belle out of the water for winter storage. They must have several jobs that need your help before you leave home."

"I haven't made up my mind entirely about leaving. In any case, it won't be 'til after Christmas. I might get something temporary and return in June."

"Have you any thoughts about marriage?"

"Yes, that's one reason to leave home. Father and I have talked of making a deal with the Armstrongs to farm more of their land. I'm not sure there's enough good land to support two farming families."

"What about maple syrup?"

"There's not much money in that. There's a short season and making syrup is a long process."

"How about planting trees at Old Drayton Farm for Christmas trees?"

"Never thought of that. That would make December a busy time. Maple syrup could fill early spring. Add a bit of farming... I don't know, it still doesn't seem like enough."

"You could cut ice and fill the ice houses for summer people. There are more summer places now. Someone might need a caretaker."

"William does some of that. We don't work well together. If I say cut the ice this way, he says, no that way. In the meantime, everyone gets cold standing around while we argue."

"I see."

"Uncle Tom says maybe he could find me a place with a business in Toronto. I don't really like Toronto."

"What about Gravenhurst? Do they need people at Ditchburn's?"

"That's an idea, but I'm not a carpenter."

"Every Muskoka man is part carpenter. You did a nice job on those shelves for your Mother's kitchen."

"Shelves are easy. Any fool can make shelves."

"I know many city folks who can't. You're still young enough to learn a craft. Think it over."

꩜

Christmas was two weeks away. As the day approached, Charles made up his mind that once the festivities were over he would take the family to Toronto for the rest of the winter. Charles and Robert had stacked a good supply of wood under both porches and in the back shed. Liza had the pantry barrels full of apples, potatoes, carrots, onions, turnips and parsnips. Garlic and herbs, hanging from pantry rafters, gave a wonderful odour. The long shelves supported glass jar battalions of jams, jellies and apple butter. Dark green acorn squashes were tucked here and there.

"It smells like Christmas in here," said Liza one day when she went in to select the right sized wooden bowl for her mince meat. It was a bit late to get started on the chopping but she and Elsie Webster had peeled all the suet. The raisins and currants were ready also.

"It looks like Christmas too." said Elsie, "See the snow falling."

"I wish there were a faster way to chop the mince meat," declared Dumpy, who forced herself to help, only because she loved mince pies.

Suddenly their nerves were jarred by a harsh, long ring from the telephone.

Only Melvin Jacob at the telephone exchange in the village could make a clamour like that. The call must be from the village or long distance.

Liza and Dumpy glanced quickly at each other with questions in their eyes.

They heard Charles go to the phone and lift the receiver.

"Hello... yes... I can't hear, the line is crackling... who?... Jack?... Ted... no, oh no... thank you... Liza knew. No one had to tell her.

"My poor Mary Lynne. Charles, we must go to her at once," Her words did not register with Charles.

"That was Thomas Beasley. Jack phoned them from the college. Baby Ted is ill. He was taken to hospital last night. The doctor expects the worst."

"Charles, how can we get there?"

She was ready to act. Charles, on the other hand, was paralysed by two griefs; the probable loss of a grandson plus the thought of missing Christmas at Lynnehurst.

Dumpy fought down a selfish sense of relief regarding baby Ted. She was neutral about Christmas.

"Charles, phone Tom Armstrong and tell him, if one of those apartments we looked at near Mary and Jack is still available, we'll take it. Do you have the addresses still?"

Her statement bounced off his brain dully, but the question alerted him and brought response.

"Addresses?"

"Yes, of the apartments near Jack and Mary. Phone Tom Armstrong."

151

"Tom Armstrong... yes..."

He was soon in charge of himself again, making notes before ringing Melvin to place the long distance call.

Liza, Elsie and Dumpy regarded the larder. Some food could be shifted to Webster and Drayton farm cellars. Some could be packed in two large hampers for Toronto. The huge bags of flour and rice could be shifted to the mouse cupboard upstairs. Very little would be left in the Lynnehurst pantry; perhaps a few herbs could remain hanging.

"It took us all fall to gather winter supplies and now, in a few days, it must go," sighed Elsie. She looked out the west window at the lake. A wind was whipping through the leaveless birches on the inner slope of Little Bluff. The dark blue lake was active with westerly waves.

"I think father can still manage to get here in his row boat. There's plenty of open water and the ice around the edge is thin. It would be easier than going all the way around by horse team."

"True. You could carry bundles more easily, too. When you go, go early in the morning before the wind gets up. Thank goodness your folks have a telephone."

The three women went ahead with their chopping of mince meat. They packed it in stone jars; one for the hamper, one for Aunt Sally, and one for the Websters.

Liza packed as many jellies as she dared carry.

On departure day they loaded several bundles and a small trunk onto Uncle John's sleigh for the horses to pull up the hill while Liza, Charles and Dumpy, weighed down in heavy winter clothing, trudged through the light covering of snow as far as the farm. Seth Talbot agreed to meet them there and transport everyone and everything to the train at MacTier. It was a cold, bumpy ride. All three Draytons regretted that they had not left on the last steamer in November.

Via Seth, Mrs. Beasley sent a small parcel of jellied meat and a sprig of English holly from a bush she had miraculously preserved in a sunny corner outside the Beasley Homestead. Mr. Beasley added a long letter from himself and his wife to his son containing messages of love and consolation. The Beasleys had lost infants in their early years together. It was part of life, but God had been good to them and would be good to Jack and Mary too.

In Toronto, the Armstrongs had achieved a great deal. An apartment had been chosen. Furniture had been removed from storage and was in place in the apartment. Enough linen and blankets had been found to make up beds. A small electric refrigerator, delivered from Eatons, was installed and full of food enough for a few days. Two loaves of homemade bread, wrapped in a fresh linen tea towel, sat on the kitchen table. The selected apartment had an electric range.

Meanwhile, Mary Lynne was tormenting herself with questions. Why do innocent babies have to suffer? What did I do wrong? What should we do now?

She refused to believe what everyone else saw as inevitable. At night Jack tried to pry her away from the hospital.

"What if he should wake at night and want me?" She insisted that the hospital let her stay. They put a bed for her near his room.

When the end came, she held Ted's lifeless form close and wailed without ceasing. The nurses called Jack's college. It seemed like hours passed before he arrived.

"Mary, darling, you have to let go of him. The doctors need to do an autopsy to find out what went wrong."

"NO," she shrieked. "Never, never, never."

Then, gazing down at the still face in her arms, she said firmly, "Darling, I will never let those barbarians cut you in little pieces. Mommy loves you, loves you, loves you. You know that, don't you? Jack, help me. We'll take him home."

"Mary, we cannot." He let her cry until she was quiet, wondering all the while what to say.

The doctor arrived in time to do the speaking. "Mrs. Beasley," he began, quietly and firmly, "every year, I see mothers as grief-tricken as you are. We want to learn more, so that fewer mothers in the future will have to lose babies. A post-mortem will teach us much. Perhaps we can save the life of someone else by what we find."

Numbly, she raised his little form to her lips for a final kiss and then handed baby Ted to the nurse.

"I'm sorry. I've been unkind to all of you. You were so good to me and to him. Forgive me."

Jack helped her into her coat. They took a taxi home.

In the days that followed, only Liza could talk to Mary. Mary cut Jack out of her grief altogether. He felt this keenly. Is a father not allowed to grieve? Friends and relatives spoke words of consolation but they seemed perfunctory. Only the letter from his parents reached Jack's inner feelings.

Liza realized what was happening to Mary and Jack.

"Mary," she said one day, "you must remember Jack. Ted was his child too. Have you ever asked him how he feels? You must encourage him to talk to you or you may lose him."

"Mother! what do you mean? Jack is a good man. He would never desert me."

"Yes, dear, he is a good man, but you might lose him as your best friend. Married love doesn't happen automatically because two good people say a vow at the wedding. You have to renew that vow in your heart constantly. You could drift apart under the same roof."

"But you and father are never apart. You just naturally are like two halves belonging together."

"We had our struggles, especially in the early years."

Liza found excuses not to visit the young Beasleys every day. She said she would be busy with the Armstrongs for awhile and gently reminded Mary how kind the cousins had been to all of them.

Dumpy adjusted to life in Toronto quickly. She enrolled herself in Shaw's Business School and began re-organizing her wardrobe to look more business-like. Charles bought concert tickets for the family.

La Petite Perdue

THE IDEA OF SPENDING CHRISTMAS AT LYNNEHURST wan not discussed between Charles and Liza the next year. Liza knew that Charles no longer had enough stamina for a Muskoka winter. They left Lynnehurst in early November on what turned out to be the last steamer scheduled for the season.

Standing on the wharf at Brown's Landing to wave good-bye was Dumpy, along with the farm cousins and Elsie Webster. Lynnehurst was shuttered and shut. Dumpy would be living at the Farm. Aunt Sally had stumbled over an old oak root while helping round up sheep. The resulting broken leg and sprained wrist rendered her helpless. May, who had taken on the job of school teacher after Ethel Chadwick's retirement, would be boarding with the Beasleys mid-week and most winter weekends.

Dumpy could fulfil the womanly needs of the farm and experience the adventure of true winter. She was not sure she wanted that adventure but, for her father's sake, she would enter into it fully so that he could relive his younger days vicariously through her.

As the steamer rounded Point Caroline, it gave a farewell toot which acted as a signal to the waving watchers. As if of one mind they turned to face their trail through the woods.

Before taking that path, William helped Elsie Webster into her waiting rowboat and towed her clear of the pier. He gave a final shove, nodding his approval as she handled the long oars and glided homeward over the waves.

Then, turning to Dumpy, he remarked, "you are brave to take on feeding our household."

"I suppose you think I don't know how to cook."

"We don't need fancy stuff but Dad and I have farmers appetites. You'll be busy peeling potatoes."

Doris glanced at her beautifully manicured hands and sighed inwardly.

"Baked potatoes are healthier than mashed."

"Umph."

"Will Robert be home for Christmas?"

"Maybe, maybe not. Ditchburns don't pay him much yet and he's putting every spare penny into the house he's building."

"When's his wedding?"

"Don't know yet."

"Don't worry about Christmas, Dumpy," put in May, "I'll be home in time to help and we can do the suet and the mince meat early one weekend."

When they reached the farmhouse, both William and May glanced at the chimney and quickened their pace. Dumpy stopped to look also. There wasn't any smoke showing. She followed her cousins indoors.

Wordlessly, Will went straight to the central box stove. He added old newspaper and kindling to the dying embers and blew to produce a flame. When the flame seemed established, he carefully selected a good piece of maple to add. In a similar way his sister was stoking the cook stove back to life.

Dumpy looked from one to the other and then to her aunt who was ensconced on the kitchen day bed. A begonia in full bloom sat on the sunny windowsill beside her. Dumpy could see signs of tears on Aunt Sally's face.

"Are you cold?"

"No, I'm warmly wrapped and well covered with these blankets."

"Something is troubling you?"

"I'm so useless! I tried to quarter these apples that Uncle John left here, but I can't even do that. The left hand fumbles; my right hand hurts if I try to hold or to push."

"Don't vex yourself. I can do it," Dumpy stooped to gather some fallen apples.

"Thank you, dear. I know you will but you have no idea how it feels to be unable. I've spent my whole life being useful. Now there's nothing."

"That's not true, Aunt Sally. I have hands and legs but I need your head to guide me through the routine here."

"Where's father?" asked Will, re-entering the kitchen.

"He said there was one lamb missing still. He has gone to look."

"There are a hundred acres out there. It may take awhile."

By tea time, the sky had clouded over. Brisk air gave way to damp chill. Aunt Sally spotted a forlorn figure emerging from the distant wood lot. She watched as John began to tread wearily across their soggy field. Slanting rays of evening sunlight caressed his shoulders, then dulled to grey gloom.

"There's your father. I don't see any lamb with him."

Will checked the firebox one more time. May moved the kettle further forward. Dumpy stirred the soup, then checked that the soup bowls were warm. Sally kept looking out the window as if keeping her eyes focused in her husband's direction could transmit energy. Half way through the field John glanced upward, sending a long look in response to his wife's gaze. He had little energy left for waving or for quickening his pace. Somehow Sally knew her mate was feeling her will power.

Momentum of slow, steady steps carried him forward.

"May, dear. Go open the gate for him."

Her father trudged through the gate without waiting for May to re-fasten the latch.

Will was at the shed door. Wordlessly, John Drayton dropped onto a bench in the shed and made no protest when May arrived to remove his boots. Slippers appeared and were quickly put on his feet. In the house, he slumped into his big chair by the stove and looked appreciatively at Dumpy, who stood with a white ironstone mug of steaming tea in her hands. John Drayton paused to absorb the warmth and comfort of his domain, then reached to accept the tea.

A few sips later, he could utter a hoarse "thank you" to May and Will as well as to his niece. More tea trickled down his throat.

"I found her."

"Where?"

"Over the cliff on a ledge."

"Alive?"

"Alive... Couldn't get there... maybe with the rowboat..."

"When?... Tonight?"

"You're not going anywhere tonight," Sally's authoritative tone of voice ended all talk.

In silence they ate their supper. May took a fragrant apple pie from the oven and began slicing.

Will ate his piece quickly and announced, "it's better to go tonight. Father, you stay with Mother. May can come with me."

"I'll come too," offered Dumpy.

"Good."

Uncle John was grateful for his son's decisions. All he said was: "You know that ledge where Aunt Liza's stubborn pine tree sticks out? I think she's there."

"Take the old lantern, too, in case our torch burns out," warned Sally.

"Wouldn't the big rowboat from Lynnehurst be steadier and have more room for her?" suggested Dumpy, "Too bad the Daisy Belle is drained and jacked up for the winter."

"Rowboat's better for going close to shore."

Dumpy was sure her flashlight would work even if Uncle John's failed, but they took matches and the kerosene lantern anyway.

Heading down the road to Lynnehurst, they needed no light at all. The darkness was not yet intense. Every inch of the road was familiar. Even where trees crowded close, they could detect the hardened wheel ruts with their feet or could look upward to see the corresponding sky path outlined between the darker tree shapes.

Will brought up the rear, three sizes of rope and a blanket over his arm. May carried an enamel pan of tempting mash, cradled in her arms. The spirit of adventure was upon all three of them.

The big boathouse doors were soon unlocked and the row boat in the water.

Dumpy and Will rowed while May looked after the safety of supplies. She did not need to steer. Dumpy and Will were well matched at the oars, Dumpy adjusting easily to Will's long stroke and responding to his every alteration in speed or direction.

Looking at them from the stern seat, May thought they made a good team.

As the Southshore rocks loomed higher and steeper, Dumpy and Will slackened their rowing to search out Aunt Liza's pine.

"I wish father were here," remarked Dumpy

"Why?"

"He'd love a rescue adventure like this."

"I'm glad he's not here," retorted Will.

Dumpy was offended and astonished, "Why?" she responded.

"If Uncle Charlie were here, I'd be reduced to ship's cabin boy and you two would be the scullery maids. "

May giggled. In spite of herself, Dumpy laughed.

"Father is used to taking charge, but you must feel sorry he's missing this fun."

"Look!" cried May, "We're going to have a moon."

William and Dumpy turned to watch a low lying cloud glowing with soft yellow light. Presently, a mellow rim rose above the cloud horizon.

"How many times have I seen this?" said Dumpy, "It's still awesome."

"Yes," said Will in a hoarse whisper, "And each time is different."

They watched, waiting until the rim evolved into a large globe that sent a path of glimmering silver over the water to the boat. May could see her cousin and brother silhouetted in the mystic light.

It makes them look young and beautiful, she thought, *He's nearly forty and she's nearly thirty. Is it still possible to be romantic at that age?*

The moon did not answer her question.

At length they focused on their quest. In the moonlight, Liza's tree stood out in bold relief. Dumpy thought she heard a bleating, then admitted it might have been her active imagination.

"Leave the torches off for awhile. We can see better by moonlight."

Every boulder along that ridge looked like a sheep recumbent. If Dumpy stared long enough, she was sure the form moved. Wherever she pointed, William said "no."

But he was happy to say "yes" when she volunteered to act as land scout. Dumpy was the smallest of the three and was known to be sure-footed. She rolled her slim skirt above her knee (but not above her bloomers) to free her limbs for action. Then, grabbing Liza's tree trunk with one hand, she hoisted herself out of the boat, which her cousins held steady for her. In spite of his prosaic disposition, Will found himself rapt in admiration as he watched his petite cousin climbing the rock-faced shore in the moonlight.

Dumpy's feelings of romantic adventure soon dissolved into frustration. The moonlight was helpful, but it also turned ordinary shapes into strange ones. She definitely heard a bleat. Where was it? She searched every possible spot, then searched each one again. At length, she went back to the boat for her torch. Previous efforts were repeated.

This time, the beam from her flashlight caught a reflection of one red eye, "Ah ha!"

"Found her?"

"Yes, but she's down behind. I can't get there... will she come to me?"

"Here's the mash."

Will handed it to Dumpy as he clambered onto a rock ledge just below her.

The tempting mash charmed a little black nose, then a head and front leg, out of the crevice. Following Will's instructions, Dumpy tied a rope round the narrow chest and pulled gently until the silly creature was fully in her arms. Dumpy held the woolly warmth close to herself. She could feel the heart beat and wondered if the animal could feel hers. Such a precious moment.

"Come on. We haven't got all night. You lift and I'll pull. This would be a job for one of those shepherd's crooks like in the Bible stories."

The poor creature resisted, but after some frantic exercises, the lamb was landed safely in the rowboat which May had manoeuvred to the necessary place.

"Hurrah!" exclaimed Dumpy.

"Are you all right?" asked William noticing scrapes on Dumpy's arms and legs.

"I've received worse scrapes," thought May, "He never asked me if I was all right."

"I feel great," exulted Doris as she pulled up her socks and pulled down the skirt, "Only my blouse and sweater are torn. Small matter. Thank goodness there are no mosquitoes at this time of year."

"It was good you came with us," said Will. His sister knew that to be his best understatement of the year.

"This has been an adventure for this wee lamb as well as for us," remarked Dumpy as she looked fondly at the woolly creature. Lets award her with a name."

"Award! She deserves a spanking for causing us all this trouble."

"But, if it hadn't been for her, we would never have come out tonight. How often do you on your side of the point see the moon bathing the lake like this? I'm going to call her La Petite Perdue."

Will wrapped La Petite Perdue in the blanket and asked Doris to sit beside her.

"You can talk soothingly to keep her quiet. Tell her one of your stories."

"Will, aren't you even going to look at the Jake?" remonstrated Dumpy, as she obediently took her place beside La Petite Perdue.

"In a minute... May, it's your turn to row with me."

Will made a quick survey to ensure that their ropes, lights, and other rescue equipment were all safely on board. He pushed the craft out from shore, gazed moonward, and became speechless. He thought the war had cured him of youth and all yearnings for thrills; now he realized his cousin was right. How many times did silvery light on the lake go unwatched? Moonlight on the fields was beautiful, too, especially at harvest, with rows of tiny haystacks throwing eerie moon shadows. But this! This was magic!

"I feel about twelve years old again," said Dumpy.

"That makes me twenty-one. No, I don't want to be twenty-one again. That would mean war is still to come."

"If you two insist on turning the clock back, I shouldn't be out this late at night. Let's go home and put me back in my crib!"

For the rest of the voyage, Dumpy's sole occupation was comforting La Petite.

Will broke the silence, "Taking this animal home must be easy compared to the time one of our cows went over that cliff. Father says they had to tow her around behind the boat."

"Did you help that time?"

"No, I was only a little fellow."

When they rounded the point, the moon was higher and looked smaller. Not much of it's glory followed them. At Brown's Landing, the three human travellers felt the night's chill.

"This is genuine cold!" Dumpy shook herself as she spoke. The proud pain of a few scratches had swelled to agonizing stiffness. She found it difficult to struggle out of the boat.

How they got La Petite Perdue home, they were never quite sure. It was a matter of carrying, tugging, and cajoling. At last, after what seemed ages, Will gratefully stowed the lost lamb in the sheep barn.

When they reached the warm farm house there was hot tea on the back of the stove. Aunt Sally lay half asleep on her day bed and Uncle John was dozing in his chair.

He woke enough to say, "Go get into your night clothes ready for bed; then come back; I'll put a shot of whisky into a mug of tea for each of you. Drink it in bed. Then don't cause any trouble 'til morning."

"We found her!"

"I know."

Singing in the Snow

The next morning was Sunday. Doris woke early to the sound of agitated whispering. She soon got the gist of it. William was trying to persuade his sister to instruct Doris that she didn't have to use the winter back house in the shed, but, should leave her commode potty with a cloth over it and he would empty it for her when he did his mother's. May was not sympathetic.

"She's not sick, and not elderly."

"She's a city girl... not used to country ways. I think...," Dumpy appeared in the hallway to settle the matter.

"I didn't come here to be pampered. I came to be useful. Please forget the whole matter. I'll be happy to use the shed."

She was later to regret her show of bravery. When it's forty below, there is white frost and ice on the inside walls of a Muskoka shed. Exercising bodily functions in those conditions is pure misery.

At breakfast, no one made the slightest reference to the shed. May was all packed, ready to return to the Beasleys. The three young people went together in the farm row boat, arriving in plenty of time for church, after which they stood around to visit with the Beasleys and other village friends before Dumpy and William headed back to the farm.

The Chadwicks were not at church. Dumpy didn't think much about their absence. Roderick had never been strong on church attendance. He'd said all of nature was his chapel. Mrs. Chadwick didn't go anywhere anymore. The girls probably found it difficult to leave.

As the weeks went by, Dumpy took to the rhythm of farm life. She rather enjoyed cooking on the wood stove. Everything, especially the slow roasted lamb, beef, or pork, tasted superior to anything from the oven of a gas or electric burner. As for Christmas, the farm in winter was ideal.

"There may have been more than one reason the Christ child chose a lowly stable for his birthplace," she remarked to Aunt Sally one morning.

The two women were cutting, peeling, chopping together with puddings, fruit cake and mince pies in mind. An array of bowls, pans and pie plates was strewn across the table and counter top.

"I often think He chose winter so that the glory of His light and the warmth of His soul would be all the more appreciated."

Aunt Sally's wrist was much improved and, likewise, her spirits.

"They say the pagans had a winter festival before Christianity reached England and that some of our customs stem from that period," replied Dumpy.

"Yes, my dear, and I imagine there was some debauchery as part of it."

"There's some of that in these modern times, too," added Doris.

"Indeed, so," continued Aunt Sally, "And there are still souls like our pagan ancestors, in need of the gift of truth and love, so simply and so beautifully wrapped in an innocent babe."

"What a beautiful way to say it."

"I thought about these things when Regina was born. She was a winter baby."

"Did you give birth in this house? Was it difficult?"

"All our babies were born here. Compared to William's birth, the others were easy."

"Did the doctor come?"

"Only for William. After two miscarriages, Uncle John thought I needed a doctor. That proved to be a mistake. That doctor didn't know much. Mrs. Beasley helped me with the other births. Regina's birth was quick. I was alone and had time to think of the Holy Family and their stable before Uncle John returned with Mrs. Beasley."

Although Aunt Sally was still using the parlour as a bedroom, they decided to decorate it as usual and have a tree. May came one weekend in December to help.

They arranged to fetch her again on Christmas Day after church.

On the twenty-fifth, there was enough snow to use the sleigh. Uncle John put bells on the harnesses and tied a red bow to the sleigh. Even Aunt Sally went with them. Uncle John and William carried her out and placed a hot ironstone 'pig' under her feet. The whole family group was swathed in hats, scarves, coats, leggings, wool socks, mittens or muffs.

They tucked blankets over their knees. The horses were stamping the ground with heavy hooves and breathing white vapour from twitching nostrils, impatient to be off.

With a wild 'Whoa,' Will mounted his seat, then gave the signal. They were off, hearts beating faster, spirits ready to make merry. Aunt Sally and Uncle John joined Dumpy's singing of one round of "Jingle Bells." William kept his mind on the trail and the animals.

"I can't believe I'm living this," said Dumpy, "This is a storybook Christmas and I'm in it!"

The church service heightened her enchantment. Caring hands, including May's, had gathered greens to make wreaths and streamers to festoon every window beside, and every beam above. In a corner beside the altar there was a noble fir, aglow with fifty miniature candles. Pails, one with water and one with sand, stood nearby, in case of need.

Doris Drayton gasped in awe, a blend of fear and admiration. The church was full to capacity. Again Dumpy noted the absence of all Chadwicks.

The congregation said prayers and sang to His glory, then stamped out into the cold, white world. Once more, Will and Uncle John carried Aunt Sally. After a brief warm-up and exchange of greetings in the Beasley's house next door, the Draytons and their sleigh were homeward bound.

A surprise awaited them. Will was the first to suspect something. He noticed a healthy column of smoke issuing from both chimneys. True, he had 'banked' all the stoves well, but why were they sending forth so much smoke? He peered down at the road before him.

"Look!" He pointed to tire marks in the snow.

"It's Robert!... It must be," Aunt Sally's voice caught in her throat.

Indeed, it was Robert. Regina was with him, as well as Hazel Jackson, his fiancee. Regina had taken the train from Toronto to Gravenhurst to come with them.

Glad cries and greetings were exchanged.

"How wonderful to have the fires going fully and the house warm. Thank you."

Aunt Sally let Robert help Will carry her in and onto the day bed.

"The best gift of all," she sighed, "is having you here."

Such a bustling and hustling, but many hands make light work. The goose, their own, of course, was roasted to perfection. The big table was ready in the dining room. Will had helped Dumpy put the extra leaves in the night before. There was a 'silence cloth' over which a snowy white linen banquet cloth was spread. A mixture of inherited sterling and wedding present plated flatware gleamed at each place. The necessary additions and extra chairs were soon in place.

"Let us sing the Doxology for grace," commanded Aunt Sally

Praise God from whom all blessings flow,
Praise Him all creatures here below,
Praise Him above, ye heavenly host,
Praise Father, Son and Holy Ghost. Amen

Not everyone could keep a tune, but together they made a "joyful noise."

To Dumpy, it seemed like the whole week was Christmas. There was a wonderful fall of snow during Christmas night, after which a brilliant sun dawned on Boxing Day. The young people grabbed toboggans and snow shoes and headed for Lynnehurst. The Lynnehurst Hill was the best for tobogganing. With many a shriek and laugh, they indulged themselves in the opportunities nature had provided.

"We're not exactly children anymore," said Dumpy to Will, "even May, but it's good to feel like children at Christmas."

Regina had to get back to her job at Eaton's. The Jacksons would need their truck, so off went that trio after a noon meal of Christmas left-overs.

The next day was sunny, too. Dumpy wanted to get pictures of Lynnehurst in the snow. She and May set out, camera in hand, right after the breakfast dishes were done. Will said he might as well come too.

"I should shovel the snow off the ice house roof and the porch roof before we get more depth."

"Do you have to do the high roof of the main house, too?"

"No, it's pitched at a good angle and more exposed to the sun. However, what slides off the main roof piles up on the porch rooves, so I have to watch them."

The following day, they took cameras and shovel to Old Drayton Farm and to Uncle Phillip's place beyond.

"I hope my pictures turn out. They will make good Christmas gifts next year."

"Will you be able to keep them secret that long?" asked Will.

"Don't confuse me with my sister, Mary," she retorted.

After they had tramped around the two houses and done the necessary shoveling, May wanted to collect some hemlock cones for her school children. Uncle Phillip had the best stand of hemlock, with plenty of branches low enough for plucking.

Dumpy and Will wandered back to Old Drayton Farm and sat on the new verandah steps to wait. Actually, the old place was now called Fort Armstrong and hardly resembled the humble log home it had once been. The Armstrongs had built a proper second floor with two dormer windows facing the lake. Boxie had declared these windows to be excellent stations for cannon, should they ever need to defend themselves from enemies coming up the lake, hence the title 'Fort.' The old downstairs was now one large living-room with a dining-room and kitchen added on the north west end.

Picking up the theme of their earlier remarks, Will suddenly said, "yes, you are quite different from Mary Lynne. In many ways, you are more mature. You should be the older one."

"You and Mary were chums when you were growing up. When you were about seventeen, I imagined you were sweet on her. She said it was childish nonsense on my part."

"You were perceptive, even then. I loved her. She entered into farm chores with me and made them seem like a real lark. She had a way of making me feel important. I was her source of knowledge and wisdom. However, I also resented her."

"What do you mean?"

"Well, the farm was fun for her. She could always leave before it became drudgery and she always left for the South before winter set in."

"I suppose you could have resented all of your city cousins."

"Strangely, no; only Mary Lynne."

"Why?"

He paused, as if to read his own thoughts carefully; then, slowly and deliberately, "I suppose, because she was my special friend. Then, because she began to spend more time with the Beasleys. It's silly, but that irritated me. Jack, Mary and I played together as children. It's odd. Alan is closer in age but I didn't play with him as much. Later, Mary, Jack and I were often together in the sailboat. In the winter, Jack was still my best friend. When Mary and Jack teamed up, it was like I'd lost my two best friends."

Doris let silence hang between them and then, answered quite simply, "I see."

"Another thing which got my goat was when Mary went to University. I wanted more education, too, but we didn't have money and I thought I was needed on the farm. Then, Mary, a mere girl, got what I wanted. It seemed such a waste; Uncle Charlie spending his money to indulge her whim. I didn't mind Jack going to college as much."

"Oh William!" Dumpy was almost crying, "Why didn't you tell us? Your folks have some money and father would have helped, so would the Armstrongs. You could have done odd jobs in Toronto."

"I guess I was too proud to talk. I didn't want charity," He turned away from her and added, "especially from your father."

"It wouldn't have been charity, just family co-operation. You do a great deal for us!"

"Yes, that's true."

Dumpy did not know where to take this conversation next but she felt they would never speak of these matters again and her curiosity got the better of her.

"You used the word 'Love.' Did you ever want to marry Mary?"

"No, we were cousins, double cousins. I didn't think about it. Then the war came along and cured me of any ideas of marriage at all."

"The war? I don't understand."

"War showed me the ugly side of the world. I don't want to bring children into it. Some claim that war brings out courage and strengthens character. That could be, but it also encourages many to lower themselves. I saw degradation, people being hurt, and animals, too. You can't know if you haven't seen. I hope you never know. I don't want to talk about it."

Seeing her brother and cousin so deep in serious talk and catching the word 'marriage', May retreated and stayed longer with the hemlocks. At last, the winter chill forced her forth again. She began to sing cheerily to warn them of her approach.

Both William and Dumpy were ready for a change of mood. They joined, happily, in singing as all three headed back to their farm home.

❦

It was a couple of days before May confided in her mother what she thought she had witnessed at Fort Armstrong. Sally became gravely concerned. She conferred with John.

"I don't believe it. William is too old to care."

"Are you too old to care?"

He let her query pass, "Please have a word with him. It wouldn't be right. They are double first cousins. Liza would be so upset."

Uncle John caught the infection of worry. Subsequently, he spoke frankly to his son in the privacy of the barn.

"Father! How could you and mother think such a thing?"

William was shocked and angry, "I don't intend to marry anyone; you know that."

"Well, you have been in her company a great deal which you seem to enjoy and well... propinquity is a powerful force."

Will stalked out of the barn, slamming the big door behind him. They didn't see him for an hour. When he turned up for dinner he ate in silence.

Doris wondered at the change in him and thought, perhaps it was a protest of her baked potatoes. She made a mental note to prepare good mashed ones in future.

Will remained morose and avoided talking to his cousin for the next few days.

"What's the matter with Will?" she asked Aunt Sally one day.

"He and his father had a little disagreement about something. It was a complete misunderstanding... Don't try to sort it out. It will pass in time."

"You and mother have similar ideas. She always says, 'least said, soonest mended.'"

༺❦༻

When it came time to take May back to the Beasleys, Will did not invite Dumpy to join them. She was just as pleased to stay behind with Aunt Sally. Niece and Aunt soon had the kitchen chores done. They had time for tatting. Aunt Sally was an excellent tatter. Dumpy was learning. She wanted to do some each day to make sure she learned the intricate pattern Aunt Sally was demonstrating.

Upon his return, Will brought a bundle of mail, some belated Christmas greetings for everyone including a specially long letter for Doris from her father. She shared bits of news: Jack Beasley was already thinking about a spring production of Pinafore. The music master was enthusiastic and ready to co-operate with the English Department on the venture. The headmaster didn't think Gilbert and Sullivan were sufficiently academic, but Jack was sure he could bring him round. The father of their favourite boy soprano was very influential with Head and could be counted on to like the choice. They were seeing a great deal of the Armstrongs and had taken in a concert at Massey Hall.

"Listen to this one! Father volunteered to do the accounts for a charity that helps blind people. The lighting was so poor in the room allotted to him that he purchased a small goose-necked lamp and an extension cord. The Chairman of the Board of Directors objected."

"My goodness, why?"

"Because of the expense!... Father pointed out that he had purchased the lamp and cord with his personal money, but the Director said the lamp would increase the electric bill of the Institute."

"I can't imagine Charlie working with people like that, charity or no charity," remarked Uncle John, who had left his repair jobs in the shed to join the family and hear the news.

"I'll leave out what he says next, but you are right. He pointed out that, as he did not wish to become blind and therefore be subjected to their type of charity, he would finish the Ledger books for that month and they could find another volunteer."

"Can accounts be kept in braille? These people could do with a blind accountant."

Dumpy continued to read silently and then, aloud, she exclaimed, "Julian and Geraldine are coming up for a visit! They want to visit in Toronto and then come to Lynnehurst. I hope the mosquitoes won't be too bad for them."

"May got quite a thick letter too," remarked Will.

"Oh?"

"It was from that American professor fellow who was up here last summer."

"Well, well."

"Do you mean Dr. Taylor?" asked Dumpy, "He was on the camping trip father organized to the Georgian Bay."

"That's the one."

"He came calling a few times, but we thought he came to see us," added Sally. He is much older than May."

"Interesting man," remarked Uncle John, "He's very knowledgeable on scientific matters. What's even better, he can explain his work in terms that I understand."

That post-Christmas bundle of mail gave the family much to talk over and to think about for several winter days.

About a week later Sally found an opportunity to speak to her son alone. She managed to convince William that the misconception about his ideas on marriage had been all in her head and that his father spoke only because she had insisted on it. Furthermore, she never betrayed his sister's role in the episode.

"You know, dear, when a person is unwell, time hangs heavy. I think I let my imagination run away with my thoughts. Please forgive me."

"Did you say anything to Doris?"

"Not a word."

The subject was never mentioned again. In time, Will was able to relax in the presence of his cousin. One cold, grey day in ice-cutting season, he persuaded Dumpy to come with him in the big sleigh to join Tom Webster and other young men at the bay. Dumpy made no pretence to help, merely enjoyed watching the procedure, talking to the horses and taking a few pictures. The crew worked all week to fill several ice houses including those at Webster's, Uncle Phillip's, Fort Armstrong, Lynnehurst and New Drayton Farm.

Doris went out several other days while the men were working. One sunny morning she ventured to the middle of the lake smiling to herself as she remembered her girlhood quest in the canoe to find the absolute middle.

Such a different world in winter, she thought to herself... *Something marvellous to behold with a cruel threat behind the glory. Like the Sirens, it tantalizes and lures.*

Shaking herself free of these thoughts she turned toward the security of Brown's Landing, allowing herself, only one glance towards Chadwick Bay which was invisible from her position. The thought of walking over the lake to surprise Henny with a visit appealed but she was afraid to venture that far. She never even thought of 'phoning.

Roderick had installed a phone but Uncle John didn't have one. The Lynnehurst phone had been disconnected for the winter.

Later, Doris was to regret her timidity. After all, if she had planned a visit, Will could have gone with her early enough one morning to allow time for returning in daylight. They could have taken a horse and sleigh over the ice. However, this proposition had not taken shape in her head. In retrospect she later realized that, as far as Chadwick Manor was concerned, she, Doris Amelia Drayton, had built a mental blockade around it.

※

In March, Will brought home another thick letter for Doris bearing a Texas postmark. It had been forwarded from Toronto. William also conveyed his sister home for the weekend. Dumpy left May visiting with Aunt Sally and took herself upstairs to read Florence's letter at leisure on the window seat in the little alcove of her bedroom.

Florence's words were lavish in expressions of bliss. She expounded on each of her five step-children. They had celebrated New Year's Day with a fiesta on the beach for the benefit of the children and several juvenile friends. A fish fry was preceded by races and games of all sorts. Benny was an immense help with all the preparations.

He'd entered into the spirit of the occasion fully.

"My dear Doris, you would almost think he was still a child himself," she enthused.

"Indeed," Dumpy's mind echoed back.

There followed, several paragraphs about life in Galveston and about people Dumpy had never met and never would meet. Florence thanked Dumpy and her family all over again for promoting her good fortune. She ended the epistle with the best news of all. There was to be another little Howard in June. This one would be Florence's very own as well as Benny's. Could there be any happier woman than "your ever grateful friend, Florence (Mrs. B.J. Howard)."

Dumpy looked up after making her way through these ten pages of scrawling handwriting. Her eyes rested upon the dark green branch of hemlock, just outside her window. Then she looked downward at a fresh fallen blanket of white snow beyond which she could see the still frozen lake. Between her and the lake, a grove of stately tree shapes sifted the golden glory of late-day sunlight. Some of it reached her window as if groping to caress her worshipping face. She stood, to better watch the sun sink, marvelling at the richness of colour the sky could display.

Then, in a whisper, "dear Florence, I wouldn't trade this for all your bambini and fiestas. Bushland and wild vistas for me, thank you very much."

Still standing, her spirits rose to new heights. The sky now held more vivid blues, more vivid yellows. The trees between stood out more boldly, the gold relief etched on their north-westerly flanks a dramatic contrast to the black of their shadowed sides. Dumpy's eyes followed the tracery of bare maple branches against the sky.

"Which is more lovely," she asked herself, "green-clad limbs billowing in summer breezes or this stark tracery in winter stillness?"

"I did not expect to be so happy here this winter. There has been something each day to make me sing."

Pinafore

LATE APRIL FOUND DUMPY MAKING PLANS TO RETURN TO TORONTO. She was eagerly looking forward to a school performance of Pinafore and to the up-coming visit from Julian and Geraldine. Aunt Sally, 'tho stiff and experiencing occasional leg pains, was 'worlds better', restored to her normal, useful routine around which her soul's happiness revolved. Clearly, Dumpy was no longer needed. Dumpy left the farm regretfully. Her room, her window, her hemlock bough were no longer hers. The little room had an empty, uncaring look. Why? The same narrow bed, the same chest of drawers, the same white-washed walls had welcomed her in November to that room. In a quaint, cosy way she had felt cherished there. Now there was only bare emptiness. Can a room have feelings? Did this one feel rejected? There was no wind that day. The hemlock stood motionless outside the still window panes.

"You'll never live here again," her mind told her, "This room will never be yours again. Good-bye, dear room; you've been good to me."

She spoke quietly. Then she thought she saw the hemlock bough bend slightly, as if waving in response.

"How could it?" she thought. "There's no wind, no breeze at all."

She picked up her overnight bag, draped her rain cape over one arm and ran quickly downstairs to hug Aunt Sally. Without a word, Dumpy left by the back shed door.

Alone, she started down the familiar lane to Lynnehurst and the wharf at Brown's Landing. Uncle John had taken her trunk earlier. Will was milking the cows behind closed barn doors. Aunt Sally waved from a window and blew her kisses.

Once aboard the steamer, Dumpy found it easier to forget the farm and its occupants. Her expectations rushed toward Toronto and reunion with her own family. Spring is a ·light-hearted time on the lakes. New life is everywhere. Seeing Lynnehurst windows shuttered did not bother her. She knew Uncle John was beginning that very day to 'open up'. She would be back soon enough.

※

Pinafore was a jubilant success. Boys, masters, parents and friends all congratulated each other. Julian de Poncier attended two of the three performances, commending Jack Beasley most highly afterwards.

"Mary Lynne," he exclaimed over Sunday dinner at the young Beasley's apartment, "do you realize that you have married a genius of stage craft?"

Without expecting a reply, he turned to Jack, "Where did you learn how?"

"I don't know; probably during the war."

"The war?"

"In the second part of the war when I was with the Forestry Corps, the 'concert' evenings in the YMCA hut were largely my responsibility. I suppose that experience helped."

"Oh? What sort of concerts did you have?"

"Everything from professional French performers who could be persuaded to come out to us, to last minute skits put on by some of our boys. We learned to improvise costumes and props."

"So a concert was drama as well as music?"

"Yes, and everything in between. I think the men enjoyed the home-made fun the most. It kept their spirits up and made for a feeling of comradeship."

"Jack," interrupted Mary, "even before that you were helping your father put on school concerts and church pageants."

"True. Probably my first appreciation of pageantry was engendered by Orangemans' Day. Year after year I watched that parade being prepared. It never failed to stir me."

"You shouldn't talk about Orangemen here, Jack. The de Ponciers were originally a Roman Catholic family."

The ever-diplomatic Julian was quick to respond, "Please don't concern yourselves; we know you are speaking of staging, not dogma. If you had grown up in Italy, you would have been excited by Catholic parades and festivals. But, I'm amazed you've had no formal training in drama.

"No, only my M.A. in English Literature which you must realize includes Shakespeare."

Doris, who also was her sister's guest that day, began to wonder what lay behind Julian's persistent questioning. Mary Lynne saw no special strategy in the conversation. She changed the subject by asking how the opera season had been in New Orleans. That topic kept them all occupied until dessert time. In fact, Mary nearly forgot to bring dessert.

It was Dumpy who eyed a large bowl of Spanish Cream on the buffet, suggestively, but to no effect.

At last, she hinted more openly, "May I help you change the plates, Mary?"

"Thank you, yes."

As the two young women bustled around the table, Doris studied her sister's figure. It was later confirmed, in confidence, that Mary was once more expecting.

The de Ponciers had six weeks at their disposal. They planned to visit Lynnehurst, but first wanted to see Montreal. Ruthie Mae and Christopher Russell had promised to show them historic sites and the French sections.

After the de Poncier departure for Montreal, Charles, Liza and Dumpy scurried around, making final arrangements for another season at Lynnehurst. The annual Michie Company provisions were ordered and on their way a few days ahead of the three Draytons. The Drayton trunks headed for Union Station to go on the morning train to Gravenhurst.

"I don't think I've forgotten anything this year," commented Liza.

"I'm sure you've done everything, dear," Charles assured her.

"I don't know if I've remembered everything," said Dumpy, "but I'm ready for a good long summer at Lynnehurst."

Ready as they all were, none of them were prepared for the news that awaited them in Muskoka.

Roderick

Dumpy could never remember why she hadn't phoned first. As soon as the steamer passed Chadwick Bay her mind started repeating the name Chadwick. The very next day, right after Tom Webster and her father had lowered Daisy Belle into the water, Doris took over the steering wheel. Mission-bound for Chadwick Manor, Doris and Daisy cut a happy caper across the lake, playful white clouds in the blue above, dancing waves in the blue below.

There was no one at the boathouse, or on Chadwick Beach as she arrived.

Dumpy thought nothing of that. She put herself through the well-known routine of mooring Daisy, all the while thinking of titbits of news she would share with Henny.

It wasn't quite four o'clock. She would be just in time for afternoon tea.

Along the path through the woods to the house flowering trillium were still abundant. Doris looked to see if the little wild orchids were thriving. She stopped to listen for bird calls. What kind of thrush was that with the haunting song? She must ask Roderick.

At Henny's garden, she stopped again to make a loving assessment. "She's behind with her planting this year; I wonder if she's been unwell; maybe I can help her."

The Chadwick women were sitting together in the gloomy parlour. They greeted her with hollow stares. Her individual greetings were returned with automatic, formal replies. When she got around to Ethel, she realized that there was a baby in a basket beside her.

"A baby! I didn't know. What name have you chosen?"

"Roderick."

"Roderick?... After his father?... That's nice," Then, glancing around... "Where is Roderick?"

She thought she heard a gasp from Hilda, but it was Ethel who answered.

"He's dead; shot himself."

"No, Ethel, he did not shoot himself. It was an accident."

"He shot himself, I tell you. He hated me. I don't know why he ever married me."

Doris Amelia Drayton felt transfixed. She could not think; she could not move.

"Please excuse me," said Mrs. Chadwick, rising from her chair-throne and leaving the room. Hilda went with her.

Doris looked first at Henrietta, then at Ethel, again back to Ethel. Henrietta spoke.

"Dear Dumpy, we thought you knew. It was in early May. Roderick left the house with father's rifle... said something about a fox... I found him later out by the... out by the bog."

"Don't tell me exactly where," A mental picture of Roderick's body lying beside the pile of logs passed through Dumpy's mind... "Oh, Henny, we never saw any foxes out there."

"He might have been chasing one that ran that way," Henny's voice spoke the words emphatically.

"The bullet went through his neck," snapped Ethel, "A man doesn't aim at a fox through his own neck."

"He tripped and fell. The gun went off accidentally!" Henny was shouting.

"They won't believe the truth. They were afraid Mr. Withers would refuse to bury him in the Church graveyard," As she spoke, Ethel glared at Dumpy.

Dumpy, still standing, instinctively drew back toward the entrance door. She had never seen anyone's eyes look so wild.

Henny broke the spell, her voice calm and controlled: "I suggested we bury him near the bog because he loved it so much. They said that wouldn't be sanitary. In the end, the Beasleys offered part of their plot. It's near that lovely old oak tree, so there's shade part of the day. I want to plant some of our trillium to mark the spot."

"Could you take me there some afternoon in the Daisy Belle?"

"Certainly! Will there be a tombstone?"

"Not yet... perhaps later."

The baby stirred fretfully. Ethel took him from the room.

Dumpy turned to Henny and said, "Let's go outside. We'll feel better out there."

Wordlessly, Henny followed Dumpy. They walked as far as the porch, then sat on the top step. Across the lake Needles Point was catching afternoon sunlight. As the two young women watched in silence every tree and rock stood out in bold relief.

Dumpy spoke first, "I'm afraid my visit's upset your mother terribly. I wish I could think of some way to ease her pain."

"It's useless. She's determined that life is ended for her. I believe she would have gone to bed forever and refused food if it hadn't been for Ethel."

"Ethel?"

"Yes, Ethel. You know Ethel can speak sharply."

"What did she say?"

"She threatened to sit in the big chair if Mother didn't appear for afternoon tea."

The thought of Ethel on the Chadwick family throne filled Dumpy's head with shock waves, "How horrid! Has that woman no feelings at all?"

"That's the way Hilda feels about it, but I say two cheers for Ethel. Her harshness succeeded where our loving coaxing was of no avail."

"When your mother dies, does Ethel become mistress of all Chadwick property?"

"That's quite possible. The will states that Ethel has the right to live here as long as she wishes, but if she chooses to leave, a sum of money is available to her on condition she signs a waver renouncing all claims on the estate. The property will go eventually to little Roderick."

"I see."

"I don't like to believe what Ethel says but sometimes I believe Roderick wanted to die. He willed himself to stay alive until he'd produced an heir... but Dumpy, why?... why?.. WHY?... why did he find life so awful?"

Henny's voice broke into sobs.

That was a question that Dumpy didn't want to hear. Wordlessly, she put her arm around her friend. While the sobbing continued, Dumpy spoke.

"Look Henny, your garden needs attention. It would do you good to work there. Tomorrow morning I'll come back in my work clothes and with a picnic. It'll be like that time we all worked in the hay field together. We can go to the graveyard afterwards if you wish."

Dumpy was still looking across the bay as the sun's rays shifted from Needles Point to the distant shore and then faded. No boat was anywhere in sight. The waves were getting higher. The sky turned grey. Where they sat, sheltered from the wind, their two bodies close together were warm. Dumpy kept her arm around Henny until her sobbing ceased. Her own feelings became more steady.

Henny finally spoke, "Doris, the wind is rising. You must go, in case we get a storm."

Henny and Dumpy walked together to the boathouse. Along the path, they chose a clump of trillium for Roderick's grave. As promised, the transplanting of the trillium got done the very next day.

Henny's garden work took several days. Together day after day, the two friends fell into their former rhythm of talking and not talking. The pain of their grief slowly eased. Dumpy began to feel that her inner turbulence had healed completely when, one morning, just before time for her to leave, Henny handed Doris a brown paper parcel tied with a scrap of grocery twine. Dumpy's name was scrawled across the top in Roderick's hand.

"Oh no!" she cried.

"I found this last night. He must have hidden it in my dresser drawer some time ago. Take it home with you," urged Henny.

"Yes... yes, of course," Her hand went forward to receive. She found a pocket for storage.

Dumpy left immediately.

After tying Daisy securely in the Lynnehurst launch house, she climbed to the top of Little Bluff. Dumpy did not want to enter Lynnehurst yet. For a while, she sat gazing lakeward before opening Roderick's parcel. Inside were two books of their favourite poetry, a small, square box and a letter. She fingered the books carefully and let her mind unravel the memories they evoked.

Instinctively, she knew what the box contained. Many a time, she had surveyed Ethel's left hand. There had never been anything there other than one gold wedding band.

"I can't.... I just can't," she said to herself.

After a few minutes, she found that she could open the little square box. As she did so, the diamond ring slipped from her grasp and fell beside a cedar root where it lay sparkling in the sunlight. She opened the letter.

My Dearest Doris,
Please keep the ring in memory of me. I bought it for you. It does not seem right that anyone else should wear it. Do you remember one time when you and Henny and I were talking about rings? You described what you thought was the perfect setting for a diamond. I wrote down your description and later had this ring made according to your direction. One summer, I realized that you were no longer a child. It was during one of our huckleberry expeditions. I thought you felt something then, too. There were other moments as well. I suppose my vanity prompted me to detect sentiments that were not there. Please forgive me for all the discomfort I have caused you.

I have made a terrible mistake. The loss of your friendship these past few years has been the severest punishment life could devise for me. Now there is only one solution left to me.

      Your Devoted "Uncle",
      Roderick

Dumpy put the letter down and looked out at the lake. The west wind was rising. She loosened her hair so that stray strands bellowed and bounced, teasing her face.

I wish it were a gale, or better still, a storm, she thought, *I want to scream but I can't.*

She picked up the ring to examine it. The setting was perfect. Dainty gold claws held the large central jewel above four clusters of tiny diamonds arranged to form an overall diamond shape when viewed from above. Exquisitely cut into several facets, all the gems reflected light to the pure delight of the beholder.

"Dear God, I never noticed. How cruel I have been."

It was then that the tears were loosened, "I must talk to someone, but who?... Mother and Father must never know... Henny? No, not Henny."

A couple of days later she sought out The Rev. Mr. Withers.

"Mr. Withers, I'm here to confess that I am a murderer. "

"My dear child," unlike Roderick, her priest had not noticed that she had grown up.

"I wish I still were a dear child. I wish I could undo the mistakes."

She showed Mr. Withers the letter and the ring. Once begun, her story unfolded rapidly and easily.

"So now, you see it is all my fault. I could have married him. It's just that he was so... so... arrogant. But I can do anything if I put my mind to it. He would be alive today. I would be the mother of little Roderick instead of that wretched woman."

"That would have been a greater sin. You are not guilty of murder but you are guilty of arrogance."

"Arrogance?"

"You were both guilty of arrogance. In your desire to have a safe friendship you were blind to the effect you were having on Roderick. You pride yourself on your good judgement, but you cannot know everything. Your self-interest blinded you just as much as his passion blinded him," almost inaudibly he added, "eyes have they and see not."

After a pause, Mr. Withers continued, "as for Ethel Chadwick, you must not look with disdain. Judge not. Perhaps, if you had been born into ignorance, misery and violence, you too, would be wretched."

"What must I do?"

"You know what to do. Give your burden to the Lord."

"I've tried, but it keeps coming back. "

"It doesn't come back. You grab it back."

Mr. Withers patted the edge of his desk thoughtfully and, as if seeking guidance, looked out his study window. He knew Doris needed a precise formula to follow, "I think you have to tell your parents. They will not be as upset as you think. You should also tell Henrietta. It will help her to understand her brother. You owe her and him that much."

"What should I do with the ring?"

"Wear it. That will be punishment fit for the crime."

"No, I can't."

"Yes, you can. When you are ready, give me a signal at the altar rail some communion Sunday. I will place my hands on you and pray briefly for healing before administering the elements to you. No one will question this. I have done so for others."

"Thank you," she said contritely, but she did not like the idea.

They said a prayer together. Dumpy left.

What the good reverend did not tell Doris was that she was the third woman to come to him confessing responsibility for Roderick's death. He smiled. Now the real culprit had come forward. Henrietta's guilt for not warning Roderick against marrying Ethel was the easiest to heal. After all, Ethel herself had made her designs quite clear.

Roderick could have found a way out. He must have been eager for married life and quite likely was spurred on by a desire to hurt Doris.

As for Ethel's threat to sue for breech of promise, Roderick could have played the delaying game or he could have let his mother in on the problem. She would have kicked the tramp right out in no uncertain terms. What evidence did Ethel have? The Chadwick women would never have witnessed on her behalf. Pride must have blinded Roderick to these possibilities.

He probably feared his mother so much that he could not confess his mistake to her.

"History repeats itself. People make mistakes. Instead of facing up to them when they are small, they make bigger mistakes to cover up. I should preach on that topic."

"I am sure," Mr. Withers continued to himself, "there was nothing Henrietta could have done to deter Roderick. I hope she'll see this clearly when Dumpy confesses. Poor Roderick. I, too, could have helped him, but he never came near me. Poor, poor Henrietta. She will always mourn for her brother."

Seth Talbot's Ford rattled past the rectory window. Cyril Withers neither looked nor gave his customary wave. He was thinking about Ethel Chadwick. The day she had knocked on his study door had been a real surprise. Ethel never came to church. She did not appear to have any religious faith or conscience whatsoever.

After talking to her, though, he found himself admiring her brand of honesty. She probably would steal or lie if it were to her advantage, but he liked the way she called a spade a spade. She didn't hide anything. Her visit was not a confession, but a statement of fact. She had forced Roderick into marriage. She had made his life miserable. By her logic, her husband should be buried in consecrated ground. It was the one thing she hoped she could do for him.

"I'm the one who will not be buried in a churchyard," It was as if Ethel was buying Roderick's right to sanctified ground by promising to have her remains unblessed. Cyril Withers wondered what Ethel would do with the rest of her life.

For several days Doris did not have a chance to speak confidentially to her parents. She felt relieved just knowing that some day she would tell them. In the meantime, Geraldine and Julian de Poncier's visit was upon them. Dumpy summoned considerable energy to keep her spirits up and to see that her friends had a good time.

On the final morning of their week-long visit while they stood on Brown's Wharf waiting for the steamer, Julian declared: "It's everything you said it would be. I'm only sorry we didn't get to go picking huckleberries."

"Next time come in July."

"I just love the canoe," said Geraldine, "especially in the evenings. Julian learned how to paddle very soon, don't you think?"

"Paddling is logical, but sailing takes more understanding. In a sailboat you go one direction when you really intend to end up at the opposite end of the lake. Perhaps I'll get on to that next time," added Julian.

Siegfried and Elizabeth

NEXT TO VISIT LYNNEHURST WERE ALAN AND MIRIAM with Siegfried and Elizabeth. Mary Lynne and Jack were not far behind. Miriam shyly confessed the happy prospect of a third child, due around Christmas. Mary Lynne was especially thrilled by the news. Her own expectation was for January.

For Siegfried and Elizabeth, Lynnehurst was a veritable fairy grandmother's castle. They loved the blocks kept in a box under the couch at the far end of the verandah. They could play with them anytime, providing the blocks were carefully put back afterwards. Elizabeth's efforts were clumsy but she liked to help by handing her brother blocks that seemed pretty to her. Even better than playing with the blocks, Siegfried liked packing them back in the box. He took his time, carefully matching similar sizes and shapes to make the most efficient use of space.

Sometimes Joshua Webster came over to play with the children. He enjoyed teasing Elizabeth who was not much older than he. She accepted his jibes with a timid smile, becoming upset only if the two boys warred with each other. This didn't happen often, only when Joshua started to destroy and re-build just when Siegfried thought it was time to pack the blocks scientifically away.

The children spent several mornings down beside Buppa's boathouse, wading or making pretend harbours. Sometimes Alan took them for small excursions in Buppa's rowboat. He felt safer rowing near the shore, either out to the end of Point Caroline or northward to Fort Armstrong to join a 'cousinly' swim time there on the old beach.

The children liked going close to the shore line on these expeditions. They named certain big rocks and looked for them on each trip.

"There's the Cuckoo Clock."

"No, it's not. Cuckoo Clock is bigger. We haven't come to it yet."

"This is a cuckoo too. We can call it Little Cuckoo."

"We're coming to Troll Bridge," a reference to a hemlock, fallen and bent over the water but still alive enough to have green branches.

Beyond Big Cuckoo was their cave, a cool, dark space between three massive rocks, back on the shore behind a level stretch of ground. Grey lichen grew on the rock walls. On top green moss supported a covering of miniature ferns. In later years, this haven became their secret castle.

Alan wanted to teach his children how to handle the oars. He found it hard to be patient with Siegfried, because Siegfried insisted on correcting the angle of his oars, each time before making a stroke. Several seconds would pass, with the boat at a standstill while the boy studied his form.

Both Siegfried and Elizabeth preferred the canoe to the rowboat. In later years they became good paddlers.

Afternoons usually found the children in the sand box. The dappled light under the trees cloaked them with colour as they created a fantasy world out of sand, twigs, bits of bark and their imagination. This particular summer, Siegfried was really too old to play in a sand box or with blocks, but he liked to do these things at Lynnehurst.

Miriam hovered near her children on a nearby bench. Mary Lynne was often with her.

The common bond of expectant motherhood brought the two women very close in friendship.

Dumpy felt superseded in her role as sister. However, as 'aunt in charge of story-telling,' she held a secure position in the affection of the children. If she and her mother were away during the day in their efforts to encourage and cheer the Chadwick women, they were always at home for bedtime rituals. Liza presided over cleanliness.

If swim times were not sufficient, she would decree full baths in the high-sided porcelain tub. The drying procedure was even more thorough. Each child, by turns, was mounted on the adjacent wooden toilet seat, while grandmother attacked any moisture with a rough linen towel. These towels, usually beige in colour with a decorative red line across the towel three inches from each end, became a trademark for Lynnehurst. Elizabeth grew up believing that no one else in the whole wide world ever used them except her grandmother.

Liza wasn't rough with the children. On the contrary, she was gentle beyond belief but, *very* thorough. No crack between toes or behind an ear was ever missed.

The children tried to hold still as directed, but were eager to flee into the bedroom, where Aunt Dumpy was already hanging the day's garments to air and pulling out the night wear. Aunt Dumpy was always quick. They knew she wanted to reach storytime as much as they did. Sometimes, the three of them huddled together in the big 'sleepy hollow' chair for a book story. Sometimes Aunt Dumpy tucked the children in their cots and told them a story of her own making. She never seemed to run out of stories to invent on the spot. After putting the bathroom 'back to rights' their grandmother joined them. Then it was prayer time for the four of them.

Alan and Miriam enjoyed the summertime freedom in the evenings. They might go out on the lake, usually in the company of Jack and Mary Lynne, or they might visit their various cousins. Sometimes they took advantage of the long twilight to explore and dream about a suitable site for a cottage of their own. Alan wanted to buy a couple of acres from Uncle John in order to build on the South Shore facing down the lake. Miriam was leery of the height of the rock face there. She thought a place in the woods nearer Lynnehurst would be safer for the children. Either way, they had a pleasant evening stroll, usually ending with a cup of cocoa and a rock cake on the verandah back at Lynnehurst. Dumpy would join them in this treat. They did not notice that she was unusually quiet and thoughtful at these times. The end of the day, which was so pleasant and relaxing for her married siblings, was the loneliest time for Dumpy. It was then, she agonized internally over the whole Roderick business.

One evening, when Jack and Mary Lynne had gone to stay at the Beasleys and Alan and Miriam were visiting the Armstrongs for the evening, Dumpy decided to talk to her parents about Roderick. It proved easier than she had expected. They seemed relieved to hear her explanation.

"Doris, you've done nothing wrong. We are, each of us, responsible for our own mistakes. Do not burden yourself with Roderick's," asserted her father, then he added in a lower voice, "I think, if you had married him, you would have made me miserable!"

Liza was thoughtful before she spoke.

"Poor boy. His women spoiled him all those years. Then he was unable to face up to difficulties. 1 hope I have not spoiled Alan."

"If you did, Miriam continues it, so he will be all right," Charles was serious, but his eyes gave a hint of a twinkle.

Turning to his daughter, he continued with, "Choosing a marriage partner is the one thing about which we must be totally selfish. You don't marry for charity and you musn't marry with the expectation of reforming your mate. Such expectations lead to unhappiness for everyone concerned."

"Charles," reproved Liza, "Doris doesn't need that lecture."

"I'm sorry. I'm upset, but at the same time, I don't want you to be upset," He reached over to give Dumpy's hand an affectionate squeeze and left the room.

Liza had more patience. She and Dumpy talked for a long time.

Finally she said, "We must see what we can do to console the Chadwick ladies. You talk to Henny and I will visit Mrs. Chadwick again. Perhaps she will relent the strictness of her mourning enough to come for afternoon tea sometime when it is just us here."

"Henny and I will be together tomorrow. We're going to scout for huckleberries up behind Needles Point."

"Good. Elsie and I will make some nice sandwiches for you and some lemonade. You can have a picnic."

"Pray for me too."

"Certainly dear."

"Henny has been more cheerful lately. I hate to open the wound for her again, but I must. Mr. Withers made that quite clear to me."

"That good man. He understands people. I wonder how long we will have him with us."

The Years Speed By

Liza didn't have long to wonder about The Rev. Mr. Withers. By the next spring, he had slept away into death. It was to be expected at his age, everyone said.

They did not, at first, realize how much they missed this saintly friend. Dumpy was sad, but secretly relieved as well. She had not made it to the altar rail for his special prayer and blessing. Now it wouldn't be necessary. Nor had she found occasion to wear the ring. She promised herself that if there were some grand occasion, she would do so. Henny had agreed the ring should not be worn every day.

Mr. Withers was replaced by a young man who walked quickly and made changes. He put a cross on the altar and lit candles. His opinions offended the Orangemen. The young ladies thought he was wonderfully handsome. Some joined the choir to have a better look. Old Mrs. Cleary couldn't make the pump organ produce the kind of music he wanted. He started a fund for a new organ.

After two years, he left. Mrs. Cleary's daughter left with him.

The next minister fitted in very well until his wife died. He sought to lift his sad spirits with alcoholic spirits. It was then that people began to miss Mr. Withers and to talk of all his good qualities.

The Beasleys, living next door to the church, were painfully aware of the disruptive church affairs. The family at Lynnehurst had other matters to capture their attention. Liza had two more grandchildren, Charles Allan Drayton and Mary Lynne Beasley, born just ten days apart. To distinguish her from her mother, little Mary Lynne was called Lynne. Jack had hoped for a son to replace Ted, but as Lynne developed, her lively ways and beautiful, black curls drew paternal love from him like a strong magnet. She favoured his mother in appearance.

The sudden death of George Whitby left Aunt Belle childless and with meagre financial resources. She sold the Montreal house and moved to an apartment in Toronto. Her summers were divided between Lynnehurst and Fort Armstrong. At both places, she made herself useful with domestic affairs. She seldom read a book but her fingers were never still. If she wasn't helping with cooking and other culinary chores, she was busy knitting baby things—woolly scarves, socks, mitts, and her speciality, the tub scrubber, this latter item made of string rather than wool. If her fingers needed a rest from knitting needles or crochet hook, she picked up a pen and became the family correspondent.

Fort Armstrong was filled with grandchildren too. Tom Jr. started the trend with twins named Thomas and Timothy and didn't ·stop until he and Stephanie had six offspring. Alice, now Mrs. William Dugdale, produced three lovely girls. Boxie, who loved flirting with as many young ladies as possible, put off marriage as long as he could. When the dazzling Angela O'Hara came into his life, he and Angela wasted no time. A gala wedding at Old Trinity Church, Toronto, was followed swiftly (or so it seemed to Liza) by home building in Rosedale and the production of a family. Boxie's business skills seemed to surpass his father's. One success led to another.

Liza tried to make the years slow down but they sped by faster and faster. One summer melded into the next; she could not remember one from another. Which spring was it that the Webster's main house burned? She and Charles, by cancelling a trip to Italy, found money for Frank and Emily. Other friends donated labour and time. Frank, who could ill afford to miss any summer's revenue, was depending more and more on the tourist trade. By summer that year the new Webster home and Lodge were ready for partial use. However, pioneer ways of community self-help were fading into modern commercial methods. Boxie did a brisk business in insurance policies that year.

Following the winter at New Drayton Farm, Doris returned to Shaw's to increase her secretarial and accounting skills. The business school had no difficulty recommending her to a well-respected business where in time she became their senior secretary. Doris felt herself to be well on the way to being the indispensable someone who could manage a company almost single-handed, while others made the social contacts and looked good in the public eye. She did not have to ask for increases in salary; they arrived unsolicited. She enjoyed being the power behind the scenes.

However, there was one large 'fly in the ointment.'

One afternoon at tea time she announced: "Father, I've decided to leave Munroe and Robinson."

"But Doris!" The words were blurted out and his face froze in a state of shock.

"Are you unhappy there?" asked Liza.

"No. The people are good. The work is interesting. I am never bored."

"What then is the matter?"

"I see the years stretching out before me. I don't want to spend them in an office, no matter how prosperous or powerful I become. More important, I do not want to spend my entire life in Toronto."

"But you have a month each year to be in Muskoka. If you want travel time, ask for some in the winter months as well."

"I could do that, but already they cannot get on without me for long absences. You have spoiled me with freedom. I do not want to be tethered to a short rope."

"Do you want to travel?... Perhaps around the world?"

"A little, maybe... I have come to realize that, for me, the only real life is a life that centres around Lynnehurst. There I have connections with nature and with family. Those are the driving forces inside me. With a good book as its transport my mind can travel. When I close the covers of the book I want to be in Lynnehurst or making preparations to be in Lynnehurst."

Liza began to understand. Charles kept silent, still nursing a disappointment.

He had dreamed of his daughter surpassing his own business successes.

Doris looked at her mother, "I would like to study the secrets of nature like Buppa did."

Turning to her father, she added, "I will also study the secrets of the stock market. Building an income through investments is a challenge that intrigues me. You, Father, have taught me sound principles. So have my experiences at Munroe and Robinson."

"Sound principles are the beginning. You need to keep informed and up to date," Charles was warming to her proposals.

"The business pages of The Globe can be read in Muskoka," Doris paused to break a piece of bread and apply butter, daintily, to a small corner, "Most of all, I think I want to enrich family life like you have done, Mother."

"Do you still hope for marriage?" asked Liza.

"That option seems closed for now, probably forever."

Another fragment of bread was processed, raised to her mouth, then lowered without reaching its intended destination. "I do not consider myself an old maid. I had opportunities. I chose to say 'no'."

"What then do you consider yourself?" Charles asked, amused by her rationalization.

"I'm a maiden aunt."

Maiden Aunt Doris Amelia Drayton accepted a teaching position at Shaw's Business College. That left her free to live at Lynnehurst four months each year, an ideal arrangement. For the aging Liza and Charles it meant a growing appreciation of their maiden daughter's presence at home.

1929

ONE SUMMER THAT LIZA COULD REMEMBER, as distinct from all the others, was that of 1929. All July and August, each house in Browns Landing settlement was filled with family and visitors. Across the lake, the hotel hired extra staff to handle their busy season and more musicians to play at weekly dances. Several impromptu Sir Roger de Coverly dances filled the verandah at Lynnehurst. The Draytons staged at least one full-fledged costume party with all the trimmings, as appreciative Aunt Belle expressed it while smacking her lips over the chocolate icing on a particularly good cake.

One evening at bed time Liza remarked to Charles that the atmosphere was like the summer before the Great War, "It's like 1914 on a bigger scale. Muskoka is bursting with cottages and hotels. I'm glad we bought Point Elizabeth. Other camping spots are disappearing fast."

He folded his day clothes over the rabbit ear chair beside the bed and reached under the pillow for his night shirt.

"I feel something is hanging over us," continued Liza. He looked at her keenly. She had said that in July of 1914, too.

"I feel something too, but it's about money, not war."

"Money?"

"You know I haven't liked the financial extravagances I've seen in the business world these past years, especially the gambling type of stock market activity. The bubble has got to burst sometime. I thought it would have happened before this."

Turning out the light he knelt to say his prayers. Liza was already kneeling on her side of the bed.

Unlike Liza and Charlie, the younger generation did not seem to have any worries. They filled their days happily in a number of ways. Mary and Jack treated willing guests to afternoons of sailing. Sometimes, little Lynne was with them, loving every new activity and adventure. Charlie still liked to sail but Liza ventured out only when the wind was moderate. Miriam, a Land-lover, kept her children ashore. She and Alan and their guests gathered at the grass tennis court and in the sand box area. The Russells, Ruthie Mae and Christopher, who were staying at Websters along with Kennard Lee and his family, were often at the Lynnehurst court, though Kennard divided his time between there and Fort Armstrong where Boxie had installed a new asphalt court. Fort Armstrong games were faster. Lynnehurst tennis provided good exercise.

It put the ladies all in a glow, as eager for a swim as their perspiring male partners. Kennard's wife had a bathing costume she had bought at a New York boutique. It attracted several side-long glances. Liza and Belle, who both tried to be polite, had misgivings.

"I suppose it's the style nowadays," murmured Belle, when she and her sister were alone together in the changing hut after one swim session.

"I'll never want anything less than this," insisted Liza, referring to her double layers of black wool, a yellow trimmed skirt over knee-length snug pants, the top of which sported a shallow, modest, scoop line around the neck and sleevelets high on her arms.

"What will we do if Eaton's stops selling our kind of bathing outfit?"

"We'll just keep mending these!"

"That's possible for you. You have only twenty more swimming years left before you're too old. I'm much younger than you."

"I think I could keep mending this black outfit for twenty-five years," Liza protested gently. Then with more assurance, "We will have to have faith, Sister. There's always a way to manage."

"Next you'll be advising me to pray about our bathing suits."

"Why not? Swimming provides us with cleanliness and joy. Surely those are godly attributes."

Belle made no response to Liza's philosophizing. Her mind did not flow as deeply as her sister's. It was soon off on another tangent, a characteristic tactic that kept Belle buoyant throughout life. No problem could hold her attention for long. Likewise, no sorrow could down her. All she asked of life was opportunities to be useful and to enjoy. After swim time, there was always tea time, a canoe ride on the lake or a card game indoors. Better still, she liked company for a good visit. Isabelle Brown Whitby was a sociable soul, with practical and creative skills as added blessings.

For Siegfried, the summer of 1929 was the summer of the raft. Never had father and son transformed odd bits of lumber so magnificently. Alan and Siegfried shared exuberant pride in their project. Did the boy become a man or did Alan become a boy again? Who can say? What we know is that some magic was at work as they laboured, rain or shine, with hammer, saw and wood. The natural affection between them was moulded into a sacred fraternity. No ship afloat had ever won such esteem from its designers as did Siegfried's raft.

Throughout the raft manufacture, Alan would check all sizing with a tape measure. Siegfried insisted on using Buppa Brown's old red level as well. The firm of Siegfried and Dad took pleasure in being trim in all respects. On launching day, Alan screwed a sturdy dock ring on one end of the completed raft while Siegfried rummaged in Buppa's old boat house for a length of rope. Then they were ready. A struggle... a few grunts... splash! The raft was in and it floated! While the launching was a private, two-person ceremony, chattering hordes of swimmers soon were upon them. Little Alan and Lynne were in the lead, the two mothers in hot pursuit.

"Look!"

"The raft is in!"

"It floated!"

"Can I get on?"

"Me too."

Alan Sr. looked questioningly at Siegfried. Siegfried was appreciative of this deference.

"Yes, let Alan and Lynne be the first to have a ride."

"Put me on first."

"No, me."

"NO!" commanded Alan Sr., "Both of you at the same time. I'll hold Alan ready; somebody take Lynne. Now... one, two, three!... There you are. Sit still. I'll pull you around with the rope."

The two children were content to be still for three minutes; then, "I can make it go with my hands."

"I can too."

In their efforts to outdo each other, Lynne lost balance and fell in. Her mother, already in the waist-high water, caught Lynne immediately. There was some spluttering, then loud wails as Mary held her child at shoulder height.

"He pushed me. "

"No dear, I don't think so."

"Yes he did," The volume of wailing increased.

Liza, seeing the little face red with anger, knew there was not much physical pain involved. "If they can cry, you know they're all right," It was one of Liza's refrains that her children and grandchildren heard on many occasions.

Little Alan, meanwhile, was seated centrally on the raft, rapt in wonderment. He sensed a state of unexplained victory.

"Alan," commanded Alan Sr., "please say you are sorry to Lynne."

"Sorry."

The adults seemed satisfied with this simple apology, but Lynne never heard it.

Her cousin continued to wonder and feel confused. He didn't think he had pushed anyone but if the adults said he had, it must be true. He was also amazed at Lynne's sobs. It was not the last time he was to be perplexed by his cousin's reaction to events in their lives.

Mary carried Lynne off to the bath house changing hut and sat her on a bench.

"You stay here, dear, until you're able to feel like a lady again," Mary withdrew, seating herself just outside on the dock.

Lynne knew that sometimes the adults got in and out of their bathing costumes in this place (her mother usually changed her in her bedroom up at Lynnehurst). She began to look around. There was another bench on the opposite wall just like the one on which she sat. Above it was a row of wooden pegs, too high for her to reach. A two-by-four ran horizontally around the little room, serving as shelf as well as support for the simple construction. Lynne searched along this shelf, hoping for some object upon which she could vent her anger. There was not so much as a bar of soap to destroy. There was a soapy smell in one corner. It made her think of grandmother.

She smiled. A ray of light from a knot hole touched her cheek. Where was the knot hole?

Lynne gazed up at the roof, seemingly so far above. It extended only half way across the shelter, allowing sun-filled air to flood the interior. Lynne could see blue sky. Feather-light clouds drifted across, inspiring her imagination to create stories.

There were no sobs now. The ugly feeling inside her, having vanished, Lynne could have remained happily where she was for much longer.

Her mother, waiting outside, was not to know of her child's absorption. She was occupied with some memories of her own childhood. Even stronger, was her desire to return to the swimming party. Consequently, when silence reigned inside for a moment or two, she deemed it possible that her daughter was sufficiently in a state of 'ladyhood' to warrant liberation.

When they returned to the others, every child present had received a turn on the raft. Now, Siegfried was in charge. He had a small paddle with him, which he employed in various ways, to study the effects. Different patterns and currents could be created in the water. The raft's movement might be clumsy compared with that of other water craft but Siegfried could make it work for him. Methodically he tried paddling on each of the four sides. As the raft was a perfect square, the results were similar.

For the rest of the summer, Siegfried was happiest when on his raft. He still enjoyed fishing expeditions in the rowboat with his father. He would help paddle on excursions to Needles Point, but the times alone with his raft were moments of bliss.

By adding more lengths of old rope he gave himself larger areas in which to experiment, venturing beyond the lea of the launch house into the reaches of the west winds. Wind was never a deterrent, only a challenge. He discovered that wind has currents within currents, all of which could change from day to day.

"Next summer, I'll add a sail to my raft," he announced to his father.

"You'll want a rudder as well. There's that old cracked one in the boathouse."

"Couldn't I just use my paddle?"

"Possibly."

Next summer never came... at least, not what Siegfried would call summer.

☙

One evening on the verandah Alan Sr. found time and opportunity to talk to his father.

"I've been talking to Boxie," he said, "He gave me ideas for expanding C.R. Drayton and Son. With another warehouse and a modernized office, we could handle twice the business."

"Son, you could expand the business, but you'd have to work harder to attract customers. You'd have more trips to Europe, less time at Lynnehurst. Have you thought about the effect on your family?"

"Once expansion has started, I could bring another partner in with me. Sales are going well. Each year, profits are larger. If business continues to grow, we could open a branch in another city, Galveston or maybe Memphis."

"'If' is a small word but it has large significance."

"True, but remember, 'nothing ventured, nothing gained.'"

"Do you remember the Bible stories about Joseph, the Provider?"

"Of course."

"Your Sunday School teacher probably emphasized the lessons about faithfulness and forgiveness."

"Yes."

"Well, there's also some business wisdom to be learned. In times of prosperity, prepare for the lean years. I have a feeling that the current boom is based on false wealth. I'm alarmed by the speculation on the Stock Exchange. The bubble is going to burst one of these days."

"You've said that before."

"It should have happened sooner. In floating the balloon further, it will mean a bigger pop when it bursts."

"What then would you advise me to do?"

"Use a portion of your profits to do necessary repairs to your buildings. Foundations should be secure, roofs solid. Then, even if business dwindles, you can hang on."

"I think the wiring needs to be replaced. More light fixtures would be a help."

"Those would be worthwhile improvements. Saunders might be able to give you some advice there."

"Father, is this why you're having Lynnehurst bat-proofed?"

"Partly," Charles smiled and gave a gentle laugh, "Your mother doesn't seem to mind, but some of the ladies are fearful of the sweepings and swoopings at night."

"Miriam is one of them."

"When Alfred Beasley told me that his business was slack this year, I decided this would be a good year to have it done."

"He's being very thorough. Do you think he'll finish before the end of July?"

"I hope so."

Lynnehurst

༺༻

1929 was something of a disappointment for Boxie. The marvellous Angela had produced a baby girl. However, Jessica was only the first child; next time there could be a boy. Boxie was called upon to admire, but he was totally excluded from the care and nurture of this precious daughter. He felt left out. However, Boxie didn't waste time feeling grieved. That summer he became a special uncle to Tom's boys, Thomas and Timothy. Together, they built a tree fort which they called "Little Fort A."

1929 was etched indelibly in Dumpy's memory as the year Ethel Chadwick joined the daytime menage at Lynnehurst. One early June day, Ethel appeared on the Lynnehurst doorstep asking to see Doris, privately. Ethel had overcome her fear of the water enough to travel by the Chadwick "D. P." when occasion demanded. Once she and Doris were seated in the glassed-in portion of the verandah, out of the way of mosquitoes, Ethel got right to the point.

"I want to learn to type and to take shorthand."

Dumpy studied the piercing eyes confronting her, but made no comment. She wanted to watch a mother phoebe guarding the nest just outside the window under the eaves, but dared not shift her attention from Ethel.

"The Chadwicks don't know I'm here," Ethel's voice continued with staccato rhythm, "I do not ask their advice. I'm determined to leave them, to leave Muskoka. If I learn how to type, I can get a job in Toronto."

"Toronto? What about Drick?"

"I will not take him. They think I ruined his father. Well, they can have his son. I don't want him; he reminds me too much of Roderick."

"Ethel! How can you say that?" Dumpy could not imagine such lack of maternal feeling.

"1 never wanted to be a mother. It was all Roderick's idea. Men are beasts."

"Surely not... Perhaps some are."

"You might as well know. Your dear Roderick was a beast. You did well to escape him."

Dumpy winced.

"Oh yes, I know all about you and him. He talked in his sleep sometimes."

Dumpy thought of several possible retorts but remained speechless. If Roderick behaved in a brutal manner to Ethel, it must have been in reaction to Ethel's vile nature.

Presently Dumpy said, "I take it you would like me to teach you business skills."

"I don't ask for a favour. I could repay you by helping Elsie with the housework. I know she was unable to get a younger woman to help her this year."

Doris began to think that the scheme might have some merit.

"Miss Drayton, you help me this summer and I promise I'll walk out of your life forever."

There was only a short pause before Dumpy replied, "I'll do my part. Just wait here while I speak to Mother about the kitchen duties."

Once the deal was struck, everyone concerned was informed of the plan. Henrietta brought Ethel over in the D.P. six mornings a week to help Elsie. Henny then carried on the delivery of her garden produce and eggs to several cottages. Five afternoons Ethel and Doris were closeted in the small office Charles had made for himself off the library in the new wing. Doris taught Ethel thirty or more minutes each day, then left her to drill the skills she'd learned. Often Doris took Ethel in Daisy Belle back to Chadwick Manor in time for afternoon tea.

Dumpy warmed up to Ethel. There were no more unpleasant references. The two women even relaxed enough with each other to exchange literary tit-bits. Roderick had taught his wife a great deal. After his death, she read every book in the Chadwick library. It was one way to escape the unwanted society of her in-laws. Now Ethel was asking to borrow books from the Lynnehurst shelves. She read quickly, returning each volume promptly.

"She'll make a crackerjack secretary for someone," proclaimed Dumpy near the end of August. I've taught her some accounting too."

᯽

1929 was the year the Montreal Browns finally had a place of their own. They bought an island on the other side of the lake, quite a distance from Brown's Landing.

A small cabin was easily and charmingly enlarged to suit their growing family. Little Tilda was now Mrs. Hansard M. Spencer. Hansard, a lawyer in Toronto, and cousin Tilda looked forward to long summer holidays at the cottage, a perfect place to bring children. Uncle Harold at age 73 was thinking of retiring. He bought a Ditchburn launch and frequently packed the whole family into it for visits to Lynnehurst. Harold Jr. had been married for some time, yet didn't feel he could leave his business for any length of time. However, his two young sons, Percy and Matthew, were part of the Brown entourage in Muskoka all July and August. Percy and Matthew certainly never forgot the summer of 1929.

Bat Party

Early one hot afternoon in late July, Alfred Beasley descended from Lynnehurst's attic and announced, with his own brand of humble pride, "Now, Mr. Drayton, I've sealed the very last crack. Every knot hole is secure. I defy any bat to squeeze through my defences."

Alfred took out a large handkerchief and patted the perspiration that glistened all over his face.

"Thank you, Mr. Beasley. I feel confident that every lady resident here and, hopefully, future generations of ladies will be grateful."

Alfred was persuaded to stay for iced tea on the front verandah with the older family members, while younger ones went for a second swim of the day. All afternoon the Lynnehurst household maintained a high level of good cheer.

The news that bats had been barred from entering Lynnehurst spread through Brown's Landing settlement and even as far as Brown's Island. After evening tea, all and sundry descended upon Lynnehurst to celebrate its liberation from bat tyranny.

Loud was the cheerful babble of voices, trying to decide between a game of charades or the Sir Roger de Coverley. Liza headed towards the piano. They had two sets of dancing while the sun descended. The sky softened with a blush of gold and pink.

"Let's have musical chairs," cried Timmy.

They did, with shouts, shrieks and a few tears on the part of the littlest ones.

Then Alan and Lynne were carted by their mothers off to bed. Sky colours gave way to twilight. Twilight deepened into darkness.

"It's crazy week," murmured Charles to Dumpy as he put his book back on the shelf.

She followed his example. They left the library to join the merrymakers.

In the hall, Dumpy stopped and pointed up the stairs, "Is that what I think it is?"

"Glory be!. There's another one. Don't say anything. Get a tennis racquet. These must be two that got locked inside and can't get out."

They each grabbed a racquet, swinging expertly.

"I got one."

"You must have missed; there are still two of them."

'That's a third one."

"Oh! There are more."

Their commotion drew the attention of the revellers on the verandah. Aunt Belle arrived first. Her shrieks brought others. Already it was obvious that there were not one or two, but several bats still inside Lynnehurst. Charles turned his racquet over to Percy. Dumpy relinquished hers to young Matthew. Cousin-uncle Boxie lifted other tennis racquets from their storage nails on the wall as weapons for Tommy and Timmy to use.

"Charge!" cried Boxie as he led the assault up the stairs where the bat population seemed densest.

Little Alan and Lynne could not be persuaded to go to sleep. Their mothers gave up, letting their pyjama-clad charges join in the fray.

Some of the women covered their heads as they retreated to the closed in section of the verandah, their chosen sanctuary. Elizabeth and her mother were there already.

Aunt Belle stayed at the scene of action. She uttered oohs, ahs, shrieks, and other useless noises. Dumpy beseeched the youngest combatants to be careful of their weapons, some of which were treasured by the tennis players of the family. She rescued her brother's favourite racquet from Tommy, finding an old, partly unstrung replacement for him.

Boxie soon realized the time had come to formulate a strategy. He and Alan as the older, more experienced corps deployed themselves below stairs to track down escapees from the youthful fury of the front line forces upstairs.

There were not enough racquets for Siegfried to have one. Instead, he went for the dustpan and hearth broom. Silently, he began collecting the carcasses for removal to the back shed, carefully dodging legs and swinging arms as he worked. Upstairs, downstairs, it didn't seem to matter. Siegfried kept steadily at his post. Charles began to help his intrepid grandson.

"What have I done," wondered Charles out loud, "I never knew we had so many bats. They must be coming in from outside, but how? Why?"

"No, Granddaddy, they were in the house all the time. They hide in the daytime and come out at night."

"That's it! Why didn't I think of that?"

"Sometimes I can't sleep," continued Siegfried, "I've seen them leaving the house at dark. I've tried to count them but there were too many."

Liza decided to leave the shelter of the glassed-in verandah to inspect the larder.

Elsie, who had a similar idea, was in the kitchen stoking up the stove.

"Elsie, it's your time off."

"It seems to me this is a special occasion. Besides, one of those creatures was in my room. I couldn't rest for thinking about it."

Elsie's room was off the kitchen. When the new wing was built and the house modernized, this space at the back of the house had been prepared for her. She had her own bathroom, too.

"I don't think there are enough rocks left," Elsie continued, "so I thought I'd bake some more. We've lots of eggs."

"I'll make tea for more iced tea. There's that raspberry squash."

"Some might like hot tea."

The oven had plenty of time to reach a good temperature. The bat excitement slowed but did not cease until well after a batch of rock cookies had been made and a large cake baked, cooled and iced.

Elizabeth, who fell asleep on the sofa, missed out on refreshments altogether.

Her father carried her up to bed, clothes and all. Alan Jr. was tempted to follow his sister but he forced himself to stay awake long enough to have cake and milk with Lynne, in the kitchen under grandmother's watchful eye. Eventually, everyone had refreshments and departed, but the bat episode was discussed and described for weeks afterwards. It went down in history as a major family legend. Boxie told Angela that his troops killed two hundred bats that night. The following year, he raised the number to three hundred. Siegfried said there were a hundred and fifty-nine. I trust Siegfried's total. After all, he'd counted them.

Uncle Philip missed the bat party. He was sceptical of his nephew Boxie's account. Next day Timmy and Tommy brought their great uncle over to see for himself. By that time, Alan and Siegfried had buried the dead in a mass grave. They let Timmy dig up enough to prove the point. Uncle Philip didn't need to see every one. He swore to believe forever, begging the boys to rebury the dead.

Watching from a window, Doris felt heavy with sadness, "Poor creatures. They didn't do anything wrong," she confided to her father.

"We'll probably be punished for our sins next summer by an invasion of mosquitoes," responded Charles.

Slide Lake

IF THE BAT PARTY WAS THE HIGHLIGHT OF JULY, 1929, a Slide Lake expedition provided the climax in August. Following family tradition, they timed it for the full moon. Originally, Charles had instigated these moonlight canoe trips as one way to keep adolescent offspring busy and out of trouble.

There were no adolescents in the 1929 fleet of canoes that set out for the two mile paddle up the big lake to an old Indian portage. The group of adults and children, mostly cousins, sang as they went along, their favourite tunes that year being from Pinafore. Someone was wailing pitifully about the lack of telephones in dungeon cells when the Dugdales cried, "Quiet!" They pointed ahead. Two loons loomed into view, then dove out of sight, only to be heard a little later laughing in the distance.

At the portage, the canoes were hauled ashore and turned over in safe resting places under trees. The adventurers followed a trail for a short way, then turned to the left for some serious climbing. Their final destination was Table Rock, the flat surface above a high cliff overlooking a small, round lake known to the early settlers as Slide Lake. The Browns and the Draytons believed this to be the very best place in all Muskoka for viewing the moon. One of the Dugdale girls asked why?

Her grandmother and her great aunts chorused in reply, "because it is, that's why!"

The older cousins laughed. They had heard that answer before.

It was a point of honour not to use a flashlight as they climbed. Flashlights had been tucked in pockets, but never had Browns or Draytons needed one at Table Rock. Charlie said they took torches only to scare away bears that might be rummaging for blueberries. If bears had ever been there, the babbling human voices were sufficient deterrent, especially Aunt Belle's "ooos" and "ahs," as she grabbed tree trunks to hoist herself higher or received friendly shoves from nephews and brothers-inlaw.

At the top, it took a few minutes for everyone to find a portion of rock surface on which to settle. They grouped in several huddles. Miriam held her small son Alan on one side, his sleepy head drooping towards her lap. Elizabeth was snuggled close on her other side. Siegfried and his father were not far away. Liza, thinking of the night Charles declared his love, put her arm through his and drew closer. An awesome beauty enveloped the whole group. Voices hushed. The Dugdale girls stopped giggling. Far below, on the glass-like surface of the small round lake, a moon path glowed. Above, in a sky of deep blue velvet, the silver globe hung so close and yet so far, a kindred creation suspended between them and the vastness of the night. Siegfried gazed, spell-bound. He tried to imagine the end of space. Every time he thought he could imagine the end, the final wall , as it were. his mind realized that there would be more space beyond that wall.

"It's impossible to know nothing," he remarked to his father.

"Some people think they know nothing."

"They can't really know nothing. I just tried."

"I don't know what you mean, but I do know that no one can know everything. I've tried that; there's always more we don't know."

"Is that where God comes in?"

"I think so."

Lynne, sitting a few yards away, was wide awake, "Is it Slide Lake because it's so smooth things slide across it?"

"No dear," replied Mary Lynne, her mother, "There used to be a log slide here."

Lynne didn't know what a log slide was. It sounded ugly. She gave up and shut her eyes.

Mary Lynne was thinking of Jack. He had already left for his new job in the south. Enrolment was dwindling at his college in Toronto, so when Julian de Poncier had written to suggest Jack apply for the Directorship of Dramatic Arts at a new university campus, he eagerly complied. The Board of Governors, of which Julian was one, hired Jack on the understanding that he would work towards a doctorate right away. Mary wondered what area Jack would choose for his studies. Julian had recommended a PhD in Education as the easiest option.

With Boxie's arm around her Angela was loving the romantic feeling of the moonlight but she wondered if it was a mistake to insist on coming. The canoe ride was lovely. Boxie and young Timmy had done the paddling while she had lounged on cushions and leaned against a carved back rest propped on the middle thwart. However, the scramble and climb through the woods had taxed her strength unmercifully.

I wonder whether this exertion will affect my milk, she thought to herself. Aloud, she whispered, "Boxie, darling, I'm feeling weak."

"Do you want to go back? We can make a sling and carry you."

"Not yet. Let me rest. Going down hill will be easier." She pulled her big sweater closer and did up the buttons. Boxie held his wife very close. The twins, Tommy and Timmy, soon tired of sitting still. Flashlights in hand, they went off to hunt for bears. Presently, a wolf howl was heard piercing the silence.

The moon-gazers on Table Rock were not fooled. They made no response but an answering howl was heard from below the cliff. Liza looked questioning at Charles.

"No, I don't think so," he said, "Sounds more like other humans out to see the moon."

In later years, Tommy and Timmy told their children and grandchildren about the time they gave wolf calls and real wolves replied. A chap named Steve Baldwin, from Ohio, told his friends about his summer in Canada, when he heard wolves on a cliff above a lake he was exploring by moonlight.

His friends asked, "what did you do?"

"I called back, just to fool them, then went back to the cottage where I was staying."

Liza decided the best way to deal with wolves in the bushes was to announce loudly, "It's time for cocoa."

Out of pockets and knapsacks came thermos jars of hot chocolate and tins of rock cookies. The twins reappeared.

Fortified with nourishment, Angela was ready for the return trip. It was Tommy's turn to help Uncle Boxie paddle. Half way down the hill, Tommy gave another wolf howl, "just for good luck."

Others lingered on Table Rock until the moon shifted and shrank. Reluctantly, they followed, sleepy heads stumbling along as best they could on the pathless descent.

The air felt distinctly cooler. A tangy blend of scents excited Dumpy's imagination.

Her nostrils could identify pine, cedar and the earth itself mingled in with something more. A perfume manufacturer could never reproduce this fragrance. Dumpy wished she could bottle some to rejuvenate herself in the dreary Toronto winters. Little did she realize that it would take more than forest fragrances to keep her going in the upcoming winter.

"Summer's almost over," sighed Aunt Belle.

"I wonder how many more years I can climb all that way," murmured Liza. Her premonition was well-grounded. She never again climbed to Table Rock.

Steamer to Heaven

AFTER THE SLIDE LAKE PARTY THE SOCIAL SEASON WAS OVER. Almost every morning, Lynnehurst inhabitants got up early to help see someone off. Liza's four grandchildren never missed a chance to watch the steamer come in to Brown's Landing. Some mornings were foggy. Charlie frequently used the bell that hung from a post on the steamer wharf. Lynne begged Aunt Dumpy to hold her up so she could pull the rope.

Even on clear mornings, she insisted.

"But Aunt Dumpy, the fog might come."

Uncle Phillip Drayton's was the first house to become empty; then Fort Armstrong. Once her children and grandchildren had departed Aunt Tilda's place seemed empty. She left. Uncle John and William got to work, quickly draining pipes and closing shutters. Aunt Sally cleaned the ice box at Fort Armstrong and dealt with food left-overs. A final cleaning was considered necessary to discourage mice. During departures Charlie helped his brother John with the shifting of luggage from wagon to wharf and from wharf to steamer.

"I did this when I was younger because I was young," Charlie reflected, "Now I do it because the younger men leave first."

Sometimes Will helped, but often farm duties kept him away. William didn't relish farewell ceremonies; too much chatter, too much sentiment expressed. Of course, everyone enjoyed the summer. Of course, they loved their cousins, aunts and uncles. Of course, they all counted the weeks until time to return. Why keep repeating these inanities, year after year?

Mary, on the other hand, was as excited as the children. She didn't want to miss out on whatever was going. Furthermore, steamers were her friends. She loved all boats, but steamers were like God, ruling their life in Muskoka. Steamers brought supplies and all things needful. Steamers brought people. Like the Lord, the steamer giveth and the steamer taketh away. Both Mary and her mother Liza assumed that, like the Lord, the steamers would go on forever. One morning after steamer departure, Charlie barely made it back to Lynnehurst before a nagging pain in his chest compelled him to slump onto the sofa in the library.

Liza noticed an ash-like pallor cover his face. Charlie had hardly ever been sick more than a day in their married life. She hastened to the kitchen to pull the kettle forward.

"Elsie, please make a cup of tea for Mr. Charles. I fear he has been overexerting himself."

On returning to the library, she realized more than a cup of tea was needed.

She asked Doris to call Dr. Evans. Liza never felt comfortable using a telephone, especially long distance. Phones made her feel restricted, cut off from the person behind the voice on the other end.

Dr. Evans recommended they keep Charles warm, "Don't let him do anything, even if he feels better. Make him rest until I get there."

They knew it could take Doctor Evans a while. Roads in Muskoka defied any efforts at speed, even for the doctor's new Pontiac.

Liza remained with her husband. She watched as he tried to sip his tea. His eyes searched hers. Wordlessly, his lips moved.

"Never mind," she assured him, taking the cup from him.

Charlie reached out to hold one of her hands. He motioned to indicate pain in his chest. She detached herself to put the cup, with its saucer, on the oval table. Charlie lay back again. Liza covered him with the afghan Aunt Belle had just finished making. She adjusted the cushions. Her grey-blue eyes remained riveted on his hazel eyes.

The children, sensing something, wanted to see their granddaddy.

Liza said, "Your grandfather needs sleep. Come, give him a kiss before you go to play."

Mary kissed him too. She and Miriam decided to take the children to Drayton Beach.

Later in the day, after Dr. Evans' visit, Siegfried and Elizabeth were allowed to see their grandfather again. That night, Dumpy gave Alan and Lynne early tea and took them upstairs for a long storytime before bed.

Miriam phoned Alan Sr. in New Orleans. Mary joined her mother at the sofa-side vigil. Charlie's eyes were closed.

Next morning, Liza felt a warm body beside her in the bed. When she blinked she encountered Lynne's brown eyes looking earnestly at her.

"Where's granddaddy?"

"He isn't here. He's gone to heaven."

"Is he coming back before Mummie and I go to see Daddy in our new house?"

"No dear, we won't see him for a very long time."

Lynne made herself cosy beside her grandmother.

"Is heaven up in the sky?" Lynne imagined she saw the steamer taking him up past clouds into blue sky. It made as much sense to her as a steamer going through fog on the blue lake. She waved her chubby hand to the ceiling of her grandparent's bedroom.

"Grandmummy, I saw Granddaddy waving to me from the steamer deck."

Liza felt comforted by the warmth of Lynne's presence. Lynne was four years old that summer.

Early in September, they buried Charles Robert Drayton beside his parents, Joseph and Caroline, in the church graveyard.

The following May, Charlie's brother John Drayton was interred nearby. When the other mourners had withdrawn, Sally and Liza remained in the graveyard.

"Sister," said Sally, "we were blessed in our husbands. We could not expect to be so blessed forever."

"Yes, Sally, at first I thought I could not have any life without Charles. It was like I was standing numb beside a big abyss. When I remembered there was life before Charles, I realized it would be possible without him."

"We have our children."

"And we have each other. Belle is also a widow. Tilda will join us someday. Like Buppa used to say, we sisters will stick together. Brown's Landing makes it possible."

Sally and Liza were not the only widows to face the depression years.

What was different about the Brown sisters was that they had a good supply of blessings and knew how to count them. They kept their eyes open to the ultimate realities of beauty, truth and love. Thus, their lives never became mean or desperate as with some others who had eyes only for material misfortunes.

What about Dumpy? How did she survive the Great Depression? She continued teaching at Shaw's, working diligently for low wages. Her investment income shrank dramatically, as did her mother's but they managed. With her brother Alan far away in New Orleans, Dumpy became the man of the family in Toronto, attending to legal matters, taxes and bills. Her investment policy was simple. You can't lose anything if you don't sell it.

Something she did try to sell was Roderick's ring, telling herself that the proceeds could be given to feed the hungry in one of Toronto's soup kitchens. To her surprise, no one wanted her ring. One pawn shop reluctantly offered ten dollars.

"It's worth far more than that," protested Dumpy.

"But Madam, no one is buying diamond rings these days."

Dumpy then felt justified in keeping the ring. By siphoning one dollar out of each month's pay, she was able to make ten donations to charity.

"Now I have bought the ring," she told herself, "It's mine, not Roderick's."

Her reasoning lightened her conscience. She began to take delight in the diamond, wearing it on special occasions.

ABOUT THE AUTHOR

Sarah Ditchburn Neal was born in Baton Rouge, Louisiana and spent her first fifteen winters on the campus of Louisiana State University before her family returned to Muskoka. At Trinity College, Toronto, she earned a B.A. degree in Modern History. Sarah has had a lifetime of summers in Muskoka. After forty-five winters in Ottawa, she and her husband Fred retired to the family homestead near Lake Rosseau.